Jade's Choice

Also by Maree Anderson:

The Crystal Warriors Series
The Crystal Warrior
Ruby's Dream
Jade's Choice
Opal's Wish

***

The Seer Trilogy
Seer's Hope
Seer's Promise
Seer's Choice

***

Lightning Rider

***

Young Adult books:

The Freaks Series
Freaks of Greenfield High
Freaks in the City

***

Liminal

***

Jade's Choice

Book Three of
The Crystal Warriors Series

Maree Anderson

ISBN-13: 978-0-9922498-9-2
ISBN-10: 0-9922498-9-9

JADE'S CHOICE
Copyright © 2012 by Maree Anderson
First print edition, 2014

Publisher: Maree Anderson

Cover Design: Rob Anderson

This novel is a work of fiction. Any names, characters, places and events portrayed in this novel are products of the author's imagination or used fictitiously. Any resemblance to actual events or places or business establishments or persons, living or dead, is coincidental.

All rights reserved; the right to reproduce this book or any portion thereof in any form whatsoever in any country whatsoever without the express permission of the author is forbidden. This book shall not, by way of trade or otherwise, be lent, resold, hired out or otherwise circulated without prior consent of the author in any form of binding or cover other than that in which it is published.

Thank you for respecting the hard work of this author.

Chapter One

Jade exhaled a shaky breath, braced herself, and walked into the light, ultra-modern hotel lobby. The doors whooshed shut behind her, cocooning her from the heat and noise outside. She rubbed her arms, desperate to maintain the pretense she was simply reacting to an abrupt transition from summer warmth to air-conditioning. Because to admit the truth was to acknowledge how damn close she was to turning on her heel and making tracks to the nearest bus stop.

Her hand crept to her neck. She rubbed the pendant between her fingers, worrying the deep green stone's smooth surface like a devout Catholic coaxing absolution from rosary beads.

Absolution. Yeah. Sure could do with a hefty dose of *that* right about now.

She managed a half dozen steps before she halted, pursing her lips against the instinctive reaction to gape. *Wow*. Color her impressed. The grand staircase mentioned on the hotel website really *was* grand. But it wouldn't do to stand there, gaping like some unsophisticated small-town girl who'd never set foot in a luxurious hotel before. It wouldn't do at all. She tossed her head, thrusting back her shoulders, and stalked over to the lifts projecting "I've seen it all before" for all she was worth.

The lift door opened. Thankfully, it was empty.

Jade's heart raced until it seemed it would leap from her

chest and take off for parts unknown. She ground the heel of her hand into her breastbone, willing her heartbeat to calm. And then, as the lift smoothly ascended, she clutched her pendant and focused—again—on the man she'd arranged to meet.

Given his accent and his formal way of speaking, she reckoned he would be in his fifties. Tall and lanky and debonair. Excruciatingly polite. Reading glasses perched on the end of his nose. Sober, pinstriped suit with a handkerchief peeping from his breast pocket. Highly polished shoes—

The lift halted. Jade checked the floor number and forced her legs into motion. Once the lift doors shut behind her, she glanced around the foyer for lurking hotel guests.

All clear. She smoothed her dress down her thighs, stroked a palm over her hair, and ran a finger across her teeth to remove any lipstick that might have migrated from her lips. Finally, she huffed into her palm and sniffed her breath. Still minty-fresh. Yay. She even managed to summon a shred of pride that her knees didn't wobble as she headed down the carpeted corridor, searching for the room number he'd given her.

Here it was.

She stared at the shiny numerals. It wasn't too late to back out.... Before she could change her mind, she rapped smartly on the door.

It opened mid-knock, as though he'd been lurking and watching for her through the peephole.

Jade skittered back a step. Her mouth went dry, skin clammy. She didn't know whether to be flattered by the thought of him watching for her arrival, or totally squicked. She stuck out her hand. "I'm Jade."

"I know." He grasped her hand, and his eyes gleamed with an emotion she was at a loss to name.

Discomfited, her gaze slid from his face. She stared over his left shoulder, where it was safer—a last-ditch attempt to distance herself from what she was about to do.

He squeezed her hand a little tighter. He seemed to be daring her to meet his gaze. She exhaled long and slow, and answered his challenge.

Bad move. Those shrewd, too-knowing blue eyes captured hers, sucking her down into fathomless depths. She couldn't look away from him. Some still functioning part of her brain reminded her she was rudely staring, prompted her to say something witty instead of standing there gawking like a lump. But glib words—or any words at all for that matter—escaped her, and she continued to gaze at him, transfixed. Only when his attention flicked to a twittering trio of designer shopping bag-laden matrons heading for the foyer, did the strange compulsion ease.

Jade blinked and shook her head to clear the fuzz from her mind. He released her hand, and she had to lock her knees, fighting a wave of dizziness. Wouldn't do to collapse to the floor and make a spectacle of herself. Doubtless he wouldn't appreciate the unwanted attention it might provoke. And, while she scrabbled for the shreds of her lost dignity, he ushered her into his suite with a courtly gesture.

The furnishings screamed money-is-no-object exclusivity. Jade inhaled the almost too-clean, slightly too-cold air, and shivered. He wasn't at all what she'd expected given their one brief, businesslike phone conversation. Blue jeans, black boots, black jacket over a white shirt—pretty trendy for an old man. And he *was* old—had to be at least seventy if those numerous, deeply seamed wrinkles were any indication.

Jade swallowed to lubricate her vocal chords. "It's nice to meet you, Mr. Stone," she finally managed to say.

Playing for time, she wandered through the sitting room area to stare out the window. The view of the Sydney Opera House, its remarkable roofline evoking a fleet of tall ships with billowing sails, stole her breath. "Wow. That's just... wow!"

Ack. How completely unsophisticated did that sound? So

much for trying to come across as worldly-wise and up for anything. She should leave now—give up this ridiculous idea. She wasn't cut out to be a... a....

The ugly word echoed in her mind, and she suppressed a flinch, hoping he couldn't tell she was dying inside, shriveling with shame. But the truth was that she'd run out of choices. She had to see this through to the end.

When she turned to face him, he didn't bother to hide that he'd been observing her closely—still was, in fact. His head was cocked to one side, brows crinkled. He'd probably figured out she had been on the brink of doing a runner.

Jade pulled herself together and threw him a practiced social smile—the one she used to put café patrons at ease, and encourage them to chatter away so she didn't have to exert herself and have a real conversation.

It usually worked a treat.

But not this time. The silence lengthened. Her facial muscles started to ache, until maintaining the bright, sunny smile became an exquisite torture.

"You have not eaten," he said.

A statement, not a question. Jade blinked. And she was wondering how on earth he could know she'd skipped breakfast when her stomach rumbled. Loudly.

"I, too, am hungry," he said. "And I am reliably informed the hotel's brasserie provides a pleasant dining experience. Or perhaps you would enjoy a pre-lunch cocktail?"

Tempting, but.... "I'll pass on the cocktail, thanks." Despite the allure of floating through the next few hours in an alcoholic haze, Jade wanted—needed—to experience this encounter honestly, with all senses engaged. If she couldn't handle intercourse with a stranger sober and fully aware, then she sure as heck wouldn't be able to look in a mirror without heaving when this was all over.

Uh oh. He was staring at her expectantly. *Think fast, Jade. Hotel restaurant and a chance to delay the inevitable? Or the privacy of this lovely suite... with what comes next hanging over you like some sword of Damocles.* Both options had their pros and cons.

"Would... would you be very offended if we ate in your room, Mr. Stone?" Sitting through a meal in a public setting, minding her Ps and Qs while making small talk, would only give the butterflies fluttering in her stomach the opportunity to morph into fang-filled creatures of the night.

"Not at all. I have discovered that room service prepare the most wonderful toasted sandwiches—"

"Sounds good to me." Jade sank into the nearest armchair and tried not to fidget as he phoned down for food. He hadn't bothered to ask her preference before ordering but she didn't call him on it. This wasn't a date. She didn't have to assert herself straight up and make it clear she wasn't some naïve little girl content to let the guy make all the decisions. If he wanted to order for her, then he could be her guest.

He finished placing the order and hung up.

Jade uncurled her fingers from her pendant. "So, Mr. Stone—"

"Peter.

"Right. Peter. Is there anything in particular you'd like to do while we're waiting for the food to arrive?"

As soon as the last word left her lips, she regretted speaking up. She widened her eyes and plastered a hopefully engaging expression on her face while she mentally cursed her big mouth. *Way to go, Jade. Your job is to sit here looking decorative for as long as he wants. Your job is to pretend you enjoy his company, not act like you want to get this over with. Your job is to keep your mouth shut, and smile no matter what he does—or asks you to do.*

One of his eyebrows quirked upward. "I am in no particular hurry," he said.

A flush scorched her cheeks. The criticism had been subtle but she'd caught it. He'd indicated over the phone he desired her services for three hours, and if he chose to spend the time sitting chatting with her in his hotel suite, who was she to complain? She shifted in her chair, biting her lip and searching for something to say to ease the tension.

He huffed a sigh. "I meant no censure," he said. "You take what people say too much to heart, Jade."

Shit. She'd revealed too much. And the ease with which he could tap into her thoughts both frightened and angered her. She couldn't afford to be frightened so she instinctively embraced the anger, but had enough presence of mind to duck her head to hide her expression while she wrestled with it.

Damn him. Where did this old guy get off thinking he could make such personal comments? He might *think* he knew her. He might imagine he'd accurately pegged her *type* given her obviously Asian heritage, her carefully applied make-up, and the flirty sundress she'd paired with matching high-heeled sandals to counter her height disadvantage. Yeah. All he saw was a little china doll, willing to take the easy way out and prostitute herself for money. But he was wrong. He had no idea who she truly was… and why she'd stooped to this.

Nor would she ever allow him to know the real Jade—she couldn't, because the real Jade hated him for wanting her. Just like she hated that she hadn't been able to find another way. And despaired, too.

"Calm yourself, child."

She hadn't heard him move but he was there, beside her, his hand clasping her wrist. And the warmth of his touch seeped into her skin, dissolving her anger, soothing the panic and despair that threatened to overwhelm her, leaving her calm and relaxed.

"I have a gift for you, Jade."

He tugged her from the refuge of the armchair. And, as she stood, it hit her like a physical blow that this was it, the defining moment of her life.

Last chance, Jade.

Could she go through with it? Could she screw a stranger—and a practically ancient one at that—for money?

Damn straight she could. She had responsibilities, and those responsibilities would only become more pressing. She needed the advice of the best specialists money could buy. She needed to supplement her meager income—sooner rather than later.

She rested her hand on his forearm and allowed him to escort her to the huge bed that she'd tried to ignore ever since she'd first stepped foot into the suite.

Peter perched on the edge of the mattress by the heap of pillows, and patted the coverlet beside him. "Sit down, Jade.

She joined him on the mattress, resisting a childlike urge to bounce up and down. So far, so good. She could do this.

But Fate had one last slap upside the head to deliver, and when she glanced at Peter, a sneering, hate-filled face superimposed itself overtop his. It was the face that haunted Jade whenever she let down her guard and a let a man get too close.

Nausea and revulsion seared her stomach. Necessity and pride were all that prevented her bolting to the bathroom and locking herself in. She wrapped both arms around her middle. Peter appeared to be a decent guy. She couldn't imagine him hurting her or degrading her. She could do this. She *would* do this. For her sister's sake.

While she took deep breaths and tried to hide that she was freaking out, Peter opened the bedside drawer and retrieved an object wrapped in gold silk.

He placed it in her lap. "This is for you, Jade. Treat him well, for he deserves a second chance at redemption."

Treat *him* well?

Jade frowned at Peter's strange choice of words, mulling them over to gauge hidden nuances and meanings. If she accepted this gift, what else was she unknowingly accepting?

Despite her unease, her gaze fell to the wrapped object in her lap. It was the size of her palm. Its weight surprised her.

Whatever-it-was felt solid and smooth beneath its silken wrapping. She unwound the strip of fine cloth—a scarf, at a guess—to reveal an egg-shaped stone of breath-stealing beauty, its polished emerald and jade hues perfectly offset by the deep gold of the scarf.

She stroked the stone's surface and it responded, warming beneath her fingertips, glowing as though polished by her feather-light caress. And then it whispered to her, and a flood of despair and long-endured horror at its fate crashed into her unprepared mind. She shared its consciousness—she had no choice in the matter. And she, too, suffered.

Jade's first instinct was to throw the stone across the room but she couldn't move a muscle, not to brush it from her lap or even to close her eyes. She was held in thrall, powerless. Even her gaze was fixed on the cursed thing.

Shit! All those cautionary tales about young girls arranging clandestine meetings with strange men they'd met online were right. But no one would ever believe *this*. And Jade hadn't the faintest idea how to escape this... this... whatever the heck held her captive.

"Do not fight him, Jade."

Fight what, exactly, goddamn it?

She concentrated, trying to divorce her own senses from the all-consuming sensation of hope now emanating from the stone. Sweat beaded her forehead, the droplets plumping and merging into fine rivulets that snaked slowly down her temples before seeping into her hairline. "What is it?" she managed to grate from between tightly clenched teeth. "What. Is. This. Thing?"

"He is your destiny, Jade," Peter said. "Do not be afraid. He will not hurt you."

Yeah, right. Peter Stone was a whack-job. He'd hypnotized her. Or... or... done some weird pressure-point nerve thingy to paralyze her. And he believed this stone had human characteristics, considered the cursed thing to be alive?

God. She was in big trouble now.

Peter reached for the pendant nestling in her cleavage. His touch was cool and impersonal on her skin as he rubbed the ingot-shaped stone briefly between his fingers, before letting it fall. She noted an expression that smacked of extreme satisfaction before he backed away, and disappeared from her narrow line of sight.

Jade's pendant hummed against her skin, as though the old man's touch had gifted it with a voice. Its sweet tones resounded in her mind, soothing her fears, quieting her instinct to resist. Its song crescendoed, and then sharpened into a questioning discord that thrummed through her body—

And was answered by the stone nestled in her lap. The full force of its power slammed into her, casting her adrift on a stormy sea of absolute resolve—the stone's resolve. *His* resolve, for she could sense him now, an undeniably male presence calling to her, demanding her surrender.

You are my savior, he said. And her world narrowed to his deep voice echoing in her mind, his thoughts probing hers as he sought entrance to her innermost secrets, his hope that she would be the key to what he so desperately sought, his belief she was his safe haven.

I am Malachite. And you…. You are mine.

She struggled, fought him. He would not own her. He would not!

Please, he whispered in the confines of her mind. *Do not leave me here. I can endure it no longer. Please!*

Via the bizarre mental linkage, Jade experienced the true horror of his prison. Roiling blackness. A pitiless nothingness that absorbed all light and consumed sensation.

Until she had linked with him, he'd been blind and deaf. When he'd howled his despair, no sound issued from his vocal cords, and he didn't know whether he'd been rendered dumb, or whether sound no longer existed in this never-ending Hell he called *Halja*.

Until she'd found him, he'd clawed and torn at his flesh but felt no pain. He hadn't known whether he still possessed a physical body in this space and time. For all he knew he had been reduced to nothing but a disembodied brain floating in the seething darkness.

Until her, there had been nothing but his own thoughts—guilt-ridden demons infected with self-loathing and despair, gnawing away at his sanity… feeding on his soul.

Please!

How could she be so cruel as to resist his plea?

She yielded. His answering roar was triumphant, and it shook her to the marrow.

Somehow, Jade got her limbs to work and struggled to her feet. The stone fell from her lap. It hit the carpet, cracked, and split in two. Abruptly freed from the stone's influence, she toppled backward, her body stiff and leaden, arms hanging uselessly by her sides.

The fall seemed to last a lifetime.

Finally, an instant before her spine smacked the mattress, a blazing corona of light captured her gaze. She bounced once, twice, still paralyzed, her brain numbed to everything except burgeoning wonder at the gray, ghostlike form materializing.

The specter was human-shaped, with glowing, glacial blue eyes. It solidified into a human man, who collapsed to the floor with a shocking *thud* that resounded in Jade's skull.

She couldn't comprehend the enormity of what she'd witnessed. A man appearing from thin air? It wasn't possible. *He* wasn't possible.

"Malachite!" The scream rent the too-quiet serenity of Peter Stone's hotel suite.

It was a woman's scream. *Her* scream.

"Jade!"

The man's hoarse shout reverberated throughout the room, careening off walls and surfaces. His pain scoured her skull, and his horror at what he had become, what he was prepared to do to gain his freedom, lanced through her soul.

The room wavered, becoming as fuzzy and indistinct as the thoughts clamoring in her beleaguered brain. And then there was nothing at all.

Chapter Two

B LOODY HELL. What on earth had hit her? The entire freakin' forward pack of the Wallabies rugby team? Jade's body throbbed and ached. Her skin prickled, hyper-sensitive to even the light, filmy material of the summery dress she wore. She tried to pry open her eyelids but her body refused to cooperate with her brain. And when her head inadvertently lolled to one side, despite her efforts, her eyelids were still closed.

Cool cotton beneath her cheek—a pillow. Textured material beneath her out-flung hands suggested the coverlet of the bed. She twitched her toes. Someone had removed her sandals. Huh. At least she wouldn't be poking holes in the hotel's horrendously expensive umpteen-thread-count bed linen.

A voice yanked her from her musings—a pissed-off-to-the-max-sounding voice. "This cannot be right," it rumbled.

Mmm. Not Peter Stone's voice. Too deep, the timbre too rich and chocolaty-smooth to be Peter's.

Jade finally coaxed her eyelids to open but everything was blurred and indistinct.

"What were you thinking, choosing this... this... fragile *child* for me?" the voice said. "I fear she will break in two if I so much as lay a finger on her."

Huh?

"Have the long centuries of your guardianship finally addled your brain, old man?"

Ouch. Now the voice was like a lash, so rife with fury that Jade imagined Peter on his knees and cowering before its wrath. But when Peter responded, he didn't sound the least bit cowed. His voice was low and calm. "My brain is as sharp as it has ever been. And you know very well that I am but a servant to the will of my goddess."

This announcement was greeted with a prolonged silence. And then, "You dare lie to my face, Guardian?"

"You know it is no lie."

"Then tell me this: What is she doing in your bed, old man? Is it the will of your goddess to now bond me to your castoffs?"

Jade didn't catch Peter's reply because everything started to go a little fuzzy around the edges again.

She must have drifted off for a short time, for she came to with a gasp. She lifted one incredibly heavy arm and managed to rub her eyes without stabbing her fingers in her eyeballs. One more blink, and a large form swam blurrily into view.

She rubbed her eyes again. And just to be absolutely certain her vision was working properly, blinked a couple of times.

Whoa. It was the phantom man. But he sure wasn't a phantom now. He was very much here. Not to mention built. And the scarred, battered leather pants and matching sleeveless vest he wore displayed his impressive physique to full advantage… if you liked that oh-so obvious "Hey, I work out a lot!" look in a man. His thick, unkempt shoulder-length hair and shit-kicker boots further enhanced his "mess with me at your peril" image. He was all taut muscles and carefully leashed strength. A lean, mean, fighting machine of a man.

The impossibility of a human being morphing into existence from thin air was a little too extreme for even Jade's fertile imagination to cope with. She thrust what she'd witnessed from her mind, refusing to believe it could have been real, firmly telling herself that he must have entered the hotel room while she was out to it.

Peter stood before the stranger, facing him as an equal. The old guy had guts, Jade would give him that.

"She is the one for you, Crystal Warrior," Peter said. "Or to be precise, she *will* be."

"Admit it, Guardian. She is a mistake. Again."

"Jade is no mistake."

Jade stifled a snort. *I should bloody well think not!*

"Jade," the stranger murmured. "A beautiful name for a beautiful girl."

Mmm. His voice coated her skin like a balm, seeping into her sore muscles and easing her hurts. And she would accept the compliment, too, she decided. She'd never been called beautiful before.

"And I require a *woman*," Mr. I'm Too Sexy For My Leather Pants declared. "Not some mere slip of a girl."

Nice one. Way to get struck off her Christmas card list.

"You are recalling Francesca," Peter said.

"Yes, I am recalling Francesca. 'Tis impossible for me to forget her. You and your demon-spawned goddess made sure of that."

"I truly believed Francesca was the one—"

"She *was* the one for me. The only one. Omnipotent sorcerer that you are, I find myself astonished that you cannot grasp that simple fact."

"I comprehend far more than you could ever know."

"Spare me your meaningless prattle, old man. When you forced Francesca to choose between us, her suffering rent my soul in two. Granted, she already had much hurt and sorrow to bear, but your gross miscalculation, your arrogance, increased her suffering twofold. What say you to that, Guardian?"

Peter's chin swiveled toward Jade, and she shuttered her eyes, faking unconsciousness. The conversation was getting really interesting. Sure, it was a bit "out there". And sure, she probably should bolt for the door, but a little voice inside her head insisted that she wait to hear this play out.

"*I* say, your suffering far exceeded hers, Malach. And I say the intentions of my goddess can be unfathomable—even to one who has served her for centuries. I do not profess to understand why Francesca was chosen for you at such a difficult time in her life. All I know is that she *was*. Just as I know that, by the grace of the goddess you so revile, you have been given a second chance."

"Perhaps."

Man, this guy was a hard sell. He wasn't giving Peter an inch.

"Or perhaps your goddess is in truth a sadistic bitch. Perhaps she is merely enjoying a second opportunity to torture me for my sins."

"Believe what you will," Peter said, with a finality in his tone that made Jade break out in goose-bumps. "Though it might please you to know both Kyan and Wulf have found joy in those chosen for them."

Jade's curiosity got the better of her again and she cracked open her eyelids.

The big man's fierce expression had softened. "I rejoice to hear my Lord Keeper Wulf has found happiness. And despite my personal feelings toward Kyan, I wish both him and his Chosen well. No human should be made to suffer as we have."

He squeezed his eyelids shut, holding his body rigid, hands fisted at his sides. And when he opened his eyes again, the purity of the anguish lurking in their pale blue depths sent icy shivers coursing down Jade's spine. "Why, Guardian?" he asked. "Why inflict me upon this girl? 'Tis foolhardy. I see not the slightest hope of redemption in such a choice."

"The choice has been made. For your own good, Malach, you must put your feelings for Francesca aside."

"I cannot."

Boy, this Francesca chick had really done a number on him.

Peter heaved a defeated sigh. "Then there is little else I can do but leave you to your fate."

Hang on, Peter was talking departure?

"No!" Jade blurted, struggling to sit. Pain bloomed in her skull, and tiny flecks of silver danced across her vision. She absently tried to brush them away. No way was Peter leaving her at the mercy of this stranger. That had so *not* been a part of their discussion.

She swung her legs off the mattress and stood, her knees wobbling, hoping she wouldn't embarrass herself by doing a face-plant onto the carpet.

Peter hastened to her side and she clutched his arm, grateful for the support. "Peter, what's going on? Who is this man? And why does he keep calling you 'Guardian'?"

Peter placed a hand on her forehead and, strangely, before she could push his hand away, the pounding headache she'd been determined to ignore eased.

"His name is—"

"Malach. Yeah, I got that." She summoned a high-wattage smile for the stranger. "I hope you won't consider it rude if I asked you to leave, Malach. Like, now? Peter and I have some, uh, unfinished business."

He crossed his arms and glowered at her. "As do I."

Uh oh. Her smile didn't seem to be working.

She shrank from that fierce, judgmental gaze, but Peter planted a hand on the small of her back and propelled her forward until she stood directly before the big man—Malach. And Peter's hand ensured there was no place to hide. The old man was a heap stronger than he appeared.

"Jade is the one for you, Malach," Peter said—insisted, really. "She may be diminutive in stature but her spirit towers with potential. If you can find the key to her heart, she will truly be your savior. As will you be hers."

Jade cringed, and ducked her head as heat crawled up her neck and painted her cheeks. God. How humiliating. Peter was offering her up to Malach as though she was the solution to all his problems—like she was some precious artifact with magical powers or something. As if. And even if she *had* been inclined to help the guy, the sad truth was that she could barely cope with her own problems let alone a stranger's.

Malach lifted her chin with gentle but insistent fingers. And, as he examined her face, she took the opportunity to do some examining of her own.

His silver-smattered raven hair suggested he was older than she'd first estimated. His skin was darkly tanned, and only highlighted those eerily pale blue eyes—eyes shadowed with painful memories that Jade suspected were best buried deep and never unearthed. Harsh lines etched his mouth, and she guessed it had been years since he'd last smiled.

His was the face of a soldier returning from war, his soul crushed by the atrocities he'd witnessed. Even his broad shoulders were slightly hunched, as though he carried a heavy, ever-present burden. Jade hadn't a clue how she could have gleaned all that merely from looking at him, but she knew beyond a doubt it was the truth. He'd suffered horribly.

She didn't realize that she'd reached out to him until his callused hand engulfed hers, preventing her from touching his face. His brows knit as he gazed into her eyes, seeking answers to questions Jade didn't know that she'd asked.

She always found it incredibly discomfiting to gaze into the eyes of a stranger. That sort of intimacy was for star-struck lovers, or longtime partners who were comfortable in their own skins—like Jade's parents had been. But now she felt no compulsion to look away, or even to yank her hand from Malach's grip. It was as though they both were frozen, and waiting for… for… *something*.

Peter's satisfied chuckle broke the spell. "And you dare question my choice, Malach? Remember, you have one month to initiate the bond. If you and Jade pass the Testing, you will be forever free of the crystal. Forever free of me, too. Is that not reason enough to embrace my choice, Crystal Warrior?"

"And if we fail?" Malach asked, his gaze never leaving Jade's face.

Peter didn't answer.

"Of course. Your goddess-damned crystal will take me again." Malach's tense body radiated frustration and anger. His hand squeezed Jade's, grinding the bones of her fingers together. She tried to wrench her hand from his grasp but he held her too tightly.

"So much for your benevolent goddess," he said, obviously trying to goad Peter. "The conniving bitch has contrived to punish you as effectively as she does me. Remember that, old man. Remember, while you endure countless centuries as Guardian of our crystals until this travesty ends. Would it not be easier to strike me down and have an end to me rather than risk another failure?"

God! Jade's skin went clammy. Her heart stuttered, and then hammered in her chest. This whole situation was getting way the heck out of control. "Now hang on a minute. No one's gonna be killing anyone, okay?"

Both men ignored her, too intent upon imposing their wills upon each other.

"Your death would not finish this, Malach, however much you might wish it," Peter said. "You are not the only victim of my curse, as you well know."

Jade blinked. "Curse? What curse?" Her Aunt Lìli was a bona fide witch. She might be able to counteract—

"How many, old man?" Malach demanded. "How many of us are still condemned to the crystals? How many of us still suffer?"

Peter left the questions unanswered. "You have been given another chance, Malach. I would advise you to welcome it with open arms and an open heart."

"Then tell me more about this Testing, Guardian. What does it entail? I would gladly venture across the sands during the Storm Season, and invite the winds to strip the flesh from my bones if it meant being free of you and your accursed crystal."

"To reveal any more is forbidden. I have already stretched the rules decreed by my goddess to breaking point, and I will not willingly risk her wrath. But I can say this: Never forget, Malach, that your fate is now irrevocably intertwined with Jade's. There is nothing you can do to change that."

Jade's hand was still caught in Malach's tight grip, forcing her to twist awkwardly to keep Peter in view. To her horror, the old man had positioned himself at the door of the suite and was reaching for the door handle. "Hey, where do you think *you're* going? We had a deal!"

"Our deal has changed, Jade. Malach is to be my—how do you say? Stand-in."

"Oh, no. I don't think so. You can't leave me with a man I barely know!" Especially not this big, sexy, scary man who made her feel things she didn't know she could feel.

"You barely know me, either, my dear," Pieter said. "And yet you were prepared to give yourself to me."

Jade spluttered a protest. "That's different, Peter. And you know it."

"My true name is *Pieter*, child. Or *Pietersite*, to be exact."

"But—"

"I must go, Jade."

"Why?" If this was all some elaborate plan so he could do a runner and stiff her with his hotel bill—

"The suite has been paid in full for the next seven nights—ample time for you both to get to know each other. However, that period can easily be extended to a full twenty-eight nights if necessary. Although—" his blue eyes twinkled "—given your passionate nature, and Malach's hunger for a true soul mate, I believe a few days will more than suffice. One more thing: When you are hungry, room service will oblige. Meals have been arranged at no cost to yourselves."

Jade went hot-cold-hot as dismay socked her a stellar sucker-punch to the gut. "Seven nights? Are you kidding me? No way am I staying here tonight, or any other night. I have a job. I have responsibilities!" She threw herself backward, using all her weight to strain against Malach's grip. He held her easily—far too easily. Her pulse rate tripped up another notch.

"It has all been dealt with," Peter said. "Mei will be well taken care of until you return—however long that may prove to be. I give you my word."

Jade quit struggling at mention of her sister. "How could you possibly know—?"

The old man's mesmerizing gaze caught and held hers, subduing her with the strength of his will.

Worry about someone dear to her nagged at the edges of Jade's mind but she couldn't hold on to the memory. She frowned, kneading the tight ache between her brows with her spare hand, and feeling strangely bereft.

Peter paused, staring at them both as though committing their images to memory. "Have faith, Malach," he said. And then he stepped into the corridor... and the door began to swing shut behind him.

MALACH'S HAND INVOLUNTARILY clenched. The little female gave a pained gasp and, realizing he was hurting her, he instinctively relaxed his grip. She exploded into motion, wrenching her hand free and rushing for the door....

Too late.

It slammed in her face. She rattled the handle. "Locked. Crap!"

Before he could caution her, she shoved the door with her shoulder. "Owww!" She massaged the shoulder and worked the joint. "Goddamn you to hell, Peter," he heard her hiss.

"I heartily second that sentiment," he said.

"Huh. I'm guessing you're no more thrilled by this situation than me."

"You would be correct."

She fixed him with a ball-shriveling glower that was completely at odds with her sweetly innocent face. "Don't try any funny business, or you'll be sorry."

"I assure you that laughing is the last thing I feel like doing at this moment."

She stared at him through slitted eyes, as though trying to discern the sincerity of his last statement. Finally she said, "You gonna stand there gawking or help me with this bloody door?"

He crossed his arms over his chest. "There is little point wasting our energies when Pieter has be-spelled it."

"The *point* is we need to get out of here." She backed up and tried another shoulder charge, only to rebound off the door with such force that she staggered.

Malach winced in sympathy. That had to have hurt. "Even if the door hadn't been be-spelled," he told her, "shoulder-barging it is fruitless given that it opens inward."

She massaged her shoulder, her lips thinning to a tight white line. "Fine. So brute force isn't gonna work."

"Correct."

She crinkled her nose, obviously racking her brains for a solution to the problem, unwilling to let pain divert her from her task.

He watched her nibbling her lip and muttering to herself, fascinated despite his ire at this appalling situation. He'd never encountered a female quite like her before. On the surface so delicate and doll-like he feared she might shatter, but inwardly stubborn and tenacious, and so forthright he didn't know whether to grin at her audacity or shake some manners into her.

She slapped her forehead with her palm. "Ooooh! Have you seen my sandals?"

When he didn't respond, she clicked her fingers at him. "Sandals. Where are they?"

"What are you babbling about, girl?"

She made no effort whatsoever to hide how unimpressed she was by his question. Most females in her situation would be watching their tongues, careful not to provoke him. He was, after all, very much larger and stronger than her. Not to mention it seemed to have escaped her that they were alone. With one very large bed.

"Typical bloody man," she muttered. "Incapable of thinking outside the square. Sandals. Dark purple strappy things? Heels about yay high?"

When he still didn't answer, she grimaced, stalked over to the bed, and crouched to peer under the coverlet. Her movements were slow and studied. Malach felt like he'd been dragged behind a horse, and he could only imagine how the severely the bonding spell must be affecting this delicately built girl. And when she straightened from her crouch gingerly, but without so much as a whimper, his estimation of her rose.

She checked inside the wardrobe.

"Bingo," she said, bending to scoop up a dainty piece of footwear. "Peter must be a neat-freak. Bet he makes the bed every morning and does the dishes before leaving his hotel room."

Malach hid a smile as her staunch façade cracked just a little and her hip-swaying gait turned into more of a stiff hobble as she headed into the kitchen area.

She fossicked in a drawer and came up with a knife.

He eyed the weapon and scanned her face for clues. He had known only one other woman of this era, and Francesca had shown no interest in weaponry—not even when he had first emerged from the crystal and scared her witless. From what he could discern from *this* young woman, he was in more danger of being lashed by her sharp tongue than stabbed the instant his back was turned. But then, females were wily creatures and it behooved a man to be on his guard.

Armed with one shoe and the knife, she confronted the

door.

"What are you planning?" he asked, curious.

"I'm going to use the heel of this sandal as a makeshift hammer while I try and pry up these hinges with the knife blade. Once I've removed the hinges, it should be a simple matter to open the door." She glared at him. "Why? Got a better idea? Because if you have, now's the time to speak up. Otherwise, shut up and let me work."

Malach sauntered over to observe the proceedings as she inserted the blade beneath the lip of the hinge, and tapped the knife handle with the heel of her sandal. It was a solid plan, and Malach had never hesitated to give praise where praise was due. Even hardened warriors responded better to syrup than vinegar. "I commend you for this idea, girl. There is some small chance the old man neglected to be-spell the hinges."

Tap. Tap. Tap. "Quit breathing over my shoulder, Mal. It's distracting." *Tap. Tap. Tap.* "And you don't have to sound so astonished that I had a good idea floating round in my tiny female brain."

He knew better than to stay close to an irate female with a potential weapon in her hand. He backed off and left her to her labors.

She sniffed. "And my name is Jade. Not 'girl'."

"Jade." He rolled the word around on his tongue. "Hmmm. I am thinking your name does not suit you overly well."

The tapping paused and she stiffened, her small body vibrating with outrage. "Not that I care what you think, but tough. That's my name: Jade. Set in stone. Like it or lump it." She blew her bangs out of her eyes and resumed pounding at the hinge.

Malach sighed. He hadn't meant to be insulting. He debated explaining what he knew of jade and its qualities, but thought better of it. Doubtless she would again take his explanation the wrong way, and bristle like a feral sand-cat protecting its kits.

It soon became obvious the hinges were not prepared to cooperate without considerable time and effort. "Let me try," he said.

"Be my guest." She handed over the knife and her makeshift hammer.

He positioned the blade and whacked the knife handle vigorously with her footwear.

"Please try not to damage my sandal. My mother got these for me in Hong Kong. They're not the real deal, of course. But they are really fine Manolo Bla—"

The heel of the sandal gave way. It dangled from the sole by a thin strip of leather.

He slanted her a glance over his shoulder. She'd pressed the heels of her hands to her eyes.

He tossed the sandal aside and snapped his fingers at her. "Bring me the other one."

If looks could kill, he'd be corpse-dust dancing on a desert breeze. "Why?" she snarled. "So you can destroy that one, too? Not effing likely. Use your own boot or something."

He clenched his jaw, praying for patience. "My boots are too big and unwieldy to be effective."

She glanced down at his feet. Her gaze skittered up his body to fix on his face. And even though he suspected it took every ounce of effort she could summon, she stared him down.

Admiration surged through him. And something else, too. Something that tightened his balls and made him want to snatch her up and kiss her breathless. And then lay her on the bed and make her his. He stalked away from her, needing space to wrestle his emotions into submission. He could ill afford to feel admiration or desire for this girl. He could ill afford to feel anything at all. He needed all his wits about him if he was to survive the magical trap in which the Crystal Guardian had ensnared them both.

"You could try sticking your head under the cold tap." Her musical voice followed him, and even though the tone was mocking, it stroked his skin and stoked his need. "With any luck it might drown your attitude."

A cold bath would be far more apt, he thought.

The tapping resumed, and from the ringing of metal on metal, Malach knew she'd resorted to whacking the hinge with the knife handle. Her muttered imprecations suggested this method wasn't working to her liking.

He retrieved the other sandal from the wardrobe and approached her. Warily.

She must have sensed his approach for she spared him a brief, ire-filled gaze. "Give me that," she said. "No way are you destroying that one, too."

He handed it over without a murmur, and kept his peace as she tapped doggedly at the hinge.

The minutes stretched. The hinge deigned to move all of a hair's breadth. From the tension in her shoulders, he knew her arms had started to ache.

"Allow me to take a turn," he said.

"No. I can do this." She tensed, as though waiting for him to elbow her aside and take over.

He sighed. "As you wish."

She whacked the knife handle with her shoe, and kept whacking until the heel started to come away from the sole. He opened his mouth to warn her but before he could utter a word, she tossed the knife aside and, with both hands, worked at the heel until it detached from the sole. Task complete, she crawled on all fours to retrieve the other sandal and yanked its dangling heel completely away from the sole, too. "Now I have a matching pair," she said.

To his chagrin, he glimpsed the sheen of tears in her eyes. And, given the way she clutched the footwear to her chest, they had been precious to her in some way. He'd known her only a short time, but she didn't strike him as the kind of female who wept over trivial things.

He thought back to her comments about the footwear. Ah.

"Your mother gave you those sandals."

She blinked rapidly to prevent the tears from falling. "Yes." Her lower lip wobbled. "She died not long afterward. Along with my dad. In a car crash."

"Then I am doubly sorry."

"They're fakes—not the real deal." She shrugged off his apology, refusing to reveal how much she was hurting to a stranger. To him.

"Jade—"

She cut him off with a sharp gesture and crawled to her feet, rubbing her back and neck, as she wandered over to the kitchenette. He knew it hurt her heart and her soul to deposit the now useless sandals in the bin. He wondered when she would give into her tears.

And how he would bear watching her cry.

He should have known better, for she came out fighting. "Peter, or Pieter, or whatever the heck your name is, if you don't come back and get me out of here right now, I'm gonna kick your bony old arse from here to fucking Perth! Do you hear me?" She heaved three deep breaths as she fought for control.

Malach tore his gaze from her breasts, so ripe and firm and high—breasts that begged a man to touch and to taste. He shrugged off her allure and took refuge in disapproval. "If you believe me impressed by such language," he said, "I would disabuse you of the notion."

"Like I give a crap about impressing *you*. I'd rather impress the bloody door." She stalked stiffly over to it, rucked her dress up her thighs, and kicked outward, snapping out her bare foot with toes bent back so as not to injure them when her foot connected with the door.

Twice more she smote the door. From her technique, and the resounding *thud!* each time her foot made contact, she'd obviously familiarized herself with some form of martial combat. "Now that, I am impressed by," he drawled.

She rounded on him, lips parted to cut him down to size. He deliberately slid his gaze to her bared thighs. And didn't attempt to hide his appreciation. The undergarments she'd flashed him were mere scraps of white lace. White. Such a virginal color. Such a lie.

She flushed pink as she let her skirt fall and smoothed it down her thighs. "Show's over. Listen up, Mal—"

"My true name is Malachite, after my crystal. Or Malach if you prefer. Not Mal."

"Whatever. I'm sure Peter thought he was doing me a really big favor by trading himself for you. But I assure you that despite his advanced years, I far prefer *him* to an egotistical jerk-off like you."

"Is that so?" Malach was tired of playing games. Too, he was tired of being manipulated and used—of having his hopes of salvation soar, only to be dashed. Sweet Mother of all gods he was tired. Pieter had hit upon the truth when he had accused Malach of courting death. One way or another, Malach wanted this travesty to end. Extracting the truth from this girl so he knew how best to handle her would be an excellent start.

Hands on hips she looked him up and down, and apparently found him lacking. "It is indeed so," she said, in a fair imitation of his voice.

By the gods, she tried his patience. He seesawed between wanting to throw her over his knee and paddle her behind, and wanting to throw her on the bed and have his way with her. If she knew how much he wanted her, how he ached to bury himself in her soft feminine flesh and feel her clenching around him, she would not be so eager to provoke him.

Or perhaps she would, given the pretext Pieter had used to bring her to this room—masquerading as a client responding to her advertisement. She was young, yes, but Malach had been propositioned by younger girls angling for the increased status of being Chosen by Lord Keeper Wulfenite's influential *tehun-*Leader, his right-hand man. And this girl was no innocent, trying out her feminine wiles for the first time, flirting and coaxing but not truly comprehending the trouble she might incite. *This* girl knew how to rouse a man's passions and make him willingly dip into his pockets to shower her with fripperies and coin.

Coin. Something Malach was sorely lacking at present. There was bound to be something of value he could offer her, however. Everyone had their price. "What did the old man have to promise to bring you here?" he asked.

Her beautiful, thickly lashed brown eyes flashed fury. "That, Mal, is none of your business."

His cock twitched. She was all heat and temper—an opposite to his coolly calm Francesca in every way.

"How many years do you have, girl?"

"What's it to you, boy?"

Heavy emphasis on *boy*. Apparently she believed two could play that game. His lips twitched. "Humor me. Or are you perhaps one of those annoying young females who coyly dissemble about their age, while seeking to entrap a man?"

"You insinuating I'm jailbait? Heck, you really know how to flatter a girl, don't you, Mal? I'm twenty, if you must know." Almost as an afterthought she murmured, "Twenty-one in a few weeks."

He cocked his head as he considered her surprising answer. "You appear at most no more than one *teh* and a half, though your attitude speaks a few extra years, perhaps."

She blinked at him. "Huh?"

"A *teh* has this many years." He held up the fingers of both hands.

"A decade. Why didn't you just say a decade? Hang on— you think I look *fifteen*? Sheesh! Just because I'm vertically challenged, doesn't mean I'm a kid. Don't they have short women where you come from?" She glared at him, and then muttered something about retracting the comment as it seemed conceivable his ancestors might well be descended from Amazons.

Rallying, she thrust back her shoulders and, for good measure, stuck out her lower lip. "Look, I'm an adult, okay? I might look younger than I truly am, but I'm fully capable of looking after myself. Got that, Mal?"

Malach sized her up. Based on her reaction, he guessed that all her adult life people had treated her as a child, subtracting years from her age and not taking her seriously because of her height and her delicate looks. And that it made her very irritated indeed. But regardless of her age, she'd been chosen for him, and if he was to have any chance at all of escaping his cursed crystal, he must finish the bonding process that Pieter had set in motion.

It would hardly be a chore to bed her. He would be lying if he claimed he didn't want her. Right now, however, he would wager sex was the last thing on her mind. He could change that, though. Easily.

"Hmmm." His gaze raked her from head to toe. "Yes. I have 'got that'. I see you are most definitely not a child."

He snaked out a hand, grabbing her waist and hauling her flush against him. He bent his head, and the instant he touched his lips to hers, Malach forgot all about holding himself apart, taking what he needed and not allowing himself to be vulnerable.

The heat between them flared. He lost himself in her. And, for a few blissful seconds, she lost herself in him, too.

"Mmmph!" She jerked back her head, but he clamped her nape with a hand and held her immobile. She kicked at him but he easily ignored the drumming of bare toes against his thighs. When she pummeled his chest with her fists, he backed her against the wall, pinning her. She was helpless. But he was helpless, too. Helpless to resist the allure of her.

When her lips softened, he licked the seam of her lips and coaxed them to open, to let him in. He stroked his tongue against hers, and when she responded he groaned, overcome with want and need.

He tore his mouth from hers. She stared at him, dazed. They were forehead to forehead, nose to nose, so close her eyes almost crossed when she tried to focus on him. "Wh-what the h-hell do you think you're d-doing?"

"Proving you will have more fun with me than with Pieter," he said, somehow managing to keep his voice steady.

"Let me go... you big... idiot!" Her breath sawed in and out of her chest.

"I intend to release you—once *you* let go of *me*." He allowed smug amusement to infuse his words.

"Wh-what do you mean?"

Smirking, he backed up a few steps, away from the wall, holding his arms out from his sides.

She glanced down. "What the—? Uh, how come I'm—? Oh. Ohhh!" She unlaced her hands from behind his neck. And when she finally became aware that her thighs were still wrapped around his waist, her cheeks flushed the shade of a ripe berry. She unclamped her legs and slid a little way down his body, stifling a squeak and reddening still more when the bulge of his leather-clad erection found a home between her spread thighs.

"Omigod. Omigod. Oh. My. God. I'm clinging to you like a randy monkey. One kiss and you've turned me into a raging slut. This is *so* not good." She wriggled and slid awkwardly to the floor. Yet again, she yanked down her dress, depriving him of another glimpse of smooth thighs that he would very much like to have wrapped around him again in the near future.

Her blush deepened, crawling down her neck. And the expression in her eyes....

Shame? He frowned. She did not act like a whore.

She speared trembling fingers through her hair and backed away, her gaze hunted. "Sure wish we could ring for—"

The panic rippling across her features receded, replaced by a triumphant grin that confused Malach still more. "Sorry to disappoint you, Mal," she said. "But I'm about to spring us from our cozy little prison. And once we're out of here, you can bugger off back to wherever, and maul some other girl."

He brushed past her, heading for the bed. "I believe I will take a nap until you get it through your pretty head that Pieter will not be so easily thwarted by a mere—" What was the device called again? Ah, yes. "Phone." He stretched out full-length on the mattress, linking his hands beneath his head and closing his eyes.

"Could have at least taken off your boots," he heard her mutter. And then, "The old guy's got some truly superb supernatural woo-woo going on, I'll give him that. But he can't keep us locked away in here against our wills. Not when we have a line to the outside world."

He slit his eyelids to watch the fun as she snatched the phone from the side table and pressed it to her ear.

"Huh. No dial tone." She replaced the phone in its cradle and picked it up again. She held it to her ear, scowled mightily, and then jabbed a few buttons. "Crap. Wonder if it could be the phone jack?"

She sank to all fours, and fiddled with a small white box fixed to the wall. When she picked up the receiver again and waited expectantly, Malach closed his eyes.

"I'm trying an outside line," she announced.

There was a tapping sound, doubtless caused by her jabbing fruitlessly at buttons again.

"Double crap. No sound. No connection. No nothing. Okay. Last try. Just to be totally sure, I'm going to ring the national emergency number."

Three jabs. A pause. And then a prolonged hiss as she hung up. "Okay, okay. You were right. He's jinxed the phone lines, too. Can't even call emergency services, so I sure hope we don't end up actually having one—an emergency, I mean. And so much for phoning room service for food. We'll have to hope the mini-bar will see us through until we find a way to get out of here."

"If I know Pieter, he will have arranged for sustenance to be provided whenever we are hungry."

"Well, I'm hungry *now*. So where's the food?"

Malach snorted.

"All right, all right. I guess food is the last thing on my mind right now. All this BS has put a temporary damper on my appetite."

He cracked an eyelid to observe her prowling up and down the rug beside the bed. She halted, and he guessed another possibility had occurred to her. "Maybe it's not as bad as we first thought," she said. "One of us is bound to get hungry soon, right?" She paused expectantly until he muttered an agreement and closed his eyes again.

"So all we have to do is stay alert until we hear room service knocking. And as soon as the hapless room-service attendant opens our door, we make a run for it. Easy-peasy, huh?"

"Perhaps. Although I am certain Pieter will have thought of that possibility, also."

"You think so?"

"I do indeed."

"Damn. I suspect you might be right." The eagerness had fled from her voice, leaving her sounding tired and defeated.

"I know one sure method of escaping this trap Pieter has devised for us," he said, opening both eyes, curious to observe her reaction to what he was about to propose.

"Oh? And what's that?"

"To do exactly what he wants."

"Which is?"

"For me to bed you."

Chapter Three

MALACH REMINDED HER of some large predator debating whether it was worth exerting himself to chase something down for dinner.

Jade backed away from him. And the bed. The farther from the bed, the better. Because when he'd kissed her, she'd been powerless to prevent her body responding and feeling things she'd only read about in books, or giggled about with her best friend. His kiss had sent a fiery ball of pure sensation pulsing through her body, resulting in damp panties and an unfamiliar throbbing between her legs. Imagining his lips pressed to hers again made her want to flee... and then beg him to chase her down and kiss her again. And even now, recalling how he had smelled—of oiled leather and exotic spices and something irresistibly male—made her head swim.

She swallowed, mouth dry, body yearning, reason warring with baser instincts... such as a wholly unfamiliar desire that could end up being her downfall if she gave in to it. "Y-You're kidding me, right?"

Malach only yawned and thankfully shuttered his compelling "come hither, little girl" gaze. "I am not making a joke."

Ulp. "Sex? With you? Peter wants me to... to...." Her throat constricted, forcing her to relax and breathe before she could speak again. "He wants us to have *sex* before we get out of here?"

Saying it aloud made it real. And she knew she couldn't allow it to happen. Sex with Peter might have been manageable—maybe, though that point was now obviously moot since Peter had made himself scarce. But sex with *Malach*? He was altogether another story, one rife with scary but oh-so-seductive consequences. She instinctively knew she wouldn't walk away from this man unscathed.

"Yes, that is correct. To be precise, three times. And then the bonding process will be complete."

She gaped at him. "Three times? You expect me to do you *three* times? I'm not inclined to do you *once*, Buster." A total lie, but he didn't have to know that. "And I'm damn sure not interested in being bound to you, so you can put that little BDSM fantasy right out of your head." She pinched the bridge of her nose. "Sheesh. I figured Peter was slightly off his rocker but this really takes the cake."

Malach yawned. "*Pieter*. His name is Pieter. But you can refer to him as the Crystal Guardian if you prefer."

"Well, *I* know him as Peter Stone."

"Peter Stone." He laughed but it wasn't a pleasant laugh. It trailed chills up and down her spine. "Ironic," he said, "considering Pieter's power over stones, and that *we* were once christened 'Stone Warriors' by your people. I've long suspected the old man of having a warped sense of humor."

Hang on…. Jade caught her bottom lip between her teeth. *Peter Stone*. She'd read somewhere that the name "Peter" was derived from a Latin word meaning "rock or stone". What parent in their right mind would call their kid "Rock Stone"? Hah. Obviously an alias. What a sucker she'd been.

Enough. Time for some answers. "What the hell is going on? Who exactly is this Crystal Guardian?"

Malach's eyelids snapped open again, and their pale blue depths sparked with heat and fury. "Who is he? He is the man who cursed my *tehun*—the men of my troop—to suffer an eternity in the crystals for which we are true-named. He is Pietersite, the Crystal Guardian, the man who holds our fate in his hands."

Jade stared at him, wide-eyed, mouth agape, until commonsense reasserted itself and full-blown, relieved laughter spilled from her. "Good one, Mal!"

Stony-faced, he regarded her until her laughter awkwardly trailed off into even more awkward silence. "All righty then. Guess you're not joking."

"No."

"Ooookay. Whatever." Surely Malach couldn't believe Pieter was some sort of supernatural guardian who'd trapped him in some hellish crystalline prison…. Could he?

How about what she'd sensed, though? That frightening, never-ending black abyss. Malach's terror and suffering—that had been real. She full-body shuddered, banishing the horror of that vivid memory to the deepest recesses of her mind where her worst nightmares lurked. A waking nightmare. That's all it had been—all it could have been. A bad dream to add to all the others she'd endured. Nothing more. It couldn't be real if she refused to believe in it.

If only there was another way to get the funds she needed for… for….

She dug her fingertips into her temples but try as she might, couldn't recall why she needed a lot of money, and fast. The reason was important, though, crucial—that much she did know. It niggled the edges of her mind. And then faded, overwhelmed by the mouthwatering vision of Malach stretched out on the bed, his hot gaze licking her from head to toe and making her knees feel like limp spaghetti. Another mental image formed in her mind. Malach and herself. Buck naked. Malach plunging himself into her willing flesh. Her kneading the hard planes of his muscular back and thrusting her hips upward, needy and wanting, urging him toward climax even as she teetered on the edge of her own.

The pure ecstasy, the sensual pleasure that consumed her vision-self's face, shocked Jade to the core. She clenched her jaw until it ached, willing the vision to fade. It was so *not* going to happen. Despite the heat pooling in her pelvis, the arousal dampening her panties, the throbbing ache of wanting more—of yearning to be filled and used by Malach's hard warrior's body—it was not going to happen.

She locked her traitorously weak knees and sought refuge in tight-lipped, clipped denial. "I'm not going to have sex with you. Not if you were the last man on earth, and our lives depended upon it. So if sex is what it takes to get us out of here, then we're both shit out of luck."

Malach's nostrils flared as though her arousal had perfumed the air. And then he narrowed his eyes and observed her minutely.

Jade fidgeted beneath that penetrating gaze. His eyes reminded her of an Arctic wolf's, pale but still so intensely blue that they shouldn't belong to any creature of this world. Alien and fey enough to pierce skin and bone and see right through to her soul. Please God, her lie wasn't glaringly obvious. She caught herself twisting the skirt of her dress between her fingers and shoved both hands behind her back.

"What were you planning on doing with Pieter in this room?" he asked. "Why did he bring you here?"

"Um, we... we had stuff to discuss. A-and we were going to order in some food. All very innocent." She felt the warmth of another blush painting her cheeks and silently cursed her inability to lie convincingly.

"Nothing Pieter has a hand in is ever innocent," Malach said. "How did he find you?"

"Cripes, you sound like a father reaming his teenage daughter about a potential date." Jade flopped into an armchair. It'd been one helluva day and she hurt all over. Well, except for her ache-free head, which had ceased pounding the moment Peter had touched it. A coincidence? Or was he really that good a spell-caster?

Good God. Spells. Curses. Supernatural woo-woo of the

worst kind. What had she gotten herself in to this time?

Exhaustion descended in a heavy, smothering wave. Right now, more than anything—well, except getting the heck out of this room and as far away from Malach as possible—she craved a warm bath, a glass of wine, and a good book. Oh, and some privacy. At a pinch, a nap would do. But no way was she going near that bed when Malach was draped all over it. That would be asking for trouble.

She shifted sideways in the chair and dangled her legs over its amply padded arm.

"How did he find you?" Malach demanded again.

"Peter—*Pieter*—rang me." After she'd placed a tasteful ad in the local newspaper, describing herself and subtly alluding to what she was offering. At least, she'd presumed it was a subtle allusion. Wasn't like she had experience in this sort of thing.

"We talked for a bit and he asked me to meet him," she continued. Hah. There'd been no "asking" on Pieter's part. He had *insisted*. Refused to take "no" for an answer. "Satisfied? Can we please drop the subject now?"

"Why did he ring you?"

Apparently not. She sniffed and folded her arms, laying on the snotty bitch routine as thick as she dared. "My relationship with Pieter is none of your concern."

Malach pushed himself up on his elbows until he could comfortably rest his shoulders against the bed's padded headboard. His gaze bored into hers, stripping her bare. Her stomach squirmed with unease and, dammit, something that felt suspiciously like anticipation.

"Anything Pieter does, and any female he chooses to spend time with, is of great concern to me."

"So he was lonely and thought spending the day with me might make him feel better. So what? Is that so wrong?" *Please don't blush. Please!*

"Interesting that he chose *you* to slake his desires."

Jade didn't appreciate the sneer that accompanied that statement. Nothing had been slaked. Not yet, anyway. And probably never would be, since it seemed unlikely that Peter—or *Pieter*, or whatever the heck his name was—would be returning to this room any time soon. "We had a *business* relationship, Mal. Nothing more. I needed money and Pieter needed—"

Actually, what the heck *had* the old guy needed? Obviously something more than merely an expensive whore. Jade pondered that for a moment. And didn't much like the conclusions she drew. She had a sneaking suspicion that she'd been used all right, just not at all in the way she'd expected.

"And Pieter needed?" Malach prompted.

"I don't know." She caught her lower lip between her teeth. How to put this delicately? "Companionship, perhaps?"

"Companionship."

Funny how the word didn't seem quite so innocuous on Malach's lips.

One eyebrow quirked upward and his lip curled. "Companions. Is that what you call prostitutes in this age?"

Jerk. He didn't have to be so mean about it. "Bloody rude, obnoxious pricks. Is that what they call men of *your* age?"

He opened his mouth—doubtless to spout some pithy retort that'd flay another layer from her dwindling self-esteem—so Jade rushed on before he could speak. "So what's with all the leather, Mal? You look like you've escaped from a male strip revue. Hmmm." She tapped her lip with a forefinger. "I reckon you'd do pretty well prancing 'round on stage, bumping and grinding for the ladies—even if you are getting a bit long in the tooth for that sort of thing."

There was a long pause while he processed her words. And if she'd expected outrage she was sorely disappointed.

"I am not some entertainer who removes his clothes in public for the pleasure of gawking females," he said, his tone dangerously mild.

"And I'm not a whore," she countered, swinging her dangling foot back and forth over the arm of the chair, her gaze fixed on her wiggling toes rather than the man before her.

Her swinging foot abruptly stilled. At least she wasn't a whore *yet*.

"Really," Malach muttered.

She darted a quick glance at him from beneath her lashes and found him staring at the ceiling.

Her stomach squirmed in an oh-my-God-he's-so-hot way. Despite his needling remarks, she was close to giving in and letting him have his wicked way with her. Too close. It was best to maintain at least the pretense of being in control. If he even suspected how much he affected her physically, it was all over.

She smiled sweetly at him, batting her eyelashes for good measure. "Frankly, Mal, I don't give a flying fuck about making things easy for you. Life's not easy. It's a bitch. And then you die."

He blinked, obviously shocked by her masterful command of the English language.

Excellent. Exactly the reaction she had hoped for.

Jade had learned years ago that foul language coming from someone who resembled a butter-wouldn't-melt-in-her-mouth little girl worked to her advantage—especially when some slime-ball mistakenly believed he had the right to feel her up because he fancied her, or believed a bunch of nasty rumors. Hit the douche-bag right between the eyes with some vile allusion to his parentage, and then beat a hasty retreat before he collected his jaw from the floor. Worked every time.

"It's like this, Mal. If you trade insults with me, you'll lose. Even though I'm a girl, I have a brain, and it's connected directly to my mouth—which I'm not afraid to use."

Malach's lips twitched ever-so-slightly upward before he schooled his expression to blankness. "I have noticed that about you."

"Really. Want to play some more? Or shall we turn our minds to something more productive, like getting out of here sometime this century."

"I have already told you how we will escape this place."

"Right. The screw-me-three-times-for-luck scenario. Yeah, how can I say this politely?" She paused for dramatic effect. "No."

"Not even if I assure you I am not lying in some misguided attempt to compromise your dubious virtue?"

"No. *Not even.*"

"Not even if Pieter has the power to keep us here for twenty-eight full days, to give us every opportunity of bonding as potential soul mates?"

Bonding? Soul mates? No way. There would be no bonding. Not with Malach. Not with any man. "Surely you realize by now that 'no' is actually a complete sentence? Well, it is. So, no."

"And what of me, Jade? You were linked to me for a time before you called me from the crystal. You experienced a little of what I suffered. Are you so willing to condemn me? Are you that heartless?"

He had her there. The suffering part, at least. Jade wasn't certain about the rest of it but *that* had certainly been real. "Sex is not the answer," she said. "It never is. And call me heartless but I am absolutely not having sex with you. There has to be another way."

"Why?" He crossed his arms over his chest.

She tried her best to ignore the way his biceps rippled. She itched to run her hands over those steely-hard bulging muscles, to squeeze and stroke and explore them. To explore him.

Focus, Jade!

"Uh, why?" Her voice was little more than a squeak. She cleared her throat. "How about because I don't know you from a bar of soap. And I have no burning desire to get to know you in any way at all, let alone in a biblical way. Don't take this wrong, Mal, but you just don't do it for me. You're not my type. Sorry."

He smiled. A sexy, predatory smile that sent all her hormones into orbit. A smugly knowing smile that suggested he knew she was lying through her teeth. "I believe you were prepared to bed Pieter for payment," he drawled. "What if I, too, offered to compensate you? Would I perhaps then be 'your type'?"

Jade stifled a whimper. Change of subject needed STAT. "Do you even have any money on your person, Mal? I don't think I see a pocket in those leather pants you've somehow managed to pour your butt into."

"I have no coin suitable for use in this world. But I have other things to offer."

Her insides melted. "Like what?" Crap! She hadn't meant to ask that question aloud. "Uh, I mean, I don't want anything you're offering."

Liar! The room seemed to shriek the word. So did his knowing expression. The sexual heat emanating from him smacked her, mingling with her own desire and provoking certain portions of her anatomy to clench and quiver. She fought the instinct to flee to the bathroom and lock herself in. Because to get to the bathroom, she would have to go past him. He could easily launch himself from the bed and grab her, and if he touched her again, she would be lost. If he kissed her again, she'd let him do whatever he wanted, because secretly, she wanted it too.

Satisfaction gleamed in his eyes.

Damn. If he guessed even a fraction of how she was feeling, how much she wanted him, it would make her humiliation a million times worse.

Hot tears pricked her eyes. She ducked her head, letting her hair swing across her cheek to hide her expression. How could her body betray her like this? How could she want him so badly? How could she want a guy she'd just met, a guy with an ego the size of Ayers Rock and some serious fashion issues to boot, to strip off her clothes and screw her 'til she screamed for mercy? Not to mention he was seriously deluded, what with the whole "I have no coin suitable for use in this world" stuff. Did he imagine he came from another planet or something?

And if all that wasn't bad enough, he had to be pushing forty—far too old for her. What the heck was wrong with her?

She tugged on the ends of her hair. She still couldn't recall why she needed money but it had to be for something important or she'd never have even considered trading sex for cash. And it was glaringly obvious Malach had no cash, and doubtless harbored fond delusions his sexual prowess would be payment enough. Still she wanted him, *craved* him.

Maybe you'll end up having the best sex you'll ever get. Maybe he'll dispel your fears once and for all. Take a risk, Jade. Take a chance. What have you got to lose?

What did she have to lose?

Only her virginity and—

A young girl's face shimmered in her mind's eye. She was so pale and wan that it tore Jade's heart to shreds. *Who—?*

The elusive memory vanished.

Jade pinched the bridge of her nose until her eyes watered. What the hell?

Stress. Yeah, that had to be it. God knew she had enough going on right now to warrant that excuse.

Repressed sexual tension? Perhaps. Her best friend Grace had always warned that suppressing her libido would come back and bite her in the bum. According to Grace, women were made for sex with real live men, and shouldn't rely on supercharged vibrators with buzzing wiggly protrusions designed to get them off in a couple of minutes flat. Not that Jade even owned a supercharged vibrator. Or any vibrator at all, for that matter.

She slumped, resting her cheek against the brocade fabric of the chair. She could almost hear Grace saying, "Go on. Since you're stuck here, you might as well indulge in a little harmless fun. And he sure looks like he knows how to please a girl."

She eyed Malach from beneath the curtain of her hair. Mmm. He sure gave the impression he was, uh, *experienced.*

"I do not think it will take much effort on my part to change your mind."

Malach's voice coated her in a warm, sensual haze. She sucked in a shaky breath, drawing his potent gaze to her breasts. Her nipples tightened and her stomach gave a funny little lurch.

He seemed keen as mustard to have his wicked way with her. All she had to do was give in and—

Jade abruptly recalled the last time a guy had been mad keen to screw her. And boy, did that memory pour ice-cold water on her steaming hot libido. Again.

Murray "The Muz" Blackwood, über-jock and most popular boy in school, had turned out to be an über-jerk who'd refused to take "No!" for an answer until Jade had followed it up with a swift punch on the nose. She'd followed *that* up by jumping out of his car, and high-tailing it all the way to Grace's house.

She had confessed all, and then sworn Grace to secrecy. She'd believed that would be the end of it. Hah. How naïve she'd been.

Grace reckoned Jade shouldn't judge all men by that one disastrous encounter, but every time Jade found a partner she believed she could go all the way with, she would reach a certain point and see *that* face again. Murray Blackwood. Blind-eyed with lust as he clamped a hand over her mouth and tried to force her thighs apart. She would close her eyes and see his sneer, hear his insults, inhale the sour smell of his arousal and relive the shame. And she would back off and run away. Again.

That encounter had been five years ago. Five whole years. So why did the terror of that almost-rape, the humiliation of the aftermath, when Murray had spread the lies that had made her a pariah, still haunt her dreams?

The irony that she, a woman more often than not scared off by the mere thought of sex, was now seriously contemplating exchanging sexual favors for money, wasn't lost on her. Desperation was a powerful motivation.

A harsh realization smacked her upside the head. Murray had won. By not allowing another man to get close to her, she'd let him win. Hell, she'd let his actions color every one of her life choices up until this very moment.

Jade had never believed she was a coward, but she understood now that she was. And it was no way to live. Well, no more. She could turn the tables right here, right now. She had been prepared to let men use her body in return for cash, but she could use them, too. It was a win-win situation.

"Jade?"

The concern in his voice shocked her. As did the fact that she sensed him standing beside her chair when she hadn't heard him move.

She blotted her tears with the heels of her hands and lifted her head to confront him, refusing to hide anymore. "You were right," she told the big man staring down at her with what she could have mistaken for a worried frown if she didn't know better.

"Right about what?"

"If all it takes to get us out of here is sex, I can do that. It's just sex, after all—nothing too life changing. Of course, if you're hungry, we can always eat first and screw later. It's all the same to me."

He rocked back on his heels, lips slightly parted, the tension thrumming through him palpable. She watched him struggle to recover his equilibrium. And when he'd done so, he didn't lunge for her and sweep her off her feet to toss her on the bed, as she'd expected. A pity. Because that would have saved her from having to think too hard about what she'd just committed to.

Instead, he stood there, waiting for something. Waiting for—

Waiting for her to make the first move.

It's just sex. It's just sex. It's. Just. Sex. Nothing to worry about. Lots of people do it. Nothing to it. Right?

Right. As Jade crawled from the chair to stand on shaky legs, her stomach audibly rumbled. God, she would kill for chocolate right now. She had a feeling she would need the energy.

Mere seconds later, there was a loud rap on the door. And then a cheery feminine voice called, "Room service!"

Chapter Four

Malach sprinted for the door and yanked on the handle. Jade gasped. Wonder of wonders, the door opened.

The twenty-something room service attendant froze, her practiced smile faltering. Jade didn't blame her, what with coming face-to-face with an extremely large man dressed like the hero of some B-grade sci-fi flick and all. And then the young woman's hesitant smile segued into something wholly appreciative and blatantly flirtatious.

Jade curled her lip with wry amusement. Obviously she wasn't the only one affected by Malach's undeniable masculine presence. Being close to him—heck, being in the same room with him.... He possessed some indefinable quality that made women ultra-aware of their femininity.

"Good afternoon, sir." The woman caught Jade's expression and toned down the flirt. "Ma'am."

"Who ordered this food?" Jade asked.

"Mr. Stone rang the order through earlier."

"Oh, right. Silly me. Of *course* he did. I'd forgotten."

"Where would you like these, ma'am? Dining table or coffee table?"

"Er... dining table, please," Jade said. The woman would have her back to the door when she deposited the tray. Better to be safe than sorry if some weird woo-woo stuff happened when they fled the room.

Malach stepped aside to let the young woman pass.

Jade sidled toward him. She kept one eye on the woman, trying her best not to signal anything was amiss, or give the impression she was about to bolt.

Malach stepped toward the threshold.

What happened next might have been comical if it hadn't been so damned frustrating and a whole lot scary. Malach lifted his foot to take his first step outside the room, and the instant before his boot contacted the corridor's carpet, he was back inside the hotel room. He tried again and the same thing happened. In the blink of an eye, he was instantly transported from one spot to the next.

Jade glanced at the room service waitress. The young woman's back was still turned while she fussed with plates and serviettes. Good enough. Although Jade sincerely doubted she would succeed where Malach had failed, she had to try.

She pushed past him and darted out the door.... Only to find herself standing inside the hotel suite again.

She didn't bother with a second attempt. What the hell was the point? She confined herself to cursing beneath her breath.

The young woman turned to her with a smile. "Will there be anything else, ma'am?"

"Would you mind checking the phone? It didn't seem to be working earlier on."

The woman dutifully picked up the receiver and tested it by ringing Reception. "It seems to be working fine, now. Anything else you'd like me to do for you, ma'am?"

"No, thanks. You've been very helpful." Jade summoned a smile, even though she truly felt like shrieking and banging her fists against the wall. She eyed the closing door as the woman exited the room, and lunged before it could shut completely. When the woman's footsteps had faded from earshot, Jade let the door click shut and immediately yanked on the handle again. No joy. It was locked.

Malach shouldered her aside, grabbed the door handle, and

gave it a fierce tug that should have pulled the door from the frame and had it crashing down on top of them. He muttered a filthy-sounding oath when the door refused to budge.

Jade stalked over to the phone and lifted the receiver. Dead, of course.

Bloody Pieter. The old bugger really did have them both at his mercy. Oh well, at least she wouldn't have to fume on an empty stomach. She lifted the fancy stainless steel cover from one of the plates and discovered a huge, gourmet steak sandwich complete with chunky potato wedges. "Reckon this must be yours, Mal. Hope so, anyway. I'm not in the mood for a monster slab of cooked cow."

Thankfully, the other cover revealed far more appetizing ham, cheese and pineapple toasted sandwiches cut in dainty triangles. Comfort food. How typical that the old man would know she could do with a heaping of comfort right now.

She retired to the couch and stretched out to eat. And think. There had to be a way out of this mess. Although… the having sex with Malach option was looking more and more, uh, *appetizing*.

She glanced at him. He'd given up glaring at the door and now sat at the dining table, chowing down on his sandwich. The man had some appetite. Unsurprising, given how much of him there was to feed.

By the time Jade finished her last sandwich she had made up her mind. Sex. With this sexy man. Right now. Her aches and pains were forgotten as she contemplated running her palms over his superbly muscled chest, imagined his abs rippling beneath her fingers. Her body had already begun to react to her fantasies with a languorous relaxing of muscles and fears, readying her for whatever came next. Whatever he might choose to do to her.

"So, Mal." She eased from the couch and stretched. And then she sauntered over to him, planting herself firmly beside his chair, waiting until he finally deigned to look up from his meal and notice her.

She gazed into his eyes. Her heart thudded and her pulse galloped. Fear and anticipation. Wanting, and a need so intense that she ached. She forced herself to moisten her lips with her tongue and smile beguilingly. "Let's screw like bunnies and get this over with."

He stood, pushing back his chair with such force it toppled to the floor.

Points to her. She'd shocked him. Again.

She worked her palm beneath his leather vest and ran her fingertips over the flat disc of his nipple. She tweaked it. He drew in a harsh, ragged breath, and she basked in a wholly feminine delight that she could provoke such a response from him.

He grasped her hand, gently but forcibly removing it from his chest, denying her further exploration. But before she could muster a protest, he grabbed her beneath her armpits to lift her until they were face-to-face. "What do you want from me, girl?"

"My name is *Jade*. And, as I was saying before the food arrived and we discovered we couldn't leave this darn hotel room, I want you to screw me. Is that okay with you, Mal? That's what you said Pieter wanted. That's what you suggested we do. So that's what we'll do." Her voice shook. It was damn hard to maintain her composure when her feet were dangling more than a few inches from the ground.

As if he'd read her mind, and wanted to emphasize her helplessness, he shook her lightly. "What is your game, Jade?"

"Game?" Her voice had been reduced to that annoying little squeak again. She cleared her throat. Her heart pounding in her chest made her dizzy, and the need thrumming through her veins made her reckless. "I'm not playing games. I'm willing to have sex with you. It won't cost you anything, either. Consider this your lucky day."

The words streamed from her mouth as though her brain

had somehow switched the process of breathing to babbling. "And isn't it better to have me willing and not putting up a fight? Not that I'd have much of a show defending myself against a hoary great, uh, strapping male like yourself, but there's always a chance I might land a good kick to your balls and render you, uh, incapable of... of... *performing*. So this is better. Safer. For you. Aren't you pleased I've decided to be so... so... um, accommodating?"

"An interesting proposition. What has changed your mind, Jade?"

"Ah, I couldn't resist you any longer. I have to have you for, uh, my sanity's sake. Wanting you is... is... driving me wild." God. She royally sucked at talking dirty. Was she laying it on too thick? Surely not. He was a man. Deep down they all believed themselves irresistible.

"So you lied when you said I had nothing to offer you. You do want me."

Jade inwardly cringed. Surely he didn't have to be convinced that she *liked* him before he'd screw her. How sad was that?

Well, actually it was rather sweet. It meant he had morals—of a sort. She realized he was waiting for a response. "Um, yes?"

"Prove it."

"Um...." Oh, God. This was going to get embarrassing in a big hurry. "Take me, baby," she cooed for all she was worth. "I'm sooo hot for you." She half-closed her eyelids, attempting a sultry, totally overcome by passion expression, and trying not to think too hard about how Malach's big hands were so very close to her breasts. How his touch warmed her skin. How much she craved that touch.

She dared a peek beneath her lashes at his expression.

Impassive. Oh. Okay. More dirty talk required. "I-I want you to lay me back on that big comfortable bed and stroke my body all over. Slowly. From head to toe. With your fingers and your mouth. Um, y-you can even use your tongue, if you like."

There. That ought to do it.

She peeped at him again.

No? Really? Sheesh.

She managed a shaky breath, refusing to dwell on how effortlessly he held her, as though she were feather-light… or how heat zinged through her veins at the mere thought of his hands stroking her bare skin.

"I want you. I want your cock inside me." That had to sound convincing—had to, because it was the truth. And then her brain caught up with her mouth and it occurred to her to wonder how big a cock he possessed. Because if the size of his hands and feet were any indication, then maybe this wasn't such a great idea after all. Maybe she should—

And then it was too late for thought. He hitched her up until he could secure an arm beneath her butt. One palm splayed across her back to urge her firmly against him. His mouth sought hers and his lips worked their subtle magic, first nibbling, then pressing harder, enticing her to open her mouth and let him in.

Her breath caught. The room swam before her eyes, the subtle pattern decorating the walls cavorting in a gleeful celebration of surrender. *Her* surrender. Her eyelids drifted closed, shutting out reality, protecting her from consequences…. For now.

He nuzzled the sensitive spot beneath her ear. "I commend you on a convincing performance." His warm breath on her skin elicited a shiver. "A pity I do not believe a single word that falls from your pretty lips."

Jade blinked, trying to focus on his words rather than the sensory havoc his caresses were wreaking on her body. "Y-you don't?"

"Nay. But it matters not whether I believe what you say when your body tells a different tale. We are caught in Pieter's web, you and I. And sex is the only way I know to ease this unholy spell that consumes our rational thoughts and spurs us to incautious acts."

His words cannoned through her brain. "You truly believe we're acting this way because of some spell Pieter supposedly cast?"

"I *know* it to be true. I witnessed him cast that spell. I felt its power engulf me and transport me to *Halja*—what you call Hell. I have suffered the consequences of its casting." He shifted her in his arms.

She glanced to one side and realized that he'd moved to the edge of the bed. The stark reality of what was about to happen slammed her. Yikes. She was finally going to have sex. On a bed and everything. With an extremely large, extremely strong, extremely hot stranger... who believed he only wanted sex with her because of a spell.

Jade's *sang froid* cracked. She prayed her voice wouldn't hint at her inner turmoil. "I'm trying my best here but I still don't get it. Why on earth would Pieter go to all the effort of casting a spell simply to make us want to have sex?"

"Pieter's spell is far more complicated than that. 'Tis a curse that imprisons me—and the other members of my *tehun*—in our namesake crystals, until such time as we are each bonded to the women destined to free us."

Back to that again. Oookay. "And this bonding happens how?"

"Simply put, 'tis initiated after the third act of sexual intercourse."

Jade blinked at him. "So doing the wild thing three times will set them—and you—free from your cursed crystals?"

"If the bonded couple subsequently pass the Testing, yes."

"Riiight. Who is Pieter trying to kid?"

"The Crystal Guardian is very serious indeed. As I have learned to my cost." He shook her gently. "Are you a simpleton? Have you not truly understood *anything* that was discussed these past few hours?"

Understanding was one thing. Wholeheartedly believing was quite another.

Jade decided it was time to rethink her options. Escaping to the bathroom was looking like a damn fine option right now. She wriggled in Malach's arms but there was no escaping him. She would have to wait until he put her down to make a run for it.

"Here's the thing, Mal. I'm pretty open-minded about supernatural stuff. An old friend of my mother's happens to be a witch. So I do believe in magic spells and the power of curses suchlike. And it appears Pieter's quite a powerful witch. Or warlock. Or whatever he wants to call himself. So a sex spell sounds doable, okay? But imprisoning a man inside a hunk of rock? Come on, let's get real here."

He began a soft chant. "Verily the crystal for which thee be named/ Shalt form the prison in which thee be bound/ To atone the sins for which thee be blamed/ 'Til thee be blessed and thy true love be found."

The words burrowed into her brain, etching themselves indelibly into her memory. Flashbacks of another time slashed through her mind. She saw another place, an alien countryside that was not her own. She saw a warrior garbed for battle mounted on a huge warhorse. His men fanned out behind him. They exuded menace. Their mouths were set in grim lines, their expressions merciless.

And was that—? Yes, it was Malach, the oldest of the assembled warriors.

Jade's consciousness focused on a prepubescent girl. The child's small body quaked. She feared for someone she loved. An old man—Pieter was his name. Her grandfather. The same man now facing down the marauders, forbidding them from entering the village. And somehow, Jade became that girl-child....

AMIE SLIPPED FROM her ma's arms and ran to help Grandda'.

She heard Ma shriek. "Amie, no!"

Amie ignored her mother and planted herself at Grandda's side. She put her fists on her hips, like Ma did when she was cross. "Don't speak to me grandda' like that, ye big bully!" she said, in her loudest grown-up voice. "Go 'way and leave us be!"

One of the mounted warriors, the flaxen-haired one who was the most handsome man Amie had ever seen, snickered.

The big warrior who was the leader snarled like a wolf. "Silence!" And then he glared at her with his strange sky-blue eyes.

"The girl-child is comely," he said, and Amie shivered when she realized he was talking about her. "Too, she shows no fear. When she comes of age, I will honor her courage by bidding for her on the Choosing Block. You show courage also, old man, so to appease this child of your blood I will spare your life."

"My life is already forfeit. But not to you Lord Keeper Wulfenite," Grandda' said.

The big warrior's eyes went very wide.

Amie's heart went pitter-patter in her chest. Grandda' had scared him! Maybe now he'd go away, and take his men with him. She stifled a moan as the warrior kneed his horse forward.

The horse shied and the warrior had to yank on the reins to control it. His men moved restlessly behind him. Maybe they were scared, too. Amie hoped so. If they were scared, it would make it easier for her grandda' to beat them.

"Much good knowing my true name will do you, old man," the warrior said. "If you insist on resisting us then so be it. The earth will drink your foolish old blood as readily as it does that of younger men."

Amie's hand flew to her mouth. What a wicked man! Her gaze darted to Grandda, but he only smiled back at her, and whispered, "You are a brave girl, my Amie. And I thank you for standing by me. Now off back to your mother. Tell her I said not to scold you too much once she recovers from her fright."

Amie did as she was bid, racing back to her ma. Ma held her tight, almost smothering her, but Amie twisted around to watch her grandda'.

He raised his hands to the skies and began to chant. "Verily the crystal for which thee be named/ Shalt form the prison in which thee be bound/ To atone the sins for which thee be blamed/ 'Til thee be blessed and thy true love be found."

The big warrior threw back his head and laughed. "Blessed? What nonsense is this, old man? Mayhap you are addle-brained, yes? Warriors such as we have no need of blessings. And as for true love? Bah. 'Tis naught but a woman's fantasy."

All the pretty stones Grandda' had set in a circle around him began to glow. The clouds turned black and the sky darkened. Lightning flashed. And then strangely colored beams shot up from the stones, making rainbows in the sky.

"What sorcery is this?" the oldest warrior asked. He was a grim-faced older man who kept to the lead warrior's right side.

Amie's gaze darted to the other men. They all looked scared. She smiled, hugging herself. She'd told her mother not to be scared, that Grandda' would protect them from these wicked marauders.

Grandda' sang a spell. "Kyanite, Malachite, Shattuckite, Okenite, Danburite. The stone thee be named for shall bind thee. I, Pietersite, bind thee."

There was a flash of light, and the sky rumbled like it was answering her grandda's song. Amie rubbed her eyes. The handsome flaxen-haired warrior, the older man, and three of the other warriors had vanished. And five of the stones were glowing. She gasped. Grandda' had sent the wicked men into the stones!

The big warrior—the leader—had heard one of his men shout and turned toward the sound. But before he could say or do anything, Grandda' named the other warriors and sucked them all into the stones.

The sky rumbled again. Amie felt her ma shiver. And then Ma shrieked with fear as the big warrior bellowed and drew his sword. He yanked his horse around to face Grandda' again, and charged at him.

Amie wanted to close her eyes but she kept them open. Grandda' had said she was brave, and brave girls didn't close their eyes to shut out the scary things.

The warrior raised his sword. Amie bit her lip against a whimper because Grandda' didn't run or try to hide as the sword came down on him. "Wulfenite," he roared, "the stone thee be named for shall bind thee. I, Pietersite, bind thee!"

The flash almost blinded Amie. And when she could see properly again, the big warrior had vanished and his sword lay on the ground....

JADE JOLTED BACK to the present. She lay on the bed in the hotel suite with Malach's body covering hers—protecting her. Or perhaps preventing her from escaping.

"You saw what happened in a vision," he said.

She nodded.

"And you believe what you saw."

It wasn't a question. She caught her lower lip between her teeth. Did she believe what she had seen? Could she believe it?

"Malachite," he whispered. "The stone thee be named for shall bind thee. I, Pietersite, bind thee. And thus I was bound, to suffer an eternity in my namesake crystal."

She shuddered, wrung out from the emotion of the shared experience, her body acknowledging the truth of her vision even as her brain fought to reject what she'd seen. She let her head loll to one side, unwilling to meet his eyes, and her gaze locked upon the broken crystal pieces nestled on Pieter's gold silk scarf. Her stomach flipped. "Th-th-that's the crystal? *Your* crystal?"

He twisted, following her gaze. "Yes. That is the crystal he used to imprison me."

"It's a malachite crystal, isn't it?"

"Yes."

She felt his gaze fix on her again and the magnetic pull of him surged through her. She became hyper-aware of his big body pressing hers into the mattress, of her thighs spread wide to accommodate him. Of her vulnerability.

She gulped. "So it's true? All of it? Everything?"

"Yes."

"And Pieter's the bad guy in all of this?"

"Not entirely."

She waited for him to elaborate but no further explanation was forthcoming. "And me?" she asked. "What's my role in this, Malach?" She couldn't demean him by calling him "Mal". Not anymore. After what she'd seen he deserved a measure of her respect.

"Your role? We shall have to wait and see what the future holds, Jade. But for now—" He cradled her face in his palms and kissed her, coaxing her lips to open, stroking her tongue with his. The heat of his body melted her apprehension, her fears and distrust of men, leaving only desire.

He pulled back to tuck a lock of her hair behind her ear, giving her time to catch her breath… and to pretend his kiss hadn't affected her as deeply as it had. If she was lucky, she might eventually hear something other than the furious pounding of her own heart. Give her a few more moments and she might be able to form real words, too.

His gaze settled on the pendant now nestled in the hollow of her throat. "Green jade," he murmured, fingering the stone. "A nice example of the stone, too."

"It's real jade? Are you sure?" She'd spotted the pendant at a market and bought it on impulse. Given its cheap price, she'd figured it was merely a pretty green stone. She squinted at the piece of jade, thankful for a reason to tear her gaze from

Malach's face and concentrate on something other than him.

"I am sure." He laid the pendant back against her breastbone. His fingertips drifted over her cleavage, sliding over the silky material of her dress to caress the swell of her breast.

Her breath hitched. "I-I didn't know what it was."

"Jade has some interesting properties."

"Oh?"

"'Tis a symbol of purity and serenity. Our priests claim 'tis a dreaming-stone which, when placed on the forehead, brings insightful dreams. It integrates mind with body, promotes self-sufficiency, releases negative thoughts and soothes the mind. I do not believe it suits you well, however."

"Yeah? The purity thing, right? Thanks a lot." Enough. If he didn't want to sleep with her because he believed she was sullied and impure, then he could go screw himself three times and see if *that* worked.

She tried to push him away and failing that, attempted to knee him in the balls. He merely pinned her arms with his hands and trapped her flailing legs beneath his. "I believe *red* jade is more your match," he said.

She glared at him. "Red jade? Never heard of it."

"'Tis said that red jade is passionate and stimulating. 'Tis associated with love, and aids the release of tension in *constructive* ways." He eyeballed her until she quit struggling. "Discounting all mention of love, shall we see how passionate and stimulating you are, Jade?"

"I-I.... Um... I don't think—"

"Now is not the time for thinking, but for feeling. What was it you said to me? Ah, yes. I am going to lay you back on this big comfortable bed and stroke your body, Jade. From head to toe. Slowly. With my hands and my mouth. And yes, even my tongue. I am going to make you beg for mercy. What say you to that, Jade?"

She couldn't bring herself to say anything at all. She stared helplessly at him—enthralled. And wondered if she would survive whatever he planned to do to her with her soul intact.

So much for her hastily donned veneer of sexual experience. It'd just shattered into itty bitty pieces.

Despite being as inexperienced as a woman could possibly be, not to mention weak from anticipation and a healthy dose of trepidation, she wanted Malach so badly she was already wet and ready for him. God. If he knew how much she wanted him it would give him far too much power over her. And the mere thought of a man like Malach wielding such power scared her spitless.

IF NOT FOR the vision of his past that had so disturbed her, Malach believed Jade would have drawn out her game a while longer. A woman of her ilk, so skilled in enticing a man while playing the innocent, could lead him on until the poor bastard knew not whether he was coming or going. Females like Jade enjoyed the power they had over men, leading them 'round by their cocks, one minute willing, the next pretending outrage at the very liberties they had encouraged.

In another time, in another place, he would have enjoyed the game, enjoyed the chase, and reveled in the opportunity to prove that, ultimately, it was *he* who controlled the game.

He supposed he should be grateful she had capitulated so easily, and they could now get this deed done. The sooner he fucked her the requisite three times, the sooner they could be free of this place and he could begin preparing for the Testing.

But as much as Malach told himself he wanted it over and done with, he couldn't deny the intensity of his body's reaction when he'd kissed her. She had been all petal-soft lips, and heated need and want that had begged him to nibble and lick and tease until she yielded. And when she'd opened her lips, and let him possess her mouth, dueled with his tongue while her pale skin flushed beneath his touch, she had almost stripped him of all control.

Almost, but not quite. He had her measure. She was a potent little package of seductive wiles—a consummate actress. He could have parted her thighs and rutted with her like a drunken bore who didn't know a female's quim from her arse. And she would have moaned and writhed and whispered in his ear that he was the best she'd ever had. He knew this, and yet still he wanted to take her slowly. He wanted to lick and stroke her until she quivered and sighed beneath his touch. He wanted to tease her and incite her, work her into a lust-fueled frenzy and make her come again and again, watch her lose control again and again until, finally, before he possessed her body he could see the true Jade, stripped of all pretense.

He stared down at her and refused to acknowledge the vulnerability and fear and longing lurking in her beautiful eyes. He refused to acknowledge those emotions because then he would have to acknowledge that deep down, he, too, suffered similar afflictions.

Malach could not afford to give Jade the upper hand. He could not afford to worry about whether he had misjudged her, or what she might want or need. Once, long ago, he had put his life in the hands of another woman from this world and where had it gotten him? A second sojourn in *Halja*, praying to Pieter's vengeful goddess to take pity on him and put an end to his suffering.

He would not allow it to happen again.

Chapter Five

MALACH HAD RAISED his torso, propping himself up on one elbow to worry at the bow of Jade's halter. When the bodice loosened, he pushed the fabric down to her waist, baring her breasts. He gazed at her, his scrutiny so intent that heat flared in her cheeks.

Embarrassed, she tried to roll over and hide herself from him, but he clamped her shoulders with his big hands and leaned in to whisper, "Do not act the shrinking virgin. We both know the truth of what you are."

Whore.

The unspoken word sliced into her soul. She squeezed her eyes tightly shut against the injustice of the label. But, then again, it was the truth, wasn't it? Before, she'd been preparing to barter sex for money. Now she was bartering sex for the chance to escape this bizarre prison… and the hope that she could finally put the past behind her.

Wet warmth laved her nipple, teasing it erect. Suction, hard and uncompromising… alternating with teeth that nibbled and then gently bit. Fierce pleasure shot to her loins. She gasped and involuntarily arched her back, pressing her breast deeper into his mouth.

He switched to the other breast, his clever tongue enticing tiny whimpers from between her tightly clamped lips. Then rough, callused fingers replaced his mouth. He rolled her nipples between his fingertips, tweaking and playing with them, before finally palming her breasts in his big hands.

He moved down her body, stripping off her dress, pressing his lips to each inch of newly exposed skin. Until, finally, the only barrier remaining was her panties.

Jade opened her eyes to stillness, and glanced down the length of her body to discover Malach sitting back on his heels. His eyes were distant. He seemed to be staring through her, as though....

As though some other woman lay in her place.

Francesca.

The woman's name floated through Jade's mind. And she knew from the hollow expression in his eyes, the flat, tight line of his lips, that Malach still mourned her.

Disappointment lanced through her soul, and hard on its heels came a wash of pity. He couldn't bring himself to forget this woman, this Francesca. And who was she, Jade, to make him? There was sexual attraction between them, sure. But no matter how intense that attraction, there was nothing more. They were both using each other. And after the using was over and done with, they would both still be hurting.

Jade levered herself into a seated position, figuring she might as well have a go at opening the dratted door again. Her movements yanked Malach back to the here-and-now and his hungry gaze locked onto hers. "Where do you think you are going?"

"Um, you kinda don't seem to be in the mood anymore? So I thought I'd— Eep!"

He ripped her panties from her body, spread her thighs, and buried his face between them. "Hey!"

His fingers parted her labia.

"What do you think you're— Aaahhh!" His tongue flicked the nub of her clit, sending electric-hot currents of pleasure spiking down her spine and through her pelvis. He teased her flesh, licking and nuzzling and sucking until she collapsed back onto the mattress, her rubbery muscles unable to hold her upright any longer.

One of his long fingers speared the heated slickness of her pussy, pressing deep, joined by another finger thrusting in and out, giving her a taste of what her body craved.

She fisted the coverlet, clutching it and clenching her jaw so as not to scream. She writhed beneath his tongue, her head thrashing from side to side and her breath coming in short sharp pants, interspersed with tiny mews of pleasure. She couldn't control her body—her reactions to everything he was doing to her, making her feel. She was shivering on the verge of climax when Malach lifted his head.

"You liked that." His breath tickled the sensitive skin of her inner thigh.

She more than merely *liked* what he'd done. The unfamiliar feelings coursing through her body were exciting, an aching, exquisite torture. Whenever Malach touched her, *wherever* he touched her, she loved it... and then despised herself for feeling any pleasure whatsoever at the hands of a man who was only using her body for his own ends. Whether it was to sate his sexual needs, or to break some spell, he was still using her. Just as she was using him. But, *dammit*, she didn't want to refuse what he offered. Right now, here, in this room, on this bed, she wanted him to screw her. And the consequences could go leap from a tall building in a single bound.

Malach climbed off the bed and stood beside it, staring down at her, the expression in his eyes unreadable. He held out a hand. "Undress me. It has been too long since I have felt a woman's touch—too long since I have felt anything at all. I want you, Jade. I need you. Skin-to-skin, with no barriers between us."

He wanted her. Needed her.

It was a devastating combination. *He* was devastating. And she couldn't resist him.

She sat up and placed her hand in his, allowing him to tug

her off the bed. The flush of embarrassment at her nakedness was soon drowned by the thrill of discovery as she loosened the leather thong lacing the front of his vest. She couldn't resist running her palms over the muscles of his chest, tracing her fingertips across the ridges of his abdomen. An age later, she tried to pull the vest off over his head—given his superior height an impossible task, until Malach bent at the waist to aid her attempts.

Jade caught her breath as she gazed at him. The width and heavy muscularity of his shoulders, arms and chest suggested more than a fleeting love affair with working out. Malach exuded raw strength and power. Give him a sword or something heavier—a battle-ax or mace, perhaps—and she had no doubt he could swing it for hours without tiring. Scars and a deep ridge of puckered flesh told her that a chunk of flesh had been torn from his left side at some stage. And she understood then that he'd battled his enemies to the death without qualm or regret. Malach would do whatever it took to survive. Like now. With her.

He stood stiff and unyielding and tightly controlled while she explored him, stroking and smoothing and kneading. And when she dared glance up at his face, his expression was a mirror of his posture. She swallowed, her mouth suddenly desert-dry, panic spiking through her veins. Was she doing something wrong? Were her tentative attempts at seduction so very clumsy?

She picked the thong lacing the fly of his trousers undone, and slipped her hand inside. She combed her fingers through his crisp pubic hair, sliding past the silky smoothness of his erect cock to cup his scrotum. As she gently squeezed the soft pouches she stole glances at his face, waiting for some reaction, some sign. But there was nothing. No darkening of his eyes, no heat in his gaze to suggest heightened sexual arousal.

Misery slapped her, and her hand inadvertently convulsed around his balls. She couldn't even do this one thing—arouse a man. She was a sexually inexperienced disaster. She was—

He exploded into motion, yanking her hand from his pants and picking her up, only to toss her atop the mattress. She bounced in a startled sprawl of limbs, eyes widening as she watched him strip. His cock jutted against his belly, as big and long and thick as she'd envisioned it to be.

Bigger.

She averted her gaze, fearful of what was to come, of what she had provoked.

He flipped her onto her belly and she went rigid as he pulled her onto her knees and spread her thighs wide.

Oh, God. Doggy-style it would be. And at least it would be easier if she didn't have to see his face screwing up all blindly Murray-like when he came. It would be easier, right? Her limbs quivered. Oh God. This was going to be a disaster. Why had she ever imagined she could go through with it?

Her head drooped until it was pillowed atop her crossed arms, leaving her butt thrust in the air, and when the coolness of the air-conditioned room caressed her exposed skin, she abruptly concluded the position left her far too vulnerable. She began to straighten her arms again, only to still at Malach's command.

"No. Stay as you were. I like the view."

Her breath hitched. "I-I h-have condoms in my bag." She felt heat washing her face again as she fought to control the wobble in her voice.

"Condoms?" Silence. And then, "Ah yes, I remember these *condoms*. I have no diseases. Do you?"

She twisted to glare at him over her shoulder. "No! Of course I don't. Do you seriously think I'd be doing this if I did? But—"

"And, in the way of your world's women, I presume you are protected against pregnancy."

"Yes." She silently thanked Grace for insisting she go on the pill. "Just in case," Grace had said—not that her friend could possibly have imagined Jade in a situation quite like this at the time. "But—"

"All will be well, Jade. You will not catch any diseases from me. I will explain it all to you in time, but for now, I have other things on my mind." Malach stroked a finger through her cleft.

Her body jerked even as her mind raced. Maybe she wouldn't be ready. Maybe she wouldn't be wet enough to take him inside her. Maybe he'd give up and— "Ahhh."

His fingers probed telltale slickness and then pushed inside her while his thumb strummed her clit. Tingling white-hot pleasure burst through her brain and her body—even her toes—as he expertly drove her toward orgasm. She came in a pulsing rush that left her gasping for breath with little silvery stars cavorting through her headspace.

Before she could flop onto her stomach in a loose-limbed, fuzzy-brained sprawl, his hands grasped her hips, holding her still. She could barely summon the strength to tense her muscles when the slick head of his cock probed her opening, parted her labial lips, and slowly pushed inside her.

"Gods," he muttered. "You are so tight 'tis like taking a virgin."

She bit her lips against a sob as a sharp, pinching pain bloomed.

Malach stilled. And then he pushed deeper, and the sensation of being steadily stretched and implacably filled became almost too much to bear. His cock was a throbbing presence that her body instinctively welcomed, and somehow accommodated, as he accustomed her to his invasion, clasping her to him with one arm wrapped around her midsection as he rocked gently within her. The pain was quickly forgotten as she teetered on the brink of pleasure… and then wholeheartedly embraced it.

With excruciating slowness, he withdrew almost completely, teasing her with the tip of his cock. He reached around her body to finger her clit until she could bear it no longer and arched her back, pressing her buttocks toward him, enticing him, wanting him—all of him—inside her.

He worked his cock a little way in and paused. "Tell me what you want, Jade."

She quivered, and then rocked back into him.

"This?" He pushed himself a little deeper inside her.

She whimpered.

"More?"

"Yes. More. Now."

He thrust all the way to the hilt inside her, so deep that his balls slapped against her tender flesh.

Instinctively she clenched her inner muscles around him. A rumbling groan tore from his throat, and a thrill coursed through her at the realization that she was *not* entirely powerless. She clenched again, tighter and stronger this time, and purred with purely female satisfaction when he groaned.

"Tell me what you want," he said, his voice hoarse. "This?" He pumped his cock into her, slowly increasing the speed and power of his thrusts, inexorably nudging her toward mindless pleasure.

"Yes," she said, and whimpered.

He tilted her hips, and the angle only intensified her pleasure as he stroked in and out, in and out, faster and faster. "And this?"

"Yes. Yes! Fuck me, damn you!" Her inner muscles spasmed around his cock as he complied, fucking her in fast, deep strokes, grinding into her and withdrawing, the sensation a sensual pulling and pushing that tipped her over into ecstasy. Heat spiraled through her, pooling in her belly, intensifying until she wanted to shriek. And, as her orgasm consumed her, she screamed his name.

With one last powerful thrust, Malach spilled himself inside her. He wrapped his arms about her waist and toppled onto his side, taking her with him. They lay on the mattress, panting, still intimately joined, for the moment incapable of moving.

"I do not consider Pieter my equal in the art of pleasuring you, Jade," Malach murmured against her hair. His hand strayed to her breast, palming it, his touch and his warmth streaking straight to the pleasure centers of her brain.

"Probably not," she managed to get out as she tried to catch her breath. "But… then again… just to make… absolutely sure… want to go again?"

He chuckled with genuine amusement, his laughter vibrating against the sensitive skin of her nape. She imagined his chiseled lips curving into an all-too-rare smile, and the vision warmed her heart.

They did "go again". Twice. And their last coupling was a gentle exploration of each other that seemed to last for hours. Perhaps it did—Jade was far too involved with the sheer wonder of the experience to bother watching the clock.

Immediately after they had both climaxed for the third time, her ears rung as though a church bell had tolled inside her head.

The echoing sound abruptly faded as Malach said, "We are bonded." He sounded faintly surprised. "The old man was right about you, damn his eyes. Now there is no turning back." He rolled off her to lie on his back and stare at the ceiling.

Jade opened her mouth to enquire what the bells meant, what this bonding stuff meant for her—for them both—but he forestalled her questions by gathering her into his arms and draping her over him like a blanket. "I need rest, Jade. Please."

Sensing he craved comfort and her understanding—even though she didn't understand anything about this—she lay her cheek against his chest and let her muscles go lax as he caressed her hair with long, gentle strokes. Despite her curiosity and the unanswered questions whirling in her brain, she drifted to sleep cradled in Malach's arms, all her worries banished for a little while by the comfort of being held and protected from anything the world might throw at her.

A SHOUT AWOKE HER. Jade lay still, her heart pounding, brain struggling to recall where she was.

The hotel.

She relaxed. Probably some drunken guest trying to find his room. And then the mound of blankets beside her heaved and bucked. She leaped from the bed and stood beside it, shivering in the dim light.

Malach howled something as he fought with the tangled covers. He struggled and thrashed until he succeeded in throwing them to the floor, and then he bolted to a seated position, his chest heaving.

Jade switched on the bedside light, illuminating the room in a soft glow. She peered at his face. His brow was slick with sweat, features twisted into a barely recognizable mask of horror and fear. Shaken, she drew back. She barely knew him, but her first impression had been of a strong man, both physically and mentally. A man utterly capable, and supremely confident of his chosen path. She had imagined him facing whatever life threw at him with courage and conviction. And, in the hours she'd spent with him since, she'd seen little to alter that first impression.

"Francesca!"

That name again. Uttered this time with heartbreaking despair and longing.

"Not the crystal again. Gods. No. Please, no!" His voice was hoarse and raw, as though he'd been screaming for hours.

A shiver that had nothing to do with standing naked in an air-conditioned room slithered down Jade's spine. It was a shiver of presentiment. Malach *had* been screaming for hours. Silently, in his mind, where no one could hear.

"I choose death! Kill me, Crystal Guardian. Kill me, you coward. Damn you, old man, why won't you kill me? Kill meeeeeeeeee!" His scream trailed off into eerie silence, punctuated only by harsh gulps as he struggled to breathe. His pale blue eyes were wide and sightless, blinded by his inner demons. His nightmare repelled even the light, capturing him in its warped version of reality. He stretched his mouth wide and screamed again.

"Malach." She leaned forward, and gently shook his arm. "It's me, Jade."

He grabbed her, his hands viselike around her upper arms, his grip bruising and punishing.

"Malach! You're hurting me!"

The pain in her voice got through to him, for his grip eased and he blinked, focusing on her face. He hauled her into his lap, first patting her face gently with his palms, and then stroking his hands over her body.

"Are you real?"

It was a broken whisper from a broken man, and her heart clenched with pity for his suffering. "Yes. I'm here, Malach. I'm real."

"Thank the gods. Thank the gods. Thank you!" He wrapped his arms around her, buried his face against her neck and rocked her like a child, all the while chanting heartfelt thanks to whatever higher powers he believed in.

Some gods. Jade didn't ever want to meet Malach's vengeful, uncaring deities. Personally, she no longer believed in God. Her beliefs had been thoroughly shaken when her parents died, but she'd cast aside the last vestiges of blind faith when… when….

Something bad had happened. Not to her. But to… to….

Gahhh! Why couldn't she remember?

She tugged Malach down to the mattress and wrapped herself around him, cradling his head against her breasts. And she lay wakeful, listening to him breathe, watching over him as best she could, offering what little comfort she could spare. She had nothing else to offer a man so obviously traumatized, and she regretted it deeply.

When Malach finally lapsed into a sound sleep, she set

about carefully extricating herself from his arms. She pulled the covers up over his hips and stood staring down at him for a long time, memorizing his face. Then she turned away, hating herself for what she was about to do.

If Pieter hadn't been feeding Malach a load of complete bollocks then maybe—just maybe....

She tiptoed over to the door and tried the handle. It opened. And stayed open until she quietly eased it shut again.

Huh. Well what d'you know? The door *had* been linked to some kind of a sex spell after all, and three times had definitely been the charm. She wondered if Aunt Lìli had ever come across such a thing. Maybe she would ask—if she could find a way to broach the subject without making her aunt suspicious.

She glanced at the wall clock. It was just gone five in the morning. Hopefully there'd be a bus to Lane Cove along soon, and if so, Jade fully intended to be on it. Snatching up her dress, she slipped into the bathroom.

As she stretched out the kinks in her spine, she noted that the aches and pains from yesterday had all but disappeared. Oh, certain unaccustomed places were sore still, but they were the kind of aches that made a thoroughly pleasured woman smile secretly to herself.

She didn't dare run the shower and risk waking Malach, so she cleaned up as best she could, scrubbing her armpits and swiping between her thighs with a damp flannel.

Her panties had been shredded beyond repair thanks to Malach, so she donned her dress and smoothed out the creases. It would have to do.

She finger-combed her hair and gave herself one final check in the mirror. Her face was scrubbed clean of makeup and the panda-circles of smudged mascara. She looked young and fresh-faced. Even her eyes sparkled. And, lack of panties aside, it wasn't obvious she'd indulged in a night of indescribably incredible sex with a stranger. For some reason she'd thought the soul-consuming passion she'd so recently experienced might have emblazoned itself upon her face.

She delved into her bag and found the bus fare she'd tucked away… along with the box of unused condoms. The cold hard reality check was like a slap in the face. She shook it off, reluctant to face the lamentable fact that she'd been talked into having unprotected sex with her first ever client.

But Malach wasn't exactly a client, was he? No, he was more like a hulking great lapse in judgment. And, just in case, she'd get herself tested for STDs.

She peeked out from the bathroom.

Safe for now. Here's hoping her luck would hold.

Heart in her mouth, she snuck past the bed, snagging her sandals from the rubbish bin as she passed. It was a bit of a hike to the bus stop and if her feet got sore, she figured even heelless they might be better than no footwear at all. She could only trust the material of her dress wasn't too transparent, and that once outside, there would be no inconvenient—and highly embarrassing—gusts of wind.

She opened the suite's door just enough to squeeze through and paused, glancing back at the sleeping man.

"Thanks, Malach," she whispered, and blew him a kiss. "Thanks for more than you could know." Then she pulled the door quietly closed behind her, shutting away this interlude of her life forever.

As she traveled down in the lift, she told herself she had no regrets at leaving him. It might have been just sex to him, but he'd treated her gently—despite believing she was an experienced prostitute. And although the unusual circumstances of their meeting left her still in the crap monetarily, she kinda hoped Malach would get shod of all this supernatural woo-woo business with Pieter and gain his freedom.

He'd suffered badly at Pieter's hands, and Francesca's too, for that matter. Whatever he'd done to bring himself to Pieter's attention, Jade believed Malach had been punished enough. He deserved some happiness in his life. And maybe, just maybe, she might have helped him heal. It was a fair trade considering he'd helped her overcome some of her hang-ups about sex.

But whatever the future held for Malach, Jade had things to do. Like finding another client. Preferably someone who, unlike Pieter, would stick around and pay her this time.

"Good morning, miss," one of the hotel staff called. She waved at him as she pushed through the hotel exit and out onto the street.

The cool morning air hit her like an almost physical blow, and a sense of urgency tore through her. Her instincts screamed at her to go straight home. Now. She knew she had to obey, but she didn't know *why*.

As she ran to the bus stop, awkwardly holding the skirt of her dress down so as not to flash anyone, she became hyper-conscious of her pendant. It felt unusually warm and heavy, dangling as always from its cheap silver chain and resting in her cleavage. Her skin tingled, and some impulse made her squint down at it.

Her vision filled with crimson.

She stumbled to a halt, gasping, almost hyperventilating from shock. With shaking hands, she raised the pendant to eye level. She squeezed her eyes shut, counted to three, and then looked again.

She wasn't seeing things. The green jade of her pendant was no more. The stone was now red. And not just any shade of red, a dark rich crimson that reminded her of freshly spilled blood.

Red jade.

The recollection seared her senses. And, as she stared at the stone, previously blocked memories crashed into her unprotected mind. She remembered why she had agreed to meet with "Mr Stone". And she remembered who she'd done it for.

Mei!

Her heart twisted. Bile rose in her throat as she suffered the anguish of discovering her sister's illness all over again. Cursing Pieter to suffer an eternity in Hell, she broke into a run.

MALACH AWOKE WITH the rising sun, as he always did—or rather, as he'd always done before the crystal had taken him. He reached out a hand for her and felt.... Nothing but cool bed linen.

He didn't bother to verify what he already knew. He was alone in the hotel room. She'd left him.

He rolled onto his back and lay staring at the ceiling. He could hardly blame her for leaving. Gods knew, witnessing a grown man scream until he was hoarse, and then sob like a child as he relived the horror of the crystal, would scare off even the most resilient of women. And Jade....

Jade pretended to be a woman who could take whatever life threw at her and toss it right back. But he'd seen the vulnerability that she tried so very hard to hide from him—a man used to gauging an opponent's weakness and ruthlessly exploiting it. Her worldly façade had cracked a little when she wept over the footwear that had been a mother's last gift to her daughter. It had cracked still more when he'd accepted her offer to bed her, and again when she'd climaxed for what he would wager was the first time in her life. And it had split wide open when she cradled him in her arms while he clutched her like a lifeline and used her presence—used *her*—to help him push back the nightmares.

Any man with a shred of decency would whisper heartfelt thanks into his pillow, and leave Jade to live her life how she pleased... and eventually forget the man who'd taken her virginity while half-believing her a whore.

But Malach was not a decent man. He was desperate. So desperate that he had vowed to take his own life rather than suffer a third imprisonment in that gods damned crystal. He was not a coward, however, so he would wait until the bitter end. And only if it seemed certain that he and Jade had little or no chance of passing the Testing, would he die by his own hand. It was a vow he'd made because he knew that once the crystal took him, even that choice would be stripped from him. Along with his sight, his hearing, his ability to feel.... But not his ability to suffer. No. Never that.

The shadows of his nightmares threatened to smother him, and he fixed an image of Jade in his mind. In the dead of night, as she'd hugged him close and soothed the fear that had gripped and emasculated him, Malach had felt something he'd never thought to feel again: Hope. Jade had given him that—a young woman he'd belittled and bullied into letting him bed her. And to Malach, hope was a gift beyond price.

He ground his fingertips into his temples to ease the insistent, escalating throb that was a symptom of his magical connection to Jade. His belly ached, too. But he welcomed the pains, knowing they were a compass of sorts, and that as soon as he exited the hotel, they would direct him to her. The Crystal Guardian left nothing to chance. Pieter would be denied rest until each member of Lord Keeper Wulfenite's troop had been redeemed—or destroyed himself in the process. Until then, the old man was just as much a victim as the men he'd imprisoned in his cursed crystals.

Jade was important to Malach and Pieter both—more important than she knew—and Malach felt a pang of guilt for what he must put her through. Even now he could picture her vividly, curled in his arms, a smile curving her lips as she'd slumbered. So innocent and trusting. So very young.

If he'd been offered the chance to bid for her on the Choosing Block, he would have left her to the likes of Kyan, a man who could charm a fennec fox from its lair, and any woman yet born—no matter how virtuous—out of her clothes. Jade was vulnerable, untried, untouched by the ugliness of the world, whereas Malach was a battle-hardened soldier. Even discounting her age, they were an ill-matched pair.

Now he had but four weeks to convince her that she loved

him.

Four weeks to learn to live again.

Four weeks to try and banish Francesca forever from his heart, and find it inside himself to truly love an exquisite, hot-tempered girl who hadn't hesitated to stand up to him and speak her mind. A girl who'd soothed him when the nightmare threatened to overwhelm him and strip him of his sanity, and who had escaped from their room while he slept, hoping not to have to face him again.

Four weeks until they faced the Testing.

He barked a laugh. So be it. The Crystal Guardian had not once suggested it would be easy.

Chapter Six

Jade's chest was heaving with exertion and her breaths reduced to short, sharp, painful pants by the time she reached her house. She unlocked the front door of the old three-bedroom family villa that she and Mei had inherited when their parents died, and sagged against the doorframe, willing herself to calm.

She stroked the old, polished wood of the doorframe and sighed, long and deep. She had looked into re-mortgaging the house to pay for private specialist care, but Mei had summarily scotched that brilliant plan, insisting the cost of going private would eat up all their funds, and they'd end up out on the streets. Ditto with Jade's suggestion they sell up and find a cheap place to rent. Mei wouldn't hear another word about it.

Mei was supposed to listen to Jade—her elder sibling—and do whatever Jade said, right? It was Jade's job to protect her sister, to get Mei through whatever life threw at her now their parents were gone. Only Jade sucked at this parenting thing, and suspected Mei was trying to protect *her*. Worse, Jade harbored the sneaking suspicion that Mei had discarded the notion of selling or mortgaging the house because she wanted Jade to have it when she was... when she was....

When she died.

Jade was not going to let her baby sister die. Not while she had a single breath left in her body.

She snuck inside, trying to act nonchalant—like she hadn't

broken a land speed record sprinting the last block from the bus stop. Or been coerced into spending the night in a hotel room and having raunchy sex with a complete stranger. Not to mention having all memories of exactly *why* she'd been prepared to sell herself in the first place temporarily wiped from her brain, and even forgotten her own *sister*!

How'n the heck could she begin to explain all that?

She couldn't. So her plan was to check on Mei, and hope for the best. If she was lucky, she'd be able to grab a shower and change before her sister woke and started demanding explanations. If she was unlucky, and Mei was already awake, she would have to hope she could pull off a convincing lie.

She managed a grand total of five steps up the hallway before she was busted.

"Finally! So nice of you to ring, Jade." Grace's cool tones seemed to lower the ambient temperature by at least five degrees. She stuck her head through the living room doorway and subjected Jade to the kind of narrow-eyed scrutiny that never failed to make a grown man quail.

Jade winced at the fierce determination in her friend's expression as Grace marched toward her. Yikes. She was in for it now. And then she registered Grace's girly pink satin pajamas and matching robe.

The imminent bollocking fled from her mind as she immediately assumed the worst. "Gracie! What are you doing here? Did Mei call you? God! How could I not have been here for her when she needed me? She's all right, isn't she? Please tell me she's all right. I'll never forgive myself for—"

"Ouch! Quit that, will you?"

Jade glanced down at her hands, aghast to find herself clutching Grace's wrists so firmly that her fingernails had gouged half-moon-shaped marks in Grace's skin.

She didn't even remember moving. She released Grace to scrub trembling hands through her hair. "Sorry, Gracie. God. I'm so sorry. Where's Mei?"

Grace rubbed her wrists. "Relax, she's fine. Still sleeping like a baby—unlike *moi*, your best friend in the entire world, who could sure as hell do with more beauty sleep." She broke off her lecture to push her glasses down her nose and peer at Jade over their electric-blue rims. "You don't look too hot," she said. "Come sit down before you fall down."

Wobbly-kneed with relief that Mei was okay, and that Grace had obviously forgiven her for going AWOL, Jade didn't press the point. She allowed Grace to propel her through the doorway and steer her toward the couch. She sank into the squishy cushions and tried to summon the energy to steel herself for the inquisition she knew would be next on Grace's agenda.

Grace plopped onto the couch beside her. "Holy moley, you look right royally shagged! Keep you busy, did he?"

"Grace!" Even the tips of Jade's ears turned fiery hot as she stared at her friend, wondering how on earth Grace had figured out what she'd gotten up to.

Calm down, Jade. Grace can't possibly know about Malach. No way.

Grace's laughter tinkled like a bell. She leaned over to chuck Jade under the chin. "Kidding! That's more like it. You needed some color in your cheeks. You were so pale I was starting to worry I'd have *two* invalids to nurse."

"Huh? I thought you said Mei was okay?"

"She is. God, Jade. You need to chill, all right?"

A spot just behind Jade's eye sockets started to throb, and she half-wished Pieter would appear and banish her headache again... right before she strangled him with her bare hands for dragging her into this whole mess and putting a mind-whammy on her.

Grace patted her hand. "You sit here and get your story straight in your head, while I get you a cuppa and some toast."

Jade warily eyed her friend. "I'm not hungry. And what d'you mean 'get my story straight'? There's nothing to get straight. I met up with my, uh, *interviewer*. We talked for a bit and then he left. End of story."

"Oh, really?"

"Yes, really. And how come you're here, Gracie? Where's Erica?"

"I'm here because she couldn't make it, and I—"

"Shit. I can't believe that Erica would let us down at the last minute like that." Jade clenched and unclenched her fists, beyond furious at herself for leaving Mei before the caregiver had arrived. But Erica had called to say she was running a bit behind, and Mei hadn't wanted Jade to be late for her "interview", and Jade couldn't see any harm in it at the time. Erica had never been a no-show before.

She chewed her thumbnail. "Why didn't Mei ring *me*?"

"Duh. You don't have a cell phone, so even if she had tried to ring you—"

"She could have left a message with the hotel's reception desk," Jade muttered, and then realized she would never have thought to check with reception because she had been so very certain Erica would show up in due course. "I told Mei I was meeting a guy at his hotel for the job interview. She knew what hotel it was—I wrote it down for her." And she'd hated lying to Mei, just as she'd hated having to lie to Grace.

"A job interview in a *hotel room*? Sometimes I wonder about you, Jade Liang. If I'd known you were planning on meeting him in his room instead of a public place like the bistro or a café, I'd have chewed you out big-time. Thank God this guy was above board, and not some serial rapist or something. Look, I know you, J. You'd have been too damn shy to front up to some stuck-up staff member at some fancy hotel reception desk and ask for messages. If you owned a cell phone, however...."

Grace had the whole "You really should listen to me" lecture down pat. "I hate it when you're right," Jade muttered. Not that a cell phone would have worked any better than the hotel suite's phone if Pieter had any say, but it sure would have helped afterward, when Jade had been so panicked about her sister.

"Anyway, Mei didn't ring *me*, I rang her," Grace was saying when Jade tuned in again "And although your little sister is quite capable of looking after herself, we decided it'd be a good idea if I came over and kept her company until you got home from your big day out." A knowing little smile tilted Grace's lips. "And just to clarify—not to mention satisfy my prurient curiosity—what was he like? He must have been something else if you stayed out all night, and didn't get a chance to ring home. C'mon, J. Spill! I'm dying, here."

Jade sucked in a deep breath and prepared to lie her butt off. No way could she tell Grace what she'd really been planning to do. Her best friend would have a fit of epic proportions. "It was nothing exciting, Gracie. I was just, uh, delayed. Got accidentally locked in the hotel suite, would you believe? And the phone wasn't working in the room, so we— I—couldn't call anyone." That much was true at least.

"I see." Grace levered herself up from the couch and stood, hands on hips, staring down her nose at Jade.

Grace might have been a statuesque, blonde, Malibu Barbie lookalike—if Malibu Barbies wore trendy glasses, that is—but her knack at dealing with her often difficult private patients was legendary, and she really knew how to make a person squirm. Jade tried her best not to cringe beneath that eagle-eyed stare but it was a losing battle.

"I had to wait until someone heard me banging on the door this morning before I could get out of the room," she finally said.

"Riiight. As I've said a thousand times before, you *really* need a cell phone."

"All right already! Preaching to the converted, here."

"I'll buy one for you."

"No. I can manage."

"J, this is no time to be stubborn. This is important. This is about your safety. Like I said before, what if he'd been a nutter?"

"He wasn't." God. She would never be able to tell Grace the truth.

"Yeah, I know. Luckily for you, you seem to have got off scot-free—if you don't count losing your panties while you were trapped overnight in that nasty hotel suite."

Jade tweaked the skirt of her dress further down her thighs and willed herself not to blush. "I don't know what you mean."

"It's not that hard to miss, given the way your dress is clinging to you. Someone stole them, huh? While you weren't looking? That's some trick."

"I, uh, really did misplace them. I had a shower and—"

"A-ha. Well, I hope you had lots of fun *misplacing* them."

Grace's smirk was far too wide and far too knowing for Jade's comfort. She frowned. Her friend's unsubtle innuendoes were starting to grate on her nerves. Grace couldn't possibly know about Malach, but surely she didn't believe Jade had seduced "Peter Stone", the man who'd "interviewed" her for a job, and spent the night with him? Surely not after the way they'd giggled about Jade's impressions after speaking to him on the phone. It'd been awful lying to Grace about the "interview", and Jade hadn't been at all sure she could pull it off, but playing increasingly outrageous "I bet Mr. Stone looks like" games had helped get her through the awkwardness.

A nasty thought smacked her. Could Grace suspect Jade's true reasons for meeting with "Mr. Stone"? Was Grace needling her, before getting stuck in with the mother of all lectures? God, what if Grace had spotted the advertisement Jade had placed in the paper, and figured out who'd placed it and why? That would be bad. Real bad.

"So, how'd you get home?"

Jade blinked, and struggled to focus on Grace's question. "Bus," she finally admitted, inwardly cringing as she waited for the inevitable explosion.

"Sheesh! You probably made the bus driver's day. Ditto the passengers, and anyone else who spotted you walking home from the bus stop. What the hell were you thinking, J? See, this is yet another reason to get a cell phone. If you'd rung me, I could have picked you up from town so you didn't have to worry about flashing everyone."

God, this was so hard. Jade itched to come clean and tell Grace all about Malach, but if she did that, the rest of the sordid truth would have to come out. Best friend or no, Jade couldn't reveal the truth about losing her virginity... and thoroughly enjoying the process. What Malach and she had shared, and the reasons behind the sharing, were private—too intimate to discuss with anyone, even her best friend. Plus, if she confessed even half the stuff she knew about Malach, Grace would be convinced she was delusional, and incapable of taking care of Mei anymore.

Grace's critical gaze had dropped to Jade's feet. She sat down abruptly, one hand fluttering over her heart. "Oh no! What happened to your sandals?"

"The heels broke. They just... snapped off. I guess they, uh, weren't up to the hike from the bus stop."

"Pity."

"Yeah.

"Maybe you can get them fixed?"

"Maybe." They both stared at her ruined sandals, unwilling to voice the sad truth: They were beyond redemption.

Jade toed off the footwear and kicked them under the couch. "Thanks for coming and staying over, Gracie. And—"

"Would you hush a minute and let me finish? Before we got sidetracked I was about to tell you that Mr. Stone rang me yesterday."

"Huh?"

"Mr. Stone? The charming old dude? He was dreadfully apologetic about making you come all the way to his hotel on the pretext of a job interview." Grace plumped up a cushion behind her back. "You're lucky he turned out to be a gentleman and didn't try anything on. If you heard the kinky stuff some of my male patients suggest I might like to try with them, you wouldn't be so complacent. When I think of the trouble you could have gotten yourself into...." Grace's brows pleated in a little frown. "You know, I couldn't for the life of me pick his accent. Where's he from?"

"Who?"

"Mr. Stone, of course."

"I-I'm not sure. He didn't say." Jade squinched her eyes shut and gave herself a thorough mental shake to clear the cobwebs from her brain. "Pieter— Uh, I mean, *Mr. Stone* rang you? Yesterday?"

"Yep. How do you think I knew to check on Mei in the first place? He reckoned you'd be out pretty late, and he was concerned about Mei being on her own, what with Erica not being able to make it. Anyway, I came over about four. Mei 'n me ordered takeaways for dinner and watched a couple of chick-flicks, and after I'd sorted Mei out it was so late I figured I'd hit the spare room rather than wait up for you."

The scenario Grace had spouted was so damn "off" that Jade found it increasingly difficult to believe Grace could remain so unconcerned. "But... but how did Mr. Stone get your number? I certainly didn't give it to him."

Grace frowned for all of five whole seconds before her expression cleared. "Oh—" she airily waved her hand "—it's all too complicated to go into right now. Suffice it say we had a lovely chat, and when he came to see me he explained *everything*."

Jade's stomach slid to her toes. Everything? That couldn't be good. *Hang on....* "He came to *see* you?"

"Yes, of course. He needed to check me out—make sure I was suitable."

"Suitable? For what?"

She must have looked as horrified as she felt because Grace laughed and rolled her eyes. "For Mei, silly. Your Mr. Stone hired me as Mei's private caregiver."

Jade's jaw sagged, but even though her mouth was open she couldn't seem to coax any words to form.

"I'm between contracts," Grace said. "So it's all set. He's hired me to look after Mei for the next month, which will free you up to squire around his nephew." She itched the bridge of her nose and pushed up her glasses. "Squiring. Is that the right word when the woman's the one doing the squiring? Doesn't sound right. *Escorting*, maybe. Though not in a sleazy way. Unless you want it to be, of course." She winked.

"His *nephew*?"

"Focus, J. His nephew. Mal-something-or-other. Geez, you really are whacked, aren't you? The guy must have danced your feet off at the clubs, huh?"

This time Grace's wink wasn't just knowing, it screamed wink-wink nudge-nudge you-go-girl! sexual innuendo. "Reckon he could've sprung for a taxi, though. Bit rude to expect you to find your own way home."

"Gracie—"

"Some guys can be so damn clueless, can't they?"

"Gracie."

"Only thinking of themselves. I bet if you'd been out on the town with Mr Stone, *he'd* have paid for—"

"Grace! What exactly did Pieter—Mr. Stone—tell you about Malach?"

"Only that he'd hired you to take his nephew, this Malach guy, out on the town. And if you both got on okay—you and Malach, I mean—he'd pay you to take him sightseeing around Sydney. But the best thing was the bit about commissioning you to paint a portrait of his nephew." Grace's eyes sparkled with barely suppressed excitement and she was practically hugging herself with delight.

"Wh-what?" Jade stuck a finger in her ear and wiggled it,

wondering if she'd heard right.

"The commission? For you to paint a portrait of his nephew."

A *commission*.

A painful yearning stabbed her. Someone *paying* her to paint a portrait for them. A dream come true—

Except it wasn't true. This commission wasn't because someone had seen Jade's work and been seduced by the passion that infused each and every brushstroke. This wasn't because her art spoke to someone at some soul-deep level—so much so, they *had* to own one of her works. This was the Crystal Guardian acting as puppet master and pulling the strings. *Her* strings. And Malach and Grace's, too.

Jade wondered if Pieter knew how much she had yearned for an opportunity like this. And how much it wounded her soul that it wasn't a real offer.

Huh. Silly. Of course he knew.

"He needs it completed within a month," Grace burbled, unaware of Jade's inner anguish. "He wants it done before Malach has to travel back to… to…. Funny, I can't quite remember where. Of course I told him you'd be happy to do it, but you were constrained by caring for your sister and might not make the deadline. We got to talking, and after I told him old Mrs. Whitney had recently passed on and I was between clients, he offered me this job. So it's all worked out for the best, really." She beamed at Jade, pleased as punch by the way everything had been arranged.

If only she knew the truth.

"You don't seem very grateful, J."

"*Grateful*?" Jade blinked back tears born of fury. She'd been offered her heart's desire, only to realize it was tainted, sordid. The absolute last thing she felt like doing was showing gratitude. "What the bloody hell for, Gracie? Should I be grateful to you for spilling details of my private life to a stranger? Should I be grateful to Mr. Stone for interfering, and thinking he knows what's best for me and Mei? And just so you know, there wasn't any *job* for him to offer you! I was managing to care for Mei just fine before Pieter bloody Stone appeared on the scene."

"Yeah. Sure you were. Like, so fine, you refuse help from your friends when you desperately need it. So fine, you're worrying yourself sick about finding the money you need to provide top-notch medical care for Mei. So fine, you never go out, never date, and don't have a bloody life at all because your whole life revolves around your sister!"

Grace's voice had risen, well on its way to a potentially earsplitting screech. But before it hit banshee-level, she took hold of her temper and clamped her lips shut. She rotated her shoulders, making a visible effort to relax. And Jade heard her muttering about "stubborn little witches" beneath her breath.

"Jade, Jade, Jade." Grace's features composed themselves into what Jade suspected her friend fondly imagined was a compassionate, motherly impression. Epic fail.

"Look at this as a gift," Grace said, her tone wheedling. "Jolly old Mr. Stone's obviously rolling in dough and he's happy to throw it around. Why shouldn't some stick to you for a change? And, judging by the state of you, his nephew is pretty hot and totally into you. So as far as *I* can tell, it's a win-win situation all 'round."

Dammit. Obviously Grace didn't merely *suspect* Jade had slept with Malach, she knew Jade had slept with Malach. And was unreasonably delighted about it into the bargain.

Jade knew from the eager light in Grace's eyes that her friend was dying to know all the gory details, but she refused to give Grace that satisfaction. For now, anyway. Knowing Grace, Jade would have to give in and spill the goods soon enough.

First things first. Grace's mind usually functioned like a well-oiled steel trap. She was the last person Jade would have expected to fall for such a contrived series of events. It seemed highly likely that Pieter, almighty Guardian of the Crystals, had worked his supernatural mojo on Grace, too. Just as he'd done to Jade, making her forget the most important person in her life: Her sister, Mei.

Jade suspected that getting Grace to understand she'd been manipulated by an expert was going to be an exercise in futility, but she had to at least try. "And you don't think, gee, I dunno, that this is all a little too convenient, Gracie? Nothing about this whole set-up screams totally weird series of coincidences and big fat ulterior motive to you? It sure as hell does to me."

"So he wants you to paint a portrait of his nephew and show the guy a good time. So he's prepared to pay through the nose for it. So he's happy to pay for Mei's care to free up your time—it's all good, right? With the money your Mr. Stone's forking out, you can take a whole month off from your café job to paint while I look after Mei. Besides, your sister and I love each other to bits so it won't be a problem, will it?"

Jade remained mute, watching her best friend's shiny-eyed, childlike eagerness with increasing frustration.

Grace ticked off each point on her fingers. "I'll live in so I can help Mei at night if she needs me. I can oversee her dietary requirements. And I can also deal to that old battleaxe of a district nurse who gives her the willies. Plus, I can take her to her hospital appointments and explain everything so she understands it. I'm fully versed in all the things you need to watch for with peritoneal dialysis—I was the one who pushed for that instead of haemodialysis, remember? So Mei could feel like she's in control instead of being reliant on you all the time. Except you're still clucking over her like an old chook. You need to quit treating her like a kid, Jade."

Jade opened her mouth to defend herself but when Grace was on a roll there was no stopping her. "This way, you won't have to schedule your entire life around Mei's needs for a while. I can take responsibility for her, and you'll be able to spend each day for an entire month doing what you've always wanted to do. Paint. Right?"

"Right." Jade choked on the word but what else could she say? Pieter had brainwashed Grace to the point where she would doubtless have been perfectly happy for Jade to be MIA for the entire freakin' month instead of merely overnight.

"Besides, I've already run it all past Mei and she's over the moon. She and I agree. It's time you started living your own life, J."

Wow. *Fait accompli much?* And, to rub salt in the wound, Grace's tone said she expected Jade's compliance to be a foregone conclusion. Or else.

Jade shook her head, feeling helpless. God save her from well-meaning best friends. And stubborn, bloody-minded younger sisters. Not to mention Machiavellian old men with powers beyond her comprehension and agendas she couldn't even begin to fathom. "I suppose you told Mr. Stone all about my stint at art school, too."

Grace nodded happily. "You'd better believe I told him. And that your tutor couldn't speak highly enough of you, and was gutted when you dropped out."

Jade's shoulders slumped. Even though she knew Grace wouldn't have been able to resist Pieter's magical compulsion, she couldn't help feeling betrayed. Her artistic aspirations were an intensely private thing that she didn't discuss with anyone.

Ever since she'd been old enough to hold a brush, she'd dabbled with various mediums, but it wasn't until she discovered portraiture that she found her passion. She'd painted a grand total of two portraits, and been informed by her tutor she had an incredible natural talent, before she'd been forced to quit art school, and permanently shelve her dreams of a painting career, to look after Mei. She hadn't picked up a brush since.

She'd told herself that in the grand scheme of things, painting was trivial. It was in her blood though—the desire to paint, the burning *need* to put brush to canvas. And her fingers still itched every time she glimpsed someone whose face cried out to be immortalized on canvas. Sometimes she would wake with her fingers cramped and aching, and know deep down in her soul that she'd been painting phantom portraits for hour after hour in her dreams. And she was beyond hurt at the thought of something so precious being discussed behind her back with a stranger.

What other secrets might Pieter have wheedled from her best friend? A clammy chill traced her spine at the mere thought of Grace blurting that Jade was—or had been until last night—a virgin… and was scared to have sex because she'd almost been date-raped, and had never fully put it behind her. Doubtless nothing about Jade's life was sacred to Pieter. She shivered and wrapped her arms about her middle.

"I know how rabid you are about keeping your God-given talent private," Grace said, peering worriedly at her. "I didn't bring it up until he mentioned it, I swear. He'd already seen your, uh— He already knew."

"What aren't you telling me, Grace? Spill right now or I'll… I'll…."

Grace perched on the arm of the couch and eyed her with one eyebrow raised in challenge. "You'll what?"

"I'll have Aunt Lìli put a really nasty curse on you." *Right after she puts one on Pieter if he's ever stupid enough to show his face again.*

Grace sniggered and lightly cuffed the back of Jade's head. "Is that the best you can come up with? Puhlease. Your Aunt Lìli loves me. She'd never curse me. Besides, I don't believe in curses."

"More fool you," Jade said. "Aunt Lìli's curses are not to be taken lightly. Remember Murray Blackwood?"

Grace's eyes rounded, and she chafed her arms through her robe. "Okay, point taken. But I can't believe you'd stoop to threatening your best friend."

"Please, Gracie, tell me the truth. I don't think I can handle any more surprises right now."

"Mr. Stone already knew you were an incredibly talented portrait painter, J," a soft voice intervened. "He knew because he's seen one of your paintings." Mei slid into the room, an ethereal wraith clad in delicate white, *broderie anglaise*-trimmed pajamas.

Jade did the mental equivalent of a face-palm. Of course Pieter would have tracked down one of her paintings. She was a fool to expect otherwise. The Crystal Guardian was nothing if not thorough. "Lemme guess. He visited you, too, and happened to see the painting in your *bedroom*?"

"No." Mei exhaled sharply through her nose. "Mr. Stone spotted one of your portraits in a gallery. He was so taken with it, he spoke to the gallery owner and tracked down the artist."

And of course the wily old bugger would have a carefully constructed cover story.

Jade finally braved Mei's gaze. Her sister's features were pale and drawn. Even the short trip from her bedroom had fatigued her. Guilt for not noticing sooner, for not blowing Grace off to check on her sister the minute she got home, washed through her.

"Baby, come sit down before you fall down."

Jade jumped to her feet, intending to put her arm around Mei and help her to the couch, but her sister brushed her off with a gesture and a scowl. "Quit babying me, J. I'm not a complete invalid—not yet, anyway."

Jade sank back onto the couch and watched Mei lower herself slowly and painfully onto the cushions of the chair opposite. It tore her heart to see Mei like this, rail-thin and washed-out, lacking even the energy to lift her feet. She was a shadow of the exuberant, athletic teenager she'd once been, almost unrecognizable as the girl in the portrait.

Lately, even a glimpse of that painting bit at Jade's soul. The contrast was almost too painful to bear. She shoved her despair aside, refusing to let Mei see even a hint of what she felt. And as she strove for composure, the significance of Mei's words struck her.

Mr. Stone spotted one of your portraits in a gallery....

"Hang on, what's one of my paintings doing in a gallery?" Jade frowned as she tried to make sense of it. She'd never sold any of her works—not the charcoals, the pen and inks, or the exuberant acrylic still-lifes. And especially not those two precious portraits, one of her parents and one of Mei.

After her parents had died, Jade had found the portrait of them too agonizing to keep around, and had given it to Aunt Lili. But she knew with every of fiber of her being that Lili would never sell that painting. And the portrait Jade had done of Mei was hanging in her sister's—

"I put the portrait you did of me up for sale."

Jade covered her horrified gasp with her hand. "Mei! What the hell possessed you?"

Her sister's eyes flashed. "The same thing that possessed *you* when you quit your studies to look after me. The same thing that possessed you when you looked in to re-mortgaging our house on the sly. The same thing that possessed you when you went for a job interview in some strange guy's hotel room, instead of doing the sensible thing and meeting him in a public place!"

Total impasse. Two prideful, strong-willed creatures facing off, each intimately aware of the other's strengths and weaknesses, neither willing to give an inch.

Jade combed her fingers through her hair, too ashamed to meet Mei's knowing gaze.

"Just because I have crappy kidneys, doesn't mean I'm deaf or dumb," Mei said.

"I'll fix us all some breakfast, shall I?" Grace eased up from her seat and prudently vanished into the kitchen.

Jade sighed. "Guess we're both as bad as each other, huh?"

Mei's answering snort said it all. "I think you beat me

hands down this time, sis'. How could you even think of putting yourself at risk like that?" Her cocoa-brown eyes sparked with anger. "I don't care how fabulous a job sounds, that was a totally dumb thing to do. Don't do it again. You hear me, Jade? I was worried sick about you until Grace filled me in."

"Right. How about I wish on a star tonight, and when I wake up tomorrow morning, instead of being a barista at Carlo's Café, I'll be CEO of my own company, with a six-figure salary, and all our financial problems will be solved. Hell, I'll just buy you a new kidney from a willing donor, and hire the best surgeons in the entire world to transplant it. How does that sound?"

"Sounds darn good to me. But in the meantime, you're being paid to do what you've always wanted to do: Paint. So suck it up and live with it."

Mei managed a wan smile after that little speech, and Jade deemed it safe to approach and beg forgiveness. She crawled over to kneel on the floor beside her sister, clenching her hands at her sides to resist the impulse to brush a sweat-dampened lock of hair back from Mei's face.

"I need you to stop worrying about me, Jade."

"I promise I'll try." An impossible task. Her current job covered utilities and basics, but despite her miserly ways, the nest egg from their parents' estate was being sucked up at an alarming rate. Things had gone rapidly downhill the instant she'd been forced to break into the principal they'd invested, rather than surviving solely on the interest.

"So you're going to accept Mr Stone's offer, right?"

Pieter's good intentions, expertly fabricated from half-truths and secrets, mantled Jade ever more heavily. "I guess I have to." For now.

A loud rap sounded on the door.

"I'll get it," Grace trilled from the kitchen. "What with you two hardly being fit for company and all. At least I'm wearing a robe." Grace strolled through the living room, wiping her hands on a tea towel as she headed for the front door.

Jade registered a murmured conversation, but didn't pay attention because her focus was wholly on her sister. "I don't really want to take on this commission thing, but it'll buy us some time, at least," she told Mei. "But there's one condition. I want your portrait back from whatever gallery you put it in. No way you're selling it to a stranger. Deal?"

Mei nodded. "Deal."

"And you've got to do whatever Grace tells you if it's regarding your health. No giving her grief about meals being too bland. Okay?"

"That's *three* conditions, but whatever."

Mei smiled and the world seemed almost bright again. Even so, Jade couldn't bring herself to relax and appreciate her good fortune. When it came down to providing the best care money could buy for her sister, she wasn't in a position to refuse Pieter's gift but couldn't help wondering where the hunky, black leather-clad fly in the ointment fit into all this. No way was Malach Pieter's *nephew*, that much Jade knew. Just like she knew there had to be some major strings attached to this whole crazy scheme. What was Pieter hoping to achieve by throwing them together?

Please God, she would be able to resist Malach next time she saw him, because there wasn't room for a man like him in her life. There wasn't room for any man.

Mei's smile faltered. She blinked slowly, and her eyes rounded, as if unable to believe what she was seeing. And Jade suddenly realized Mei was looking past her, over her shoulder.

She turned, half-expecting to see Grace standing behind her, doing something daft to try to make Mei laugh. But it wasn't Grace. It was the last person she had expected to see.

Chapter Seven

Instinctively, Jade lurched to her feet, and was forced to lock her knees to prevent herself from swaying like a drunkard. Or falling flat on her face with shock and dismay.

The man standing in the doorway took one step, and Jade's limbs turned to jelly. Two steps, and her knees gave way. In a blur of movement, he was there, his hands snaking out to grasp her forearms and hold her upright. "Wh-what are you doing *here*?" she whispered.

Grace materialized in the doorway, fanning herself with her hands and pretending to swoon. "That's Malach," she told Mei. "Your sister's *date* from last night."

Jade tore her gaze from Malach's face in time to see her best friend mouthing, "He's so hot!" accompanied by more ostentatious fanning of hands. "This is Mei," Grace said.

"I am pleased to meet you," Jade heard him say. "I am called Malach."

Jade's attention skipped back to her sister. Mei's gaze darted first to Malach and back to Jade. Her eyes brimmed with tears and she was biting her lower lip.

Jade's stomach twisted into a knot. She knew her sister well enough to understand that Mei grieved for lost possibilities, for boyfriends and lovers she might never have. And Jade grieved with her.

"Mei!" All the anguish and despair, all the futile rage she'd tried so hard to suppress since Mei's diagnosis, throbbed in her voice. She tried to wrench herself from Malach's grip but it was Grace who hurried to Mei's side, gathered Mei into her arms, comforted Mei while she sobbed as if her heart was breaking. Grace didn't intend to be cruel by seamlessly usurping Jade's role as mother, sister, confidante. But even though Jade knew it was grossly unfair, it would have been easy to hate her friend right now… if not for the fact she hated Pieter more for what he'd done to them.

She rounded on Malach, glaring up at him. "What are you doing here?"

"We need to talk."

Only now did she register his modern attire of a black shirt, worn jeans and black boots. Goodness knows where he'd gotten the clothes—or the small suitcase he'd abandoned by the door when he'd rushed to her side. Pieter must have waved his magic wand from afar again.

She blinked, focusing on the man himself. And silently admitted that she preferred him in leather—not that he didn't look fine in jeans and a shirt. In fact he looked good in modern clothes, really good. But in his original garb he oozed strength and confidence.

She could sure do with some strength and confidence right now. A sigh eked from her lips. "So talk," she said.

"In private."

Jade lifted her chin. "Here will do just fine. There's nothing you can say to me that Mei and Grace can't hear, too."

He quirked an eyebrow. "Are you sure about that, Jade?"

"Of course I'm sure."

He cut right to the chase. Unfortunately. "Why did you neglect to tell me you were a virgin before I bedded you?"

Damning heat flamed her face, and she wished she were anywhere but here. The situation would only escalate if she tried to deny it, so she bit her tongue. Snatching a breath, she darted a glance at Mei and Grace.

As she'd feared, their eyes were saucer-round. Grace's expression segued to "I knew it!" triumph. Mei blotted her tears and smiled at Jade, trying so hard to be brave and not reveal how much she was hurting. If her health continued to deteriorate at this rate, she might not live long enough to *date* a boy, let alone lose her virginity.

God. Mei was only seventeen. So young, with so much of her life left to live. Jade wished again—as she'd done so many times—that she was Mei's genetic sister. Then there would have been a much higher chance of being a donor match for Mei. Her heart ached anew as she relived the anguish of a family secret blown wide open in cruelest of circumstances. That Jade hadn't been a match had been shock enough. But to then discover that it wasn't merely the worst possible luck, but because Mei had been adopted? It'd been a helluva way to learn the truth.

The ever-present, simmering anger at her parents for hiding the truth welled up. And then, realizing from Mei's anguished expression that her sister knew exactly what Jade was thinking, Jade leashed her anger and banished it to seethe and fester in a tiny corner of her mind.

"I've changed my mind," she said, attempting to free herself from Malach's confining grip.

"A woman's prerogative," he agreed.

"We'll finish this conversation in private, and—"

"Your bedroom's free." Grace's voice squeaked with poorly hidden delight. She'd been nagging Jade to get laid for the past year, and now Jade had taken the plunge, Grace seemed hellbent on encouraging her to enjoy herself. Thoroughly.

"Your bedroom sounds like an excellent place," Malach said. His suggestive tone speared straight to Jade's currently underwear-free zone, which made the entire situation ten times more shocking.

"Oh, and while you're there, J, you might want to grab another pair of knickers." Grace only grinned at Jade's outraged expression. "You know, just to help him keep his mind on your... discussion."

And then Grace switched her focus to Malach, her gaze boring into him. They sized each other up and nodded, both in perfect accord.

Omigod. Jade's face flamed anew.

Mei stared at the flimsy skirt of Jade's dress through slitted eyes. She loosed a strangled squawk, clapping her hands over her mouth when she put two and two together. Her eyes sparkled as she caught Jade's gaze.

Jade groaned, knowing that a detailed blow-by-blow account of her recently acquired sex-life would soon be on the agenda for a demanding audience of two.

Malach finally deigned to release her arms and she flounced from the room—make that *attempted* to flounce, while holding the skirt of her dress tightly around her butt and thighs. Her exit was accompanied by the muffled giggles of her so-called innocent little sister and the not-so-muffled laughter of her so-called best friend.

The instigator of this whole humiliating situation trailed after her. He followed her into her bedroom and, without a by-your-leave, made himself at home by kicking off his boots and lounging on the bed while Jade rooted in a drawer for underwear.

She bent to step into her undies, and then abruptly realized she had an interested by-lounger. And, from the heat of his gaze, he was very interested indeed.

She blushed—again!—and straightened, crumpling the panties in her fist and hiding them behind her back. "You, stay put. No following me or pawing through my underwear or... or... anything else while I'm gone. I'll be right back."

"I will be waiting."

And didn't that sound like a promise? She fled to the bathroom, making sure to lock the door behind her.

After she'd donned her underwear, hampered by noodle-knees and trembling hands, Jade examined her face in the mirror. Slashes of hectic color washed her cheeks, boldly highlighting her inner turmoil... and an excitement she didn't want to feel.

This would not do. She splashed cold water on her face and willed herself to calm down before daring another glance at her reflection.

Better. On the surface, she looked in complete control—like someone who could deal with a man like Malach. Here's hoping she could pull it off.

She'd almost convinced herself it would be best to accept Pieter's manipulations and go with the flow. But now, confronted with the man she was supposedly bonded to, she did a hasty about face. She firmly informed her reflection that no way was she buying into this month-long contract Pieter was peddling without proof it wasn't some elaborate scam. If the old man was going to pay her to paint Malach's portrait, and pay Grace for Mei's care, then he could show her the money.

Oh, that's right: There was no money. Because the old man had done a runner. Ergo, the only sensible thing left to do was to march into her bedroom and inform Malach the cold hard facts—tell him that she didn't believe everything Pieter had told them, and he shouldn't, either. And once she'd gotten that out of the way, she was going to tell Malach right to his face he had to go. He had to leave her alone or... or....

Or she couldn't be responsible for her actions.

Ah, crap. Grace was right. Years of deprivation had addled her brain. Now she'd had a taste of sex she wanted more. To be quite specific, she wanted more of *Malach*. But as loudly as her newfound libido called, Mei was the most important person in Jade's life right now. She couldn't afford to be distracted by a man—however wonderful a lover he might be. She and Mei would have to manage without Pieter's dubious brand of "assistance". Somehow.

She threw back her shoulders, left the sanctuary of the

bathroom, and marched into her bedroom.

Malach's gaze locked onto hers and all Jade's bravado and reasoned arguments fled. Who was she trying to kid? Malach had her right where he wanted her. One glance from those "come to bed and I'll lick you all over" eyes and she was a goner. She'd let him do whatever he wanted again. And again. And again.

"I missed you this morning." His softly spoken words completely disarmed her.

"I-I'm sorry. I should have left you a note."

"A note would have been little use as I have not had an opportunity to learn to read your tongue. So, tell me, Jade, why did you sneak away like a thief in the night before I awoke?"

"I had things to do. Important things. Things that couldn't wait."

His piercing gaze softened. "Your sister. From the look of her skin and eyes, she is very unwell. 'Tis a serious ailment, then?"

"Yes."

"I am sorry."

"Me, too."

"It was unfair of Pieter to suppress your memories of her. If I had known—"

"If you'd known about Mei, you'd have what? Bashed through the door of our hotel suite with your head? That would really have made everything so much better—you with a broken head, and me having to put up with your moaning and groaning."

His lips compressed. "I am a warrior. I have oft-times ridden into battle with broken bones and other such minor injuries. I do not moan and groan when 'tis simply a matter of ignoring the pain until such time as the injury may be safely tended."

Jade rolled her eyes, but it was a struggle to find the sarcasm that she usually hid behind. "Riiight. Well, good for you and all your other idiot warrior mates. Look, we were stuck in that room, and there wasn't anything either of us could do about it. And hey, my—what did Pieter call it again? Oh yeah. My 'passionate nature' meant we spent a grand total of one night imprisoned before I spread my legs and invited you to screw me the required three times. Pieter must be laughing all the way to... to... wherever the hell the old bugger took off to when he left."

Malach forked a hand through his hair and sighed. "There is no shame in having your character so easily divined by the Crystal Guardian. Pieter has spent centuries observing us. Moreover, he has the assistance of his precious goddess. Mere mortals could never hope to thwart him."

A ton of questions danced through her head but tales of goddesses and centuries-old men wreaking havoc upon mere mortals would have to wait. "About this portrait thing. I don't think it's such a good idea. I mean, I'm sure Pieter will offer me a fair price and all, but what I need is—"

"This?" Malach lifted his hips from the bed to yank a fat envelope from the back waistband of his jeans. He tossed it to her.

She stared at the writing on the envelope. *Jade Liang*. That was her, all right.

She tore open the seal and gasped. Oh. My. God. It was stuffed full of money. Large denominations. And for a heady moment, she indulged in rose-tinted visions of never having to worry about money again. Buying a decent bed for Mei. Not having to buy budget brands and obsessively watch her pennies at the supermarket....

Then reality clouted her a good one. If she was lucky, it would cover the expenses if—*when*—a suitable donor kidney was found for Mei. There wouldn't be anything left over for new beds.

She swallowed, trying to work up enough moisture to speak without croaking. "Where did you get this?"

"I found it at the foot of the bed when I awoke this morning. Along with the clothes I now wear, and other items I need to make my way in this world. Even a temporary abode has been made available for my use—though I have been unable to yet discover where it might be situated." He shrugged. "Doubtless it will be revealed in time. Everything is Pieter's doing. And, knowing the old man as I do, you will find a note of explanation with the currency."

She peered inside the envelope. There was indeed a note, written in the same spidery, elaborately scripted hand.

> *My dearest Jade,*
>
> *Enclosed is $25,000 in cash, being your fee for completing a portrait of Malach. He is a complex man and I have faith that you will treat him with the compassion he deserves. Remember, he is the unwilling victim of my machinations, so if you must assign blame then 'tis I who should shoulder it.*
>
> *There is nothing to compel you to complete my request, nothing to prevent you from "taking the money and running" as you would say. Goddess knows, neither Malach nor I would blame you for that. But I hope you will see fit to fulfill this commission.*
>
> *Please know that regardless of your decision, for four full weeks Mei will have the benefit of the care that I promised. Knowing your suspicious nature, I must assure you that full payment for her care has already been made available to your friend Grace.*
>
> *I would also humbly beg that you promise me one thing: That when the time comes you will make your choice for the right reasons. Obligation is ever a poor substitute for love.*

It was signed with a *P*.

Twenty-five thousand freaking dollars? Jade wrung her

hands. Damn Pieter. She could no more boot Malach out on his ear and keep the money, than she could blame him for her current troubles. And how could she refuse to take Pieter's money and deny Mei the care she so desperately needed?

Jade refolded the note and stuffed it back in the envelope before tossing it onto her dressing table. She paced the room, staring at the worn carpet. Of course she'd keep the cash. And of course she'd paint the damn portrait. She would ensure it was the best work she was capable of, too.

"Sneaky, manipulative old bastard."

She didn't realize she'd spoken the words aloud until Malach's muttered agreement drifted to her ears. "You have no idea," he said.

She stopped pacing and swiveled to face him. "How about you fill me in then, Malach? Tell me everything you know about the Crystal Guardian. In fact, tell me everything from the beginning. I can't promise I'll believe all of it, but I can promise I'll listen."

"Ignorance is oft-times a state of bliss, Jade."

"Yeah, I'm sure. But I reckon I deserve an explanation. And since Pieter has conveniently vanished, you're it."

"'Tis not a brief tale," he warned.

She shrugged. "So?"

"So, do you not care what your sister and your friend will think?"

"Whatever do you mean?"

His lips curved. "You and I, Jade. In your bedroom. And time is passing."

"Oh. Right." She cooled her heated cheeks with her palms. She'd done far too much blushing since meeting Malach. "Right now, I don't much care what either of them think. I need to find out what the hell is going on."

Malach's grin widened. "Of course we could add some fuel to the fire."

Now it was her turn to grin. "Nice try. Just the story. No

funny business."

He placed a hand on his chest. "My manly pride has been completely crushed by your lack of desire. How will I go on?"

"Oh, puhlease. Spare me the theatrics and get on with it, will you? I haven't got all day." She curled up in the armchair she'd squeezed into a corner of her room, and prepared to be amazed.

MALACH STRETCHED OUT on Jade's bed. Such luxury. Far more comfortable than a bedroll. "This is my favorite of all your world's innovations," he said.

Jade screwed up her nose in such an endearing fashion that he wanted to smile, even though this coming conversation was nothing to smile about. "You've gotta be kidding me," she said. "That lumpy old thing?"

He nodded.

"So, you have mattresses where you come from?"

She probably imagined she was being subtle, trying to draw him out to reveal his past. Ironic, given that he would happily converse with her. For so long his world had been a sensationless silent prison, and to Malach, hearing Jade's voice, being able to hear his own voice for that matter, seemed a precious gift.

"A bedroll is common, but those with permanent abodes may avail themselves of a down-filled mattress. Of course, such luxuries usually require servants to battle the ever-present grains of sand, which, despite all effort to the contrary, inevitably invade the bed linens. Hence, we warriors have a dubbed a bed such as yours a 'scratcher'."

Jade's lips curved. "Nice one."

Malach's heart gave a bizarre little lurch. It warmed his soul to see her like this—carefree, without the weight of her worries burdening her slim shoulders. The warmth curdled in gut. She would not be carefree after his explanation.

"Tell me more about your world, Malach. I need to understand it."

From her intense expression—the way she was trying to see into his soul—Malach surmised what she truly needed was to understand *him*.

He carefully shuttered his expression. Bad enough she had witnessed his nightmare and been forced to comfort him. He did not wish her to know the full extent of the fear and desperation that drove him. He did not want to see pity in her eyes. After two sojourns in the crystal, the only thing he had left was his pride. And pride dictated that he only get down on his knees and beg this young woman to save him from the crystal if there were no other choice.

"I will tell you all, Jade, but as for whether it remains accurate? Who knows. Centuries have passed since the first time the Guardian's curse befell me, and only the gods know if the world I knew still exists. I hope that my people adapted and moved forward with the passing of time. The alternative—that myself, and others of my troop that Pieter imprisoned, are all that remains of my people—I do not wish to contemplate."

A visible shudder coursed through Jade's slender form and she chafed her arms. Malach regretted the loss of her smile. Easier for her to have remained ignorant. Easier for him, too, if he held all the cards while she was unaware of the true ramifications of her decisions. But he refused to manipulate her. If she chose to help him escape his curse, better that she did so with eyes wide open.

"What do your people call themselves?"

"We are *Styrians*, 'Riders of the Storms'. We call ourselves this in deference to the violent storm season that drives us from our tented cities to seek shelter in caves for three to four months of each year."

He went on to describe the harsh, sand-blasted land with vast tracts of near-desert, peopled by various tribes that were overseen by Lord Keepers. He noted the glimmer of fascination in Jade's eyes, and wondered whether his "exotic" background might be the key to her surprising responsiveness when he had bedded her. He'd witnessed many a woman pursue a man she considered mysterious and aloof.

"You mentioned gods," she said. "Are they cruel, your gods?"

He observed her closely. A loaded question if he were not mistaken.

"Personally, I believe all gods are cruel," she said when he didn't answer. "They punish those who're good, and reward those who're selfish and self-serving. I don't believe in God. Once I did, but not anymore. Not since—" She broke off to stare stony-eyed at the wall.

Not since her sister's illness had manifested, he would wager. Alas, he could offer her little comfort. "Our gods, too, are harsh beings who demand much of us. But the Mother of them all—the only goddess in our pantheon—is for the most part a benevolent being. She is the one we beg to keep our hides intact when we ride into battle."

He thought he heard a muffled snort. "I, too, no longer believe in gods or goddesses," he said. "I renounced them long ago." *When my Lord Keeper and his troop were condemned to a torment without surcease for the crime of following orders.*

The tension in her eased, replaced by such intense curiosity that Malach was reminded of his younger self, when he'd burned to know the secret the priests strove to hide from the general populace. Styrians had a saying: "Curiosity killed the *carakul*", and just like the tufted-eared feline predator that couldn't resist investigating cunningly placed snares and traps, Malach had stuck his nose where he shouldn't have. Malach's curiosity had borne fruit, however, unlike one unfortunate feline whose pelt he'd gifted to Wulf, his Lord Keeper.

He had not understood back then how bitter the fruit of knowledge would prove to be. Once he'd learned of the priests' folly, and the curse they'd inadvertently inflicted upon his people, he'd despaired. And wished with all his heart that he had remained ignorant and unsuspecting.

"Are you certain you wish to know more, Jade? Knowledge has power, yes. But too often the burden of knowledge is a fearsome one."

Her gaze fixed on his, determined and unwavering. "I want to know everything about you. I'm sick of secrets—even when they're kept for the best of intentions they do more harm than good." She made a rolling gesture with her hand. "If you truly want me to believe you're from another world, then keep talking. I'll tell you when to stop."

It was hardly a bothersome chore to regale a beautiful, intelligent girl with his life story. Malach described his day-to-day life as a tehun-Leader, and the nine men under his command. He told her tales of Lord Keeper Wulf, and how the man had earned his fearsome reputation both on the battlefield, and off. He explained the way his people cooked, what they ate. And when she queried an unfamiliar word, he explained that his favorite drink was an aromatic beverage made by grinding beans and infusing them in boiling water.

"Sounds very much like coffee," she said.

"Ah, yes. I have drunk your *coffee*. And 'tis indeed a similar beverage to *gahvay*."

"What did you wear? All leather—like the clothes you wore when I first met you?"

"Sand-lizard leathers are for warriors. No sensible man or woman would wear such clothing when going about their daily lives. The fashions of my time were lightweight cloths, dyed to resemble the crystals for which our warriors are named."

How long was she going to pretend she did not believe the evidence he laid before her? Did she truly believe him laboring under a psychotic delusion, and that his former life and former world did not exist? He'd felt her consciousness join with his in the moments before he'd escaped his malachite prison. He knew she'd shared his thoughts, experienced everything that he had for that brief moment. He knew she'd been sent a vision, and witnessed the Crystal Guardian casting his curse. How could she not believe?

As if she'd read his mind, she uttered a terse little laugh. "Humor me, Malach. If you're going to trip up, it'll be when you're regaling me with insignificant, everyday details."

He suppressed a sigh. Stubborn creature. There was nothing for him to "trip up" on given he was only telling her the truth.

"Tell me about this naming thing—after the crystals, I mean."

Malach stretched out a crick in his neck and bunched the pillow more comfortably beneath his head. "After a young man proves himself worthy to be elevated to warrior-status, he is ceremonially renamed after a crystal—what some call *gems* or *stones*. Each crystal is selected by the priests for certain attributes that best complement the man it is to be matched with."

"Your crystal is malachite, right?"

"Yes."

"So what're the qualities of malachite, then?"

"'Tis a stone that must be handled with caution because in its natural form it is toxic. The priests believe it is still evolving—still growing and learning its powers." He challenged her with his gaze, daring her to poke fun at his claim... as Wulf's kinsman, Kyan, had once poked fun at Malach's efforts to make sense of the scrolls he'd stolen from the priests.

She nodded, accepting his claims without demur. "I don't know much about the properties of crystals. I'll have to do some research. Can't believe I didn't think of it before."

"Why?"

"There might be a crystal that could help Mei."

"A very good idea. 'Tis well worth attempting. Perhaps I could assist your research."

"Thanks."

She hadn't been lying, then, when she'd told him she believed in magic. Nor had she tried to find some other explanation for the be-spelled door of their hotel room. So why did she not believe him now?

He masked his frustration. She had her reasons. And if he wanted her cooperation, he must respect them. "Malachite is not only an important protection stone, 'tis a stone of transformation, encouraging risk-taking and change, and releasing inhibitions."

He noticed the flush blooming in her cheeks and knew she was remembering certain events from the previous night, when she had been most delightfully uninhibited.

"Malachite has other useful qualities, but mostly the priests use it for scrying and healing," he finished.

She stared at him, nibbling her lower lip, a slight frown pleating her brows. He could almost hear her thoughts, her wonder that he had been matched to *this* stone.

"I am a man of many talents and hidden depths," he said, straight-faced, wondering if she would understand his subtle attempt at humor.

She gave him amused eyes. "I'll say. And what happens once you're matched to your stones? Does the earth, like, move or something?"

"An entire mountain collapsed the instant I was renamed for my chosen stone."

Her eyes went huge. "Wow! Really?"

"No."

It took a few moments for her to realize he was having fun at her expense. "No more of that or I'll have Aunt Lìli turn you into a toad," she told him. "And you'd better believe she can do it, too."

"I would like to meet this fearsome witch."

"You say that now. And you think *I'm* giving you a hard time with all my questions? Well, I've got nothing on Aunt Lìli. She'll turn you inside out and make you beg for mercy."

She paused, obviously waiting. And then she said, "Carry on. I think we're just getting to the good bit."

"During the ceremony, our priests cast a spell to imbue the crystal with the warrior's essence. Afterward, the priests hide the crystal in a secret place known only to themselves, where it is guarded both physically and by means of magic spells." He went on to explain that once the naming ceremony was complete, the warrior retained his new name until his deathbed. And after a warrior's death, his crystal would be chosen for another fledgling warrior. "These ceremonies have been performed as far back as we can remember—thousands of years so our priests claim. Thus, the more ancient the crystal, the more warriors it has linked with, and the more power it possesses."

Jade's gaze turned calculating. "What about the crystal that imprisoned you? The one Pieter trapped you in? Would that be as powerful as your original crystal?"

He immediately deduced the reasoning behind her question. "Perhaps. But before you consider using it to aid your sister, remember that not only has it broken in two, 'twas also cursed so it could be used to imprison a man. 'Twas never Pieter's intention to use it for protection or transformation. Intentions are powerful thing, Jade. I would be uneasy about using a broken, warped crystal to aid an ailing loved one."

Jade blew out a breath that conveyed weary acceptance. "Yeah, you're right. It could make things worse. Damn that old man."

"Pieter is indeed damned. Never fear on that account."

Someone rapped on the door.

"Come in!" Jade called.

The woman called Grace opened the door and peered around the doorframe. From her expectant expression and her subsequent moue of disappointment, Malach guessed she expected him to be in the middle of ravishing Jade. His balls tightened and his cock twitched at the mere thought. He raised his knee to hide his arousal from Grace's knowing gaze.

"Everything all right in here?"

"Yes," Jade said. "Of course everything's all right. Is Mei okay?"

"Of course Mei's okay," Grace said, mimicking Jade's snappish tone.

"Sorry."

"I know, J. No need to apologize."

Jade mustered a weary smile for her friend. "What do you want, Gracie?"

Grace endeavored to appear innocent. And failed. Malach didn't believe the woman knew the meaning of the word. "Oh, just wondering if you wanted a cuppa or something," she said.

Malach opened his mouth to say that he would very much appreciate a "cuppa or something"—especially if it was *coffee* and accompanied by food. But Jade was having none of it. "We won't be much longer, Gracie. Just have a few more things to sort out."

"I bet you do. Don't blow this, okay?"

"Go away, Gracie."

It was said without heat and Grace did not appear to take offense. "Okay. I'm outta here. But if you need me, you know where I am."

Malach waited until the woman left the room and had closed the door behind her. "I would get to the crux of my tale, if you have no further questions."

"Getting tired of talking, huh? Knew I'd wear you down sooner or later."

Malach thought about all the ways he would like Jade to "wear him down"... and then cursed beneath his breath. This girl—no, this young woman, for she had proven last night that she was no little girl—had him acting like a stripling who'd recently discovered the wonders of a woman's body, and could think of nothing else.

"Under the Keepership of great leaders like my Lord Keeper Wulfenite, the fiefs prospered as never before—save for the curse that continued to plague my people."

"A disease?"

"Nay, not a disease. The unforeseen backlash from a prideful spell cast many centuries ago."

"A spell?" Her eyes went saucer-round.

"Yes. Our priests had spied upon your world and coveted its riches. They discovered how to open a portal between the two worlds, and claimed the portents were favorable for a crossing during the next alignment of the planets. They ordered the Lord Keepers to send their fiercest and most loyal warriors to plunder your world, but the Lord Keepers were wary. There is a long and bloody history of disputes amongst our tribes. Raiding and in-fighting is a way of life, and costs many a brash young man his life. The Lord Keepers were reluctant to risk their warriors, and staunch in their efforts to adhere to the old ways. But the priests played their trump card and finally had their way—as they always do."

"What did they do?"

Malach laughed sourly. "They withheld the precious metals they conjured from beneath the earth—metals used to forge our weapons. And without the means to forge swords and thus present each new warrior with his fief-gift, the very fabric of our society shredded like the finest linen left to the storm's mercy."

"Some trump card."

"Indeed. The priests insisted there were no more precious metals to be had, that our land was depleted and not even their powerful spells could replenish the lack. But we all knew the truth. And without weapons, our warriors could not defend themselves, or their fiefs, from the outlander raiders whose coming the priests so conveniently foretold."

"Manipulative bastards. Pity the warriors didn't have my Aunt Lili going into bat for them. She would have cursed those priests with a crotch itch that would have driven them to distraction."

Malach laughed, genuinely this time. "My Lord Keeper Wulfenite would appreciate your ready wit, Jade." He resumed his tale. "There was one man with the balls to stand up to the priests. Lord Keeper Ceruss discovered the one thing the priests desired above all else, and in turn, he denied it to them."

Jade's eyes shone as she motioned eagerly for him to continue.

"The priests do not take women to their beds. They believe intercourse drains their essence and weakens them."

Her delicately arched eyebrows peaked. "They're eunuchs?"

"Eunuchs? I do not know this word."

"Men who've been, uh, gelded. Like you do to stallions you don't want to breed to mares."

Malach winced and bore her laughter like a man. "No. Our priests are not gelded, merely sworn to celibacy. Thus, to replenish their ranks, they require boys willing to forgo a warrior's life and dedicate themselves to a higher calling. Traditionally, boys who are not truly warrior material are encouraged to take this option. And in rare cases, boys will freely choose the Priests' Way, as 'tis called. Although the permission of the boy's Lord Keeper is required by law, such choice has always been respected, and only rarely is a boy denied."

Jade clapped her hands. "Oh, I see where this is going."

Malach was sure she did. She was an intelligent young woman. He'd always preferred intelligent females, unlike Kyan, who preferred them witless and giggly. "Ceruss petitioned every fief's Lord Keeper to deny permission for boys to choose the Priests' Way. He argued that if hordes of raiders were coming to pillage and destroy, as the priests had foretold, then every boy was needed to train as a warrior and swell the ranks—even those ill-suited to a warrior's life."

"Clever man. I bet that went down like a ton of bricks."

"For an entire *teh*—"

"That's ten years, right?"

"Yes. For ten years Ceruss prevailed, and no boys were dedicated to the Priests' Way. Until, finally, the priests offered something in return that not even Ceruss could resist."

Jade leaned forward in her chair. "What?"

"Invulnerability."

Chapter Eight

Jade chewed her thumbnail, pondering that possibility—or impossibility, depending on how far she was prepared to suspend belief. "This Lord Cerry-whatsit truly believed the priests could cast a spell to make all the warriors invulnerable?"

"He did—as did we all."

"And?"

"And, our priests erred. Their spell somehow skewed, bestowing instead immunity to all illness and disease, save rare ailments caused by the injudicious casting of spells."

Riiight. Hence Malach not worrying about using condoms.

"Even unintentional, the result was considered a gift beyond compare, and we rejoiced. Unfortunately, this same gift had an unforeseen side effect. From then on, our women only bore sons." He paused, allowing her to assimilate what he had revealed.

"A spell achieved something *that* amazing? Really?"

"Indeed. Do you not believe in spells and curses, Jade?"

She opened her mouth, only to shut it with a snap. Even if she chose to stick her head in the sand, and refused to believe all the evidence that'd been piling up since yesterday, she could hardly refute Aunt Lìlí's abilities.

Lìlí's curses worked. You only had to ask Murray. After what he'd pulled and the lies he'd spread, he had been idiotic enough to spot Jade and Mei and their mother at the shopping center, and call Jade a "Chink slut"… among other nasty racial slurs he'd yelled at the top of his voice. Lìli had coaxed the story from Jade's mother, and Jade later learned that Lìli had taken it upon herself to confront Murray face-to-face. Whether he confessed all, or whether Lìli read his mind, ultimately didn't matter. Lìli had cursed him—both literally *and* figuratively as it turned out.

The following weekend, Murray contracted a case of the mumps. Rumor had it his balls had swelled to the size of oranges, and eventually his parents were informed that the disease had made him sterile. Nothing too unusual in that, perhaps. Mumps could be pretty nasty if contracted by an adult male, and infertility often resulted. But the kicker was, Murray had already had a dose of mumps as a child and was supposedly immune.

Okay, when it came to Malach's claims Jade couldn't quite suspend belief, but she was getting there. "So your women only bore sons."

"Yes."

"Ever?"

"From that day forward there were no female infants born. And so it has been for centuries according to the temple records I acquired."

"Whoa."

The far-reaching consequences caused by a serious imbalance of males to females were common knowledge. Everyone knew of countries or cultures where female babies were disposed of because sons were needed to inherit. Young girls were taken as wives, and then cast aside or sold if they failed to bear sons for their husbands. Wives and daughters, considered little more than possessions to be bartered, were maltreated and even murdered at the whim of their men-folk. Female circumcision, women kept as virtual prisoners, women denied education or even basic medical care, selective abortion if the fetus was female… the list went on. It was barbaric and unconscionable, and it still happened.

But a society only *ever* giving birth to male babies? That was bad. Real bad. "Your people began to die out, didn't they? Once all the women of your world all became too old to bear any more children, there were no children born at all. Your population began to diminish. So what did you do?"

"How do you know we did anything at all?" Malach countered, capturing her gaze. She tried to read his face but it was a perfect, irritating blank.

"Oh, come on. Credit me with some brains, at least. You say this happened centuries ago. Your people must have gotten hold of women from somewhere or they would have completely died out in a couple of generations. What did you do? Steal women from other tribes?"

"Not exactly. The effects of the spell were global. All the tribes suffered the same problem, meaning there were soon few available women to steal. So our priests opened portals to your world, as they had originally planned."

"And sent through bands of marauders. Only instead of looting precious metals, they took women, right?"

"Precisely. Over the centuries, we regularly raided your earth and stole your women."

"Hang on.... Why did you need to keep stealing women? Surely once you had a large enough breeding pool you'd stop? The women you stole would have babies and everything would be hunky dory again. Right?"

Malach's blank expression segued to grimness. "For some reason that not even the priests could fathom, once your women settled in our world they, too, bore only male infants. And so, the raiding continued."

"Which is how *you* eventually ended up on Earth."

He nodded.

Jade put two and two together and came up with one pissed off Crystal Guardian defending his village from Styrian raiders. "And that's where you came across Pieter. He had magical powers of his own, and he stood against you when you tried to take the women of his village."

Malach nodded.

"And Pieter didn't care that you were following orders, and desperate to save your people." The reality of what she'd seen in the vision hit home. "Oh my God. That's why he cursed the entire troop. What I saw—it *was* real."

"I was tehun-Leader, the second in command to Lord Keeper Wulfenite, our fief's leader. Wulf was accompanied by two tehuns, along with the priest assigned to each. The priests and one tehun remained in camp to guard the women we had already taken and to keep watch. Thus it was Lord Keeper Wulf and one tehun—eleven men in total—who confronted Pieter in his village that day."

"Eleven men." Jade pressed a fist to her abdomen, fighting horror. "Please tell me the priests and the remaining troop escaped back to your world with their captives?"

He shrugged. "Likely so, but only Pieter would know for sure."

"And you say centuries have passed." Jade wondered if there were others from Malach's troop roaming the world.

While Malach related his impressions of the living conditions and the primitive technology used by the people at the time of his last raid, something he'd said niggled at her. *Centuries have passed since the first time the Guardian's curse befell me....*

Since the *first* time.

Everything—all the little clues she'd missed until now—snapped into sharp focus.

Malach's familiarity with Pieter.

Malach claiming she was a... a.... How had he termed it? "A mistake. Again."

This mysterious Francesca, who'd had such a lasting and devastating effect on Malach.

Jade almost choked on the breath she'd gulped. Freaking

heck. She wasn't the first woman chosen for him. *Francesca* had been first. And given his easy acceptance of modern technologies that should have freaked him out, like flush toilets, running water, and electricity, more than likely Malach's first bonding attempt hadn't been that long ago, either.

He must have noted her frozen-faced shock for he paused mid-sentence.

"This isn't the first time you've been here, in this time—*my time*—is it, Malach?"

He inclined his head in a parody of a bow. "Very good, Jade. There is a worthy brain inside that delectable feminine package."

"Don't patronize me," she said. "You've been matched and bonded before. That's how you know what's going on. Otherwise, you'd be as much in the dark about all this stuff as I am. Tell me about Francesca."

"No."

"Why not?"

His lips thinned. "Because 'tis no business of yours." He launched himself from the bed and stomped over to her chair. He placed a hand either side of her and loomed, glaring down at her. "Do you hear me quizzing you about your past lovers?"

The anger blazing in his eyes stole her breath. She somehow managed to summon a snort—a pretty pathetic excuse for one, but a snort nevertheless. "Only because you know full well I never had a lover until you came along."

And she suspected he'd ruined her for any future lovers she might have—not that she'd ever admit that to him in a million years. Her hand crept to her pendant, drawing Malach's gaze.

His eyes narrowed. "What is this?" He pointed to her pendant. "Why have you discarded your namesake stone?"

"This?" She held it up and brandished it at him. "I haven't discarded it at all. I imagine it's more of Pieter's magic."

"Explain. Please," he added, noting her frown at his arrogant command.

"This morning I felt an urgent compulsion to get home, but I didn't know why. And then I glanced down at it and the green jade had changed to *this*. Red jade, I presume?"

He reached out to finger the pendant and he was so close his breath skimmed her skin, sending tingles down her spine. "Yes," he said. "'Tis red jade."

It was on the tip of her tongue to remind him that he'd said green jade wasn't an appropriate gem for her, and ask if now he knew her a little better, red jade might be more her style. Then she remembered what he'd said about red jade, that it was passionate and stimulating, and decided it was far too provocative a statement.

"And when it changed to red jade, I remembered everything. I remembered Mei and… and—" She wished she could look away, hide herself from his gaze. "And why I'd decided to meet with Pieter."

"To let him use you in exchange for a fee."

She glared at him. "No need to pussyfoot 'round. I was going to play the prostitute, all right? Sell myself for money."

"To help Mei."

"Yes. I was desperate. Is that so wrong?"

He sighed. "No, Jade. 'Tis not so wrong. 'Tis a true expression of your love for your sister that you were prepared to go to such lengths. And I owe you an apology."

"Huh?" She picked her jaw up off the metaphorical floor. "For what?"

He cupped her face in his big hands, and his eyes glinted with some strong emotion as he gazed at her. "For branding you a whore based on circumstantial evidence. For taking your virginity without the tenderness and care that were your due. For using your sweet body to help me feel human—to help me *feel* again."

Tears stung her eyes. He was so terribly wounded, this man she'd given herself to, and his soul was scarred along with his body. He'd been tortured and deprived of all hope not once, but twice. And she was his only hope of escape. "Was being trapped in the crystal truly that awful?"

"'Twas beyond any nightmare you could imagine."

"And Francesca?" Jade whispered her name and felt a shiver ghost down her spine. "It must be dreadfully painful—her being long dead and buried, while you haven't aged a jot."

He released her and drew back, frowning. "What leads you to believe she is dead?"

"Well, the way you speak of her, I thought—" Jade shrugged, uncomfortable with the intensity in his voice, in his expression. "I'm sorry."

"Surely I would know if she no longer lived." He spoke as though to himself, and then he blinked, seeming to recall he had an audience of one. "I believe I would have felt our connection break if Francesca had passed from this world to the next. What year is this?"

"Twenty-twelve." Jade nibbled her lower lip. What if Francesca was still alive? Where did that leave her and Malach?

He backed away to sit on the edge of the bed. "I believe she would be nearing her fifth teh—fifty years old, by your reckoning."

Jade let her gaze drift from his face, down his body, and back up to his face again. She wasn't perving, merely estimating his age. Ah, who was she trying to kid? She liked looking at him. "And you'd be what, a little over forty? Forty-five, max?"

"Forty-one."

Twenty-odd years older than her. That should have bothered Jade, but it simply wasn't important. "So Francesca's less than a decade older than you. That's nothing. Unless you happen to have issues about older women."

"Nay. I am many things, but I am not a man who is attracted by a woman's looks alone. People love whom they will, and age should not factor. I gave my heart to Francesca once, and she still holds it in her hands."

A tendril of jealousy tried to strangle Jade's good intentions, and she briefly considered not voicing what she was thinking. But she couldn't bring herself to be so selfish and petty. Malach deserved some hope—a chance at happiness, at least. "So, if this Francesca is the love of your life, as you claim—"

"'Tis no claim. 'Tis the truth."

"Fine. Then if she *is* still alive—and there's a very good chance she is—what's to stop you from finding her again and living happily ever after?"

Malach gaped at her, his pale blue eyes wide with what she presumed was utter astonishment. And, as she watched, they lit from within with a large dollop of burgeoning hope.

She wished she could feel good about giving him that hope, but all she felt was aching sadness, as though she'd lost something precious.

Ridiculous. She should be smugly congratulating herself for thinking up such a clever scheme. If she could get Malach back with Francesca, it'd be perfect....

Wouldn't it?

A little voice inside her protested that it wouldn't be perfect. It would hurt. It would be gut-wrenching. And she would hate imagining Malach with another woman. This illogical reaction wasn't helped any by Malach appearing paralyzed by her words, capable of little more than staring at her like she'd dropped out of the sky from another planet.

She mentally shook herself. Enough. "Come on, Malach. Snap out of it. You, living happy ever after with Francesca, the love of your life. What's not to like about that?" She wasn't proud of the sarcasm lacing her tone but hey, she'd never claimed to be perfect.

Malach blinked slowly, and dropped his gaze, unwilling for her to be privy to whatever he was feeling. "It would be—"

"Pretty easy to track her down, I imagine. These days most people have an internet presence—whether they intend to or not. Do you know what country she lived in?"

"I remember her calling herself a rarity, an American with a—" He frowned. "A *pass* for traveling the world."

"Passport. Hmmm. Anything else? State? Name of the town or city?"

He shook his head. "When I first emerged from the crystal, I was bewildered and confused—in a state akin to the daze a warrior experiences when he is taken by the battle-rage, and after the battle is done discovers himself still breathing. My entire focus was the woman who had called me from the crystal. I recall I was in her abode and that she was not alone. It transpired she had a child asleep in another room. I vividly recall the child's name because at the time, I thought it unusual that the woman who called me from my crystal had rejected her own crystal-name, only to name her daughter after a crystal."

"What was Francesca's crystal-name?"

"Her given name was Beryl, but she insisted on being known by her second name."

Jade screwed up her nose. "I can't say I blame her for that. Regardless of how pretty a gem *beryl* might be, as a girl's name it's a bit old-fashioned."

"Beryl is a stone of uncommon beauty. It suited her— better than Francesca, I think."

Francesca would *have* to be gorgeous, of course. She couldn't have been plain and dumpy and unremarkable. Jade disliked the woman already. She changed the subject. "And her daughter's name?"

"Chalcedony."

"Now that's a pretty name."

"Yes. I had the impression the girl was very young. I recall—" He paused, his expression turning cold and hard.

Jade knew him too well by now. It was a mask he hid behind, and she suspected he believed displaying any strong emotion was a weakness.

"Her husband was seriously ill," he finally said. "He had been given mere months to live."

Jade huffed a loud breath. "She was *married*?"

"Yes. She was caring for him. She would not allow me to stay in her home, so she provided me with paid lodgings and spare clothing. She visited me with food and supplies until I was taken by the crystal."

"And her husband was *dying*?"

"Yes. That is what she told me."

"Bloody hell. Pieter's so-called omnipotent goddess really stuffed up big time with *that* match. Talk about bad timing and emotional baggage and really, really bad, uh, timing." She thought hard for a moment. "I don't suppose you know the name of the hotel or motel or wherever it was you were staying?"

"No. She transported me to the abode by a... a... *car* in the dead of night. And she extracted my promise to stay inside and unseen. I understood her need for secrecy and complied with her requests."

"For an entire month?"

"For four weeks, yes. She visited every few days—whenever she could get away. I was content with what she offered me."

Curiosity pricked. "Did you and Francesca... you know... have sex?" If they had bonded, why weren't they together now? What had gone wrong?

Her chest constricted, making drawing breath more of an effort, and she had to force herself to relax... and unclench her fists. She didn't want to think about Malach doing the things he'd done last night to *Francesca*—or any other woman for that matter.

"Twice." Malach's sharp reply cut through Jade's increasingly dark and twisted thoughts. "Despite our mutual attraction, I respected her decision and did not press her further."

Francesca had balked at the crucial third, uh, *intimate* encounter, and managed to resist jumping Malach's bones for an entire month? A tough woman this Francesca. Or perhaps simply determined not to screw up her life any more than it had already been screwed up thanks to Pieter selecting her for a Crystal Warrior.

Jade abruptly realized Malach's jaw was working, like he was clenching his teeth. He was clearly unhappy with this line of questioning, which must be dredging up painful memories better left buried. Poor guy. She was being an insensitive bitch.

"At the very least we should be able to track down a phone number and possibly an address," she offered, hoping to give him something to focus on other than the past... and the horrifying prospect of imprisonment in the crystal a third time.

Arctic-blue eyes, awash with hope, sought hers. "I could talk to her on the phone?" he asked.

She heard the hope in his voice and her heartstrings twinged. She cleared her throat, swallowing an upwelling of unreasonable, painful jealousy. "Quite possibly, yes. If her number's listed, it might even be as simple as ringing International Directory Services. What's her full name?"

"Beryl Francesca Laureano. You would do this for me, Jade? Help me find Francesca?"

"Of course. Why wouldn't I?"

Because you should keep Malach for yourself. You could easily fall for a man like him, so why shouldn't you have him?

Jade banished that nasty little voice in her head and refused to heed it. "And then, once this month-long deadline business is up and I've finished your portrait, you can find a way to be with Francesca again. Presuming she hasn't remarried or something."

As soon as she'd uttered the words she wished she could take them back. She hadn't meant to be cruel. And now she was forced to watch, up close and personal, as a man's hopes shattered. The light in Malach's eyes dulled and he seemed to age before her eyes.

"She might not be married," she offered in a lame attempt to make amends. "She may still be single and available. Don't give up hope."

But he had. He'd covered his face in his hands and slumped forward, with his elbows resting on his thighs.

She hated what she'd done to him—hated herself for the pain she'd caused him. She scrambled to kneel before him, grasping his wrists, desperate for him to listen. "Malach? Look at me. Don't give up."

He raised his head and the despair shadowing his eyes made her flinch. "'Tis not the possibility Francesca has remarried that concerns me. I must be honest with you, Jade, for you deserve no less. If we do not pass whatever Test the Crystal Guardian devises, I will once more be condemned to the hell of the crystal. I have vowed to die by my own hand rather than be imprisoned a third time, but I fear to the depths of my soul that the old man's curse will take even that choice from me."

A shiver of unease slid down Jade's spine. "Hold on. Run that last bit by me again. Pieter mentioned a 'test' back at the hotel, I think. And in his letter, too. What exactly is this Testing business?"

"I know not exactly what it entails because last time no Testing took place. The eve of the four-week deadline, I recall being restless and unable to sleep. And then, between one blink and the next, the crystal had taken me again. I now realize that was due to the bond between Francesca and I remaining incomplete."

She squeezed his wrists, projecting reassurance. "Okay. We can do this. All we have to do is pass this Test and free you from the crystal's influence. And afterward, I'll help you find Francesca. Simple."

He laughed, but it was a stark, raw sound. "I do not believe it will be at all simple, Jade. This time Pieter's goddess has chosen *you* for me. If Francesca and I were fated to be together, surely his goddess would have sent me to *her* instead of you."

"Oh. Good point. So you think we're stuck with each other, huh? Whether we like it or not?" Deep inside, that selfish little voice rejoiced.

"I am afraid so. I am truly sorry, Jade."

She shrugged off his apology.

His troubled gaze caught hers. "I believe it bodes ill that we are so very willing to give each other up, despite the bond having been activated. In mere weeks our bond will be Tested by forces beyond our ken. How do we expect to succeed if we do not truly love each other, if we do not truly wish to spend our lives together?"

Spending the rest of her life with Malach? *Truly* falling in love with him? Yikes. Neither were possibilities Jade had considered. Falling in love with any man, let alone a man from another world twenty years her senior, wasn't a possibility she *could* consider when Mei must remain her first, and only, priority.

Crap. They were so screwed. "I guess having terrific sex multiple times isn't gonna be enough, huh?"

Malach's attempt at a smile came across as more of a grimace. "I do not believe so."

The silence stretched until she could bear it no longer. She slapped her palms on her thighs and pushed to her feet. "No point fretting about this. I'll think of something. There's gotta be a way around it. But for now, we've got work to do."

Malach dragged his fingers through his hair. "And what work would that be?"

"Well, if I'm to justify earning this twenty-five grand, I'd better get started right away on some preliminary sketches. I've got to work tomorrow, so time isn't on my side. Hope you're feeling model-worthy." Her mind flooded with visions of ordering Malach to contort himself into various poses. Funny how he was invariably nude...

She gave herself a mental shake. She was supposed to be painting a *portrait*. Of his *face*. There was no reason for him to remove his clothes. Unfortunately.

She made an effort to pull herself together. Like, before Malach commented on the dopey expression on her face and asked what was up… and she blurted exactly what she would like to be up.

"How about you simply—" she fluttered her hands at him "—I don't know, do what you'd usually do and I'll follow you around for a bit."

Malach's eyebrows knit in a bemused frown. He didn't have a clue what she was talking about.

"I need to observe you and do some sketches before I paint you," she said. "Otherwise, I won't see the essence of who you are. I don't want to paint a static portrait—anyone who fancies themselves an artist could do that. I want the *real* you captured on canvas."

He quirked a brow. "This is important to you?"

"Yes. Otherwise, why bother? I may as well just snap a photo of you, enlarge it, and copy it onto canvas. Where's the artistry in that?"

"Very well. Where do you wish me to begin 'doing what I usually do'?"

She wrinkled her nose. Good question. Despite his modern attire, Malach exuded "other-wordly" vibes. His accent and often overly formal way of speaking, and especially his eerie capacity to be so very still and then explode into motion, marked him as alien. Different. He would command attention merely by entering a room.

Jade felt the sharp tension forming behind her eyes that signaled the onset of a headache. What the heck was she going to do with him for four entire weeks?

"Okay, what would you normally be doing at this hour of the morning?"

His right hand clutched at his hip, as though reaching for

something familiar. And then his big body stiffened, tension vibrating in every muscle. His gaze flicked to her face and he shuttered his expression, closing her out. His palm smoothed down his denim-clad thigh, and when he opened his eyes, he was in full command again. "I would be engaging in swordplay."

"Right. Swordplay. Of course you would. Sorry, but that's so *not* going to be an option. Anything else?"

"Honing my weapon."

Jade's eyes crossed and she sucked a sharp breath. His weapon.... Ohhh, he meant the sharp, dangerous one that killed people, rather than a certain portion of his anatomy he'd recently used with devastating effect. She bit her lips and hauled her wandering mind from the gutter. "Anything else?"

"Exercising my mount."

She shook her head. "Not going to happen."

"Hand-to-hand combat."

She opened her mouth to automatically nix that suggestion, too, when an idea bloomed. "How good are you at hand-to-hand combat?"

"As I mentioned previously, I was a tehun-Leader."

Evidently that was supposed to be self-explanatory. Oookay. "I'm guessing you're pretty good, then?"

"Yes."

No false modesty, simply absolute belief in his own abilities.

"I might just be able to do something about that one. Leave it with me, okay?"

If the eager light in his eyes was any indication, she'd sure piqued his interest. She decided to put him out of his misery. "I'm not promising anything, but I might be able to get you a few sessions with someone who could teach you a thing or two. If you're as good as you think you are."

"I am."

Mmm. She wondered if Grandmaster Dai-soon, Lili's old

friend, would agree. Or whether Malach would be treated to a harsh lesson in humility sometime in the near future. She made a mental note to take along her sketchbook. For a man as innately confident and physically competent as Malach, a serving of humble pie might make for some interesting inner conflicts that would translate powerfully onto canvas.

Her stomach chose that moment to rumble loudly, reminding her that she'd neglected to eat breakfast. "Hungry?"

He nodded.

"C'mon then."

As she wandered back into the lounge with Malach trailing behind, Jade caught the delicious aroma of fresh made coffee.

She discovered Mei lounging on the divan by the bay window. "Breakfast's ready," Mei announced, licking toast crumbs from her fingers. "Grace said to help yourselves. She figured we'd have an extra so she's made plenty."

Bless you, Grace. Jade grabbed Malach's arm and towed him into the kitchen where they found their Angel of Mercy smearing hot buttered toast with honey.

Yum! Her favorite. Jade made a grab for the toast, only to have her hand smacked.

"Oi! Hands off. Get your own." Grace cut her gaze to Malach and smiled sweetly at him. "What do you fancy?"

Malach pulled up mid-step. "Ah.... What do I fancy?" The gaze he slid to Jade's was pleading.

She hid a grin. "Man up. You're on your own."

Grace rolled her eyes. "To eat, I mean."

"In truth, I am not certain." Malach inhaled deeply, his nostrils flaring. As though pulled by unseen forces, he followed his nose—literally—to the freshly plunged coffee sitting on the bench. He picked up the plunger and sniffed appreciatively. "Ahhh."

"Um, you're not thinking of drinking it straight from the plunger, are you?" Grace's shrill voice suggested she was harboring visions of second-degree burns.

Malach snorted. "Nay. I remember Francesca steeping this beverage in such a way. She called it a 'press'."

"I think some Americans call it a French press," Grace said.

"I recall it was not as good a brew as *gahvay*, but beggars can ill afford to be selective." He snagged a spare mug from the bench, and poured it full of coffee.

Jade watched him inhale, drawing the aroma deep into his lungs. Then he gulped a mouthful of the hot black coffee and sighed with pleasure. He took another gulp. And then another. And Jade stood there, mesmerized by the pleasure in his expression as he savored the bitter brew.

"Ahem!"

Jade's gaze shot to Grace, who'd obviously been watching Jade watching Malach for she grinned and winked... at Malach, who'd polished off his caffeine fix and was now observing them both. A smile played across his lips.

Jade felt a familiar heat creeping up her face. Desperate to divert the attention from her blush she blurted, "Pour me a cup of that, will you, Malach?"

He inclined his head. "How do you take... it?"

That slight pause told her the double entendre was entirely deliberate.

Grace snickered. "As if you don't know already," she muttered.

This time Jade's flush was so hot she felt like she'd copped a really bad dose of sunburn.

"She takes 'it' with milk," Grace said. "And no sugar, because she's sweet enough already. Don't you think so, Malach?"

"Indeed." He held Jade's gaze for a long moment before he topped up the contents of the mug with milk and offered it to her.

"Aw, she's blushing like a schoolgirl," Grace said, smearing another piece of toast with honey.

Jade snatched the mug from Malach's hands and plonked it

on the table, sloshing hot coffee over her fingers. "Yeow!"

Before she could shake off the hot droplets, Malach had grabbed her hand. He checked the burn, and then raised her hand to his lips. He sucked her forefinger and index finger into his mouth, all the while holding her gaze with pale blue eyes that had turned wild and stormy.

Jade couldn't look away. And it wasn't merely her fingers and face that burned. Her whole body felt hot and achy as he drew her fingers deeper into his mouth, suckling them.

Jade vaguely noted Grace's throaty chuckle. "Not precisely the recommended way to heal a burn," she said.

Malach released Jade's fingers from his mouth. Turning her hand palm up, he licked the heat-reddened ball of her thumb. The lick became a kiss—a feather-light caress that somehow seemed directly connected to the pleasure-centers of her brain.

God. How did he *do* that? How could he affect her so damned much?

She wrenched her hand from his grasp and shook it. And then she snatched the piece of toast Grace had raised to her mouth, grabbed her own mug of coffee, and bolted for the lounge.

Mei's nose crinkled as Jade skidded to a halt. "You all right, J?"

Jade nodded, too breathless to speak.

"Make sure you run cold water on that burn!" Grace called from the kitchen.

"You burned yourself?"

"It's nothing. Just a splash of coffee. See?" Jade perched on the end of the divan and crammed the pilfered toast into her mouth so she could hold the hand out for inspection.

Mei turned Jade's hand this way and that. "Doesn't look serious. You sure you're okay? You look all hot and bothered."

Jade nodded again, and tugged her hand free to deal with the toast before it dripped honey down her chin. She'd just begun to regain a degree of equilibrium when Grace's raised voice captured her attention.

"I'm Jade's best friend, Malach. Which means I'm very protective of her. Consider yourself duly warned. So. About last night. You obviously had sex with her, and I only have one thing to say to you."

Jade froze, too appalled to move.

"And what might that be?"

God. She couldn't believe Malach had been dumb enough to ask.

"Hurt her and I'll have your dangly bits."

"My dangly bits?"

"Your testicles. I'll geld you with whatever blunt instrument is handy, and force-feed them to you for breakfast."

"I believe that is considerably more than *one* thing."

"I'm not bluffing. I have medical training. Understand?"

"Understood."

Oh. My. God. Jade strained her ears, expecting Grace to have a lot more to say on the subject, but when silence reigned, she didn't know whether to be relieved or horrified.

Mei touched her arm. Jade jumped. She'd completely forgotten her sister was listening in, too.

"That went quite well, I think," Mei said, straight-faced.

"I… uh…. Yes, it did. I have something I, uh, have to do now." Jade fled for the sanctuary of her bedroom. She closed the door behind her and sank onto her bed. Miraculously, she'd not spilled a single drop of coffee. Her hands shook as she sipped from the mug and ate the rest of her toast, heedless of crumbs. But by the time she'd drained the mug, she had a plan.

Keeping one ear out for her sister, Jade snuck into Mei's bedroom and powered up their father's ancient laptop. As she drummed her fingers, waiting for the clunky dial-up internet connection to do its thing, she wondered how Malach was going to react if she managed to find Francesca's phone number.

Would he want to speak to the woman?

Would *she* want him this time around?

It was weird, thinking about handing Malach over to the woman who'd rejected him, and gotten him into this mess in the first place.

And what if bringing Malach and Francesca together before the Testing took place doomed Malach and Jade to failure, and he was again condemned to the crystal?

So many questions.

She refused to dwell on her own personal stake in this whole crazy scenario. Namely, how she truly felt about the man she'd been chosen to redeem. She told herself it was a non-issue. She couldn't possibly be falling for Malach after only one night, right? Her growing obsession with him was simply a result of the incredible sex they'd had, right?

Right.

The laptop's overworked fan had at last eased to a less irritating whine. Jade took that as her cue, and Googled *Beryl Francesca Laureano*.

Aha. The results mentioned a woman by that name who'd co-owned a shop called *Mind, Body, Spirit*. Mmm. Sounded promising. It sure fit with a woman who'd named her daughter "Chalcedony" after a crystal.

According to the website, the shop sold New Age stuff, and was situated in an obscure little town somewhere in the States. All the links were broken, though, and both a Google search and a whitepages.com search on the shop proved fruitless. Maybe it had closed down.

She scanned the Google results some more and found a link to a People Finder website. After a mucking round with various name combinations, Jade finally came up with a possible suspect. There was a Mrs B. Francesca Laureano-Owens listed jointly with a Clive E. Owens.

Married? Uh oh. That couldn't be good.

There was a phone number available, but Jade would have to pay a fee for a search report. She made a face and took a punt. Googling Clive E. Owens revealed that he owned Owens Dental... and his company had a website.

Score!

She paused, chewing her thumbnail, her right hand hovering uncertainly over the website link. Should she or shouldn't she? Taking this further might be the best thing she could do for Malach. Or it could ruin any chance he had of passing the Testing and freeing himself from the curse.

She clicked the link, and waited what seemed like an eternity for the website to load.

The homepage launched straight into a video complete with cheesy audio. "Your smile is forever! A sparkling smile reflects confidence, youth, vitality," blah blah blah.

Jade snorted, and scrolled through the "complete range of oral and dental care services, all under one roof". With luck there would be some photos of the owners and their colleagues—what better way to advertise your dental business, than by flashing your own perfect pearly-whites all over your website?

Sure enough, when she clicked on the "about us" page link there he was: Clive E. Owens, in all his dazzling white-toothed glory.

Clive was an okay-looking guy. Francesca had pretty good taste in men—if indeed this guy was married to Malach's Francesca.

Jade fossicked around a bit more and discovered links to a "smile survey", as well as PDFs of monthly newsletters. Boy, this guy really went all out with his marketing. She clicked on the latest newsletter headed "Owens Dental celebrates milestone" and came face-to-face with a photo of Clive and his wife smiling widely for the camera during a company dinner.

Bingo. According to the caption it was definitely his wife: *Dr. Clive Owens and his wife, Francesca Laureano-Owens.*

Malach's Francesca....

It was her. Jade knew it absolutely.

She clicked on the link to give her a larger version of the photo, and examined the woman who'd broken Malach's heart.

Jade hated her on sight. Slim and blonde. Attractive in a cool, touch-me-not Nordic way. She looked to be in her early forties. Hah. What was the bet she embraced plastic surgery as enthusiastically as teeth-whitening treatments.

Jade sensed movement behind her and quickly closed the links.

"I wondered where you had disappeared to." Malach placed a plate of toast on the desk beside her.

"I'm comparing prices for some of the art supplies I'll need." The lie tripped too easily off her tongue. At this rate she was going to end up a ruddy expert at dissembling—like Pieter.

"Have you eaten enough breakfast?" she asked.

He nodded.

"Good. Let's go." She crammed a slice of toast into her mouth.

"What is so pressing that you do not have time to even shower or change?"

Good point. Jade held a hand over her mouth and mumbled around the remaining toast crumbs. "We need to sort out this falling irrevocably in love business so we can pass the Testing with flying colors."

"I agree. But how? Love is not an emotion one can conjure at will, Jade."

She swallowed and cleared her throat. "Yeah, I'm well aware of that. Otherwise I would tell myself you're definitely The One, and we wouldn't have this problem."

"And could I be?"

"Be what?"

"The one."

How was she going to get out of this, uh, *one*? Best to keep it light. "Well, if love was only about the sex, then yeah. You could definitely be The One. I thought we were very, um, compatible in that area."

His grin was the slightest bit smug, but the expression in his eyes didn't match. It was too serious. "I agree. If love is about compatibility when a man beds a woman, then you could be the one for me."

"Really?"

"Really."

"That's so sweet. It's probably the sweetest thing any guy's ever said to me. So thanks."

"You are welcome, Jade. Unfortunately, I do not think Pieter's goddess will be satisfied with expressions of physical lust. If she were, I am certain the Crystal Guardian would have long ago shed his burdens and we would all be free."

"Yeah. Me, too. But I reckon I have the perfect solution to that sticky little problem." She held out her hands and he obligingly yanked her to her feet.

"And what might that be?" he asked.

"We'll pay my Aunt Lìli a visit. By the way, I might not have mentioned that she's not my real aunt, but an old friend of my mother's."

"The witch, correct?"

"Yep. The very same."

His hands tightened around hers. "After what I have experienced, I am the last man to disbelieve anyone's claim that they can perform powerful magic. But remember, Jade, we are ultimately attempting to fool a *goddess*. I do not believe a witch's spell will suffice in this case."

"Chill, Malach. My idea is so damned simple it can't possibly fail." Jade grinned at him. "I'm going to make sure we pass the Testing by having Lìli cast a temporary love spell on us."

Chapter Nine

MALACH SILENTLY ACCOMPANIED Jade the short distance to the whimsically named Fig Tree Street. She led him up the path to Lìli's house and rapped on the front door. As she waited, she couldn't help hopping from foot to foot, unable to dampen her growing agitation as she wondered how Lìli would respond to their plea for help. Despite what she'd intimated to Malach, she knew it wouldn't be easy convincing her aunt to compromise her principles and be-spell them. And God help her if Lìli ever discovered what Jade been poised to do to find more money for Mei's treatment....

Sweat oozed down her spine. Her stomach performed some impressive gymnastics. Cursing beneath her breath, she slammed up her strongest mental barriers. Why hadn't she considered Lìli's uncanny ability to ferret out the truth before now? Her only chance would be if her aunt was too distracted by Malach to catch a hint of Jade's sordid little secret.

By the time Lìli arrived at the front door, Jade had willed herself to some semblance of calm—enough to kiss her aunt's cheek and greet with a hug her like she always did. "*Nǐ hǎo, Lìli Yíyi. Nǐ shēntǐ hǎo ma?*" For Malach's benefit she repeated the greeting in English. "How are you, Aunt Lìli?"

"Jade!" Lìli beamed at her. And then her gaze slid past Jade to lock onto Malach. "*Zhè wèi xiānshēng shì shuí? Who is this gentleman?*"

"*Zhè shì wǒ péngyǒu.*" Jade deliberately made her relationship with Malach very clear by introducing him as a 'friend'. "His name is—"

"*Tā shì nǐ nán péngyǒu,*" Lìli corrected. "Your boyfriend." Heavy emphasis on the "boy" in boyfriend.

Beneath Lìli's uncompromising stare, Jade's composure faltered. "No he isn't," she said quickly. And, thinking she might have offended Malach, quickly added, "I mean, not exactly. Um, sort of—like, temporarily?"

Lìli's lips pursed with disapproval.

Uh oh. "What I mean is—" Oh, crap!

Malach saved her further humiliation by bowing to Lìli, introducing himself, and expressing his great pleasure at meeting a dear friend of the Liang family.

It had been exactly the right thing for him to do. Or exactly the wrong thing, depending on your point of view.

After Jade's parents died, in the absence of any close relatives Lìli had taken Mei and Jade under her wing, and nominated herself surrogate matriarch of the Liang family. Lìli took this self-imposed position very seriously indeed, even referring to Jade and Mei as her nieces. And, as always happened whenever potential husband-material crossed her path, Lìli instantly summed Malach up, and her gaze lit with a kind of speculative eagerness that made Jade cringe.

Lìli's shrewd gaze slanted to Jade. She cackled with delight, grabbed Malach's arm, and led him into the house, leaving Jade to trail along behind. Lìli always had been a terrible flirt.

"*Nǐ cóng nǎ lǐ lái?*" Jade heard Lìli demanding. "Where are you from, Malach?" Jade inhaled sharply and held her breath, wondering how on earth he would respond... and what her aunt's reaction might be if the truth slipped out.

"I am a warrior of the Styrian people," Malach said.

Jade somehow managed to resist a classic face-palm gesture, and racked her brains for some way to salvage the situation. God. They should have concocted a cover story before—

"I belong to the Shifting Sands fief."

Ah, crap. Too late. She waited for Lìli to start in on Malach.

"A Storm-Rider, heh?"

Jade gasped, and a shiver goosed her skin as Malach stiffened and went very still. The potential for violence crackled in the air

Lìli threw up a hand in a sharp, no-nonsense gesture to halt the questions that had bubbled to Jade's lips.

Jade bit the inside of her cheek, knowing her aunt would reveal as much or as little as she deemed fit—when she was darn well good and ready, and not a moment before. And if Lìli chose *not* to enlighten them, there was nothing either of them could do about it. Lìli could be as stubborn as a hungry seagull determined to crack a cockle on a rock.

"You know of my people," Malach said.

"I know many things, young man."

"How?" He loomed over Lìli in a menacing way. And Jade was torn between the desire to step between them to protect Lìli from Malach's anger, and unholy delight that he'd put her aunt on the spot by asking the hard question. She opted for the latter. Lìli was more than capable of taking care of herself. Go Malach!

"I know of those dubbed 'the Stone Warriors' from my dreams," Lìli answered, seeming unfazed by any implied threat emanating from the large and possibly dangerous man Jade had brought into her home.

"Are you a practitioner of magic like our priests?"

"Faugh!" Lìli hissed, obviously offended. "Do not insult me by comparing me to those imbeciles. I am what your people would term a Wise Woman. Unlike your priests, we refuse to despoil *our* gifts with arrogance and self-serving acts."

To Jade's astonishment, Malach dropped to one knee and bowed his head. "I most humbly apologize for the insult, Wise One."

"Oh, get up, get up! On your feet, Malach. You do not kneel to me." Lìli's protest was token at best, Jade decided, observing the delighted sparkle in her aunt's nut-brown eyes. Lìli was secretly flattered and pleased that Malach had shown her such deference.

Malach rose fluidly to his feet and stood, loose-limbed and completely at ease, while Lìli gave him a thorough head-to-toe once-over that would have made a lesser man's balls shrivel to raisins. She even went so far as to squeeze his bicep and hoot her appreciation.

"Lìli Yíyi, when are you going to learn to keep your hands to yourself?" Jade blurted.

Over Lìli's head, Malach grinned at Jade, waggling his eyebrows to indicate that he didn't mind being woman-handled—even if this particular woman was a sexagenarian.

"A strong man. A warrior. *Hěn hǎo!* Good, good. An older, more experienced man will be very good for my headstrong, stubborn niece."

"Lìli Yíyi!" Jade covered her eyes and moaned, but Lìli took no notice and shooed her into the kitchen with instructions to fetch food and drinks.

"I will be talking to your *nán péngyǒu* in the garden, Niece. Do not take too long with refreshments." And so saying, Lìli repossessed Malach's arm and directed him through to the garden.

Jade pressed her hands against her hot cheeks in a vain effort to cool them. "He's *not* my boyfriend," she grumbled at their departing backs.

As quickly as humanly possible, she decanted homemade lemonade into a jug and arranged it on a tray along with glass tumblers, serviettes, and a plate of homemade biscuits. Through the kitchen windowpane, she spied on Lìli and Malach in the backyard garden. They had perched on spindly-legged chairs set around the ancient glass-topped table that wobbled precariously on the uneven patch of cobblestones.

And they were deep in conversation.

Jade would have given her left hand to listen in on what they were saying. She grabbed the tray and carried it through to the garden to lay it on the table. "Well," she said brightly, "you two seem to have a lot to talk about."

Silence greeted her observation. Darn. So much for subtlety. She decided to be blunt. "That was an invitation to fill me in on what you've been talking about, by the way."

More silence. Followed by the sort of unblinking regard disapproving parents bestow upon a child who's just committed a public faux pas.

Jade sighed inwardly and gave up. She sat and poured herself a glass of cordial. "Lemonade, Malach? It's homemade."

"Your aunt has been enlightening me," Malach told her.

"About what?"

"About you, Jade. And yes, I would like to try this beverage, if you please."

Jade stared aghast at her aunt. "Please say you haven't been telling tales about me as a bratty kid?"

Lìli looked down her nose at Jade—no mean feat considering she was even shorter than both Jade and Mei. "I only tell him what he needs to know."

What sort of a cryptic statement was *that*? Jade crossed her arms over her chest. "And what does he need to know, exactly?" She knew she sounded irritated, but tough. It wasn't fair to leave her out of the loop.

"Never you mind, Niece. Now stop pouting and pour the lemonade for our guest."

Inwardly seething, Jade did as she was bid. There was little point arguing. Lìli always won. It was a given—much like the sun rising every morning. She handed Malach his glass and forced her lips into a saccharine smile. "Would you like a choc-chip macadamia cookie, Malach, dearest?"

"Please."

He was trying hard not to grin, damn him.

Don't get too used to this level of service, Malach, she thought at him. *I don't do happy homemaker.*

"Jade." Lìli's tone was chiding, as though she had plucked Jade's thoughts directly from her mind—something Lìli managed with discomfiting regularity and even more discomfiting accuracy.

"Lemonade, Lìli Yíyi?" When Lìli nodded, Jade poured and handed her aunt the tumbler. Then she made the mistake of opening her mouth, intending to get straight to the point of her visit.

"I'd like a cookie, too, Niece. If it's not too much trouble."

Lìli's eyes twinkled as Jade inhaled sharply through her nose in an attempt to hold the frayed edges of her temper together.

"Everyone happy?" Jade asked. "No one have a hankering for anything else? Green tea, perhaps? Or fruitcake? If there's none left in the cupboard, I can pop down to the corner store and get some. Or perhaps, Lìli Yíyi, you would prefer me to head back into the kitchen and bake you a cake from scratch? That'd get me out of your hair for an hour, so you two could discuss me some more."

Lìli smiled indulgently. "Retract your claws and drink up, *Xiǎo Māo*. If you behave, I will give you what you think you need."

"What's that supposed to mean?" Jade bristled, preparing to do battle. "Just for once, Lìli Yíyi, do you think you could talk in something other than obscure riddles?"

Malach's brows knit into a frown. "What does 'she-ow mah-oh' mean?"

Lìli chortled. "*Xiǎo Māo* means Little Cat. It has been my pet name for Jade since childhood. It suits her, heh?" She leaned over to pat Malach's hand, and winked at him in a conspiratorial manner.

Oh my God. What next? Naked baby pictures?

Malach leaned back in his chair, balancing it precariously

on its back legs as he raked Jade with an assessing glance. "It suits her very much," he drawled.

Jade's brain chose that exact moment to vividly replay sex-session number two in glorious Technicolor detail—the session where she'd gotten a bit carried away and raked her nails down Malach's back before biting his shoulder to muffle her cries. She raised her glass to her lips in a lame attempt to hide her heightened color from her aunt, and glared at Malach over the rim.

He took no heed of her warning. Instead, he guffawed, his eyes glinting with amusement. And then he rolled one shoulder beneath his shirt in such a pronounced and careful way, that Jade had no doubts he'd been recalling the exact same moment.

She blushed from the roots of her hair, all the way down her cleavage. His grin widened.

Grrrr! She hoped her teeth marks and those scratches stung like blazes.

Lìli set her tumbler down on the tabletop with more force than was strictly necessary. Jade quickly schooled her expression and set her thoughts to less intimate matters. If Lìli couldn't truly read minds—and Jade was ninety-nine-point-nine percent convinced she *could*—at the very least her aunt was über-perceptive. To Lìli, people were like an open book, and Jade was no exception. The absolute last thing she needed was to sit through an embarrassing Q and A session about Malach's potential virility. Followed by a lively discussion about the possibility of Jade providing Lìli with babies to spoil in the very near future.

She dared a glance at her aunt.

Lìli's gaze flit between Jade and Malach. Her expression shrieked disaster for Jade's continued status as a single woman. It was what Jade called Lìli's "matchmaking look", a calculating, narrow-eyed, searching beyond the here-and-now expression she got when she was envisioning two people as a couple.

Jade chafed her arms and fought the desire to sprint for the hills.

Lìli's face creased into a satisfied smile.

Uh oh. Jade knew *that* look, too. She'd last witnessed it when Lìli had informed some despairing mama her spinster daughter would be married within the year, and then gone on to describe the lucky man with what would later turn out to be scary accuracy. Jade had also seen that expression on one memorable occasion when she and her aunt had met at the mall for tea. Lìli had taken one look at the hollow-eyed businessman sitting opposite, and announced he would find happiness with the waitress who'd brought his order.

He had. They were still together so far as Jade knew.

And now Lìli had decided Malach was The One for Jade, and that Jade was The One for him. Didn't matter what Jade or Malach—or even Pieter's goddess—might think. When it came to affairs of the heart, Lìli knew best and she reigned supreme. Her reputation amongst the local Chinese community was stellar, to say the least.

Pity she refused any payment for her services. She would have amassed a small fortune by now. But Lìli's impressive record was about to take a nosedive. And her aunt was so *not* going to be at all happy about that.

Jade needed to tell her aunt that she and Malach didn't have a hope in hell of working out as a couple because he was desperately in love with a married woman. But she couldn't—not in front of Malach. She wanted him to know happiness for a few short weeks before his whole world came tumbling down. Again.

She would let Aunt Lìli in on the secret later. And maybe it would be better to not "find" Francesca at all. With Lìli's help, they would get through the Testing and Malach would finally be free. That was all that mattered. Malach need never know that Francesca had remarried.

Lìlì's gaze sharpened, boring into Jade, sifting through her deepest secrets.

Please don't let her spill the beans. Jade sipped her drink and concentrated of the taste of the lemonade, the perfect balance of tartness and sweetness exploding on her tongue.

Lìlì's piercing expression softened and she turned her focus to Malach.

Jade sagged with relief.

A huge smile split her aunt's face. "I will do it," she said. "I will help you to love each other."

"Urg!" Jade choked on a mouthful of lemonade, coughing and spluttering until Malach helpfully pounded her back. Gasping, she waved him away. "You will?"

Lìlì nodded, looking so tremendously pleased with herself Jade's suspicions were immediately aroused.

"What's the catch?"

"Catch?"

Jade closed her eyes and counted to five beneath her breath. "Magic—especially magic used for self-gain—always has its price."

"Very good, Niece. It seems you do listen to me sometimes."

Jade caught herself before she could roll her eyes. Her aunt wouldn't appreciate that gesture at all. "Of course I listen to you, Lìlì Yíyi. But I thought I was going to have to do some serious convincing to get you to do this for us. How come you gave in so easily?"

Lìlì only smiled. She had that whole terribly stereotypical inscrutable Chinese thing going on, damn her.

"How come?"

"If it harms none, do what you will," Lìlì quoted.

"You're telling me that casting a love spell over two people who wouldn't fall in love under normal circumstances, *isn't* interfering with the natural order of things? Surely that's at least one definition of harmful."

Lìli's smile never faltered. "Not in this case, Niece." She hugged her midsection and rocked in her chair, as though cherishing a delightful secret that would be revealed in the fullness of time.

Jade really, *really* hated when her aunt did that. "But we haven't even told you why we desperately need your help to fall in love yet." A thought struck her, and she swiveled to confront Malach. "You couldn't possibly have told her everything you told me during the short time I was fart-arsing 'round in the kitchen. What did you leave out?"

"Such language." Lìli clucked her displeasure.

Malach held his hands out at his sides, pleading ignorance. "I told your aunt nothing of our predicament, Jade."

"I know everything I need to know about you and Malach, Niece," Lìli insisted.

"How?" Jade lifted her chin in challenge.

"I have my ways."

"But—"

"Do you want me to cast this spell or not, Jade?"

"Yes, but—"

"Are you convinced it is the only way to help this worthy man escape his curse?"

"Yes. I wouldn't ask otherwise. But—"

"And are you willing to accept whatever consequences may befall you as a result of my spell?"

"Yes. But—"

Lìli muttered such a rude imprecation that Jade couldn't credit her ears. Shocked into silence, she could only watch helplessly while her aunt pinned Malach with a stare fit to flay skin from bones. "And you, Malach? Will you accept the consequences?"

He inclined his head respectfully. "I will."

Jade's final protest came out as the merest squeak.

"Enough." Lìli rose to her feet. "Remain here while I prepare for the spell." She shuffled off toward the house.

"You're going to perform it now?" Jade called after her.

Lili turned back and frowned. "There is no time like the present, Niece."

"But—"

Lili raised one eyebrow.

"Nothing," Jade muttered, self-preservation finally kicking in and saving her from a lecture on manners.

"Good." Lili presented Jade with her back and continued on her way.

Jade switched her focus to Malach, who had topped up his lemonade from the jug before grabbing another cookie. Huh. She supposed she should be grateful he was serving himself and not expecting her to do it.

"These are very tasty," he said.

"Old family recipe."

"Ah."

Jade brooded. It'd been far too easy to convince Lili to compromise her principles and risk some cosmic backlash. And if Jade could have thought of any other way to pass this coming Testing with flying colors, she would have grabbed it with both hands and run with it.

There is another way, a little voice informed her.

Yeah. Right. Falling in love wasn't an option for either of them. A love *spell* was their only choice. And if Lili had been a witch with few scruples, and Jade didn't care for her aunt so much, she wouldn't be fretting right now.

Lili was a practitioner of natural magic. She could harness the energies of such things as crystals, metals, herbs, planetary and lunar influences. And the reason Lili could "see" the potential for love was because she'd learned to interpret the premonitions, dreams and hunches people so often chose to ignore. Combine the two abilities, and Jade's aunt was a force to be reckoned with.

Lili was the real deal, and she did have scruples—oodles of them. She believed her abilities were a God-given gift and that she had a duty to use them wisely and well. Her code of ethics was strictly nonnegotiable—aside from one notable lapse named Murray Blackwood that haunted Lìli to this day.

It had taken Jade years to realize that Lìli felt a deep, abiding shame at having used her gifts to exact revenge. She believed herself wholly responsible for Murray's sterility, and that her actions had directly affected his destiny. Murray might have eventually fathered children, and his offspring would have made decisions and committed acts that were an integral part of nature's grand design. She'd vowed to never do such a thing again, regardless of the provocation.

She'd been true to her word.... Until Mei.

Fuelled by frustration and despair, Jade had once accused her aunt of being a coward for not at least *trying* to cure Mei. Lìli had responded, "Do you not think I pray every single day for that miracle? Do you not understand I would sacrifice my own life if it would help her?" The tears that had spilled down her cheeks, the pain and despair etched on her face.... Jade had known then that her aunt *had* tried. And failed. And only God knew what the cost had been.

She cupped her chin in her hands, worrying, wishing she'd found another solution that left her aunt out of it. A simple love spell—could Lìli pull it off? Was it truly as simple as it sounded? How bad might the backlash be?

For the life of her, Jade didn't know. What she *did* know was that she and Malach needed to be totally, convincingly in love, or they would fail the Testing. And Malach would be catapulted back to a hell of the Crystal Guardian's making—at the mercy of an embittered old man denied eternal rest until he'd put everything to rights. And if that wasn't a perfect example of magic going horribly wrong....

Jade shuddered, and poured herself another glass of lemonade in the vain hopes the tart-sweet beverage would dislodge the huge lump choking her throat.

Chapter Ten

They'd been summoned.

Malach leaned over to whisper in Jade's ear. "What is she doing?"

His warm breath tickled her neck, and parts further south reacted. Her lashes fluttered closed as she inhaled the potent, alluring scent of male—of him. She willed herself not to bury her face in his neck, not to lick and bite and taste. "She's meditating on how best to bring the elements into play, and have them grant our, uh, desire."

"Ah."

Jade watched him watching Lìlì, who stood motionless, gazing intently at the items displayed atop the camphorwood chest in the center of her sitting room. She dug her fingernails into her palms and tried to ignore her rampaging hormones. She didn't think Lìlì would be too pleased to have her meditation interrupted by her niece doing wicked things to Malach.

But then again.... Maybe Lìlì would be thrilled to bits and have them both married before they could blink.

"Is that carved wooden chest imbued with her magic?" Malach asked.

His lips had brushed the sensitive skin beneath her earlobe as he spoke. Lord, give her strength.

Jade swallowed. "The chest is her altar. And those items she's placed on top of it represent the... the—" She exhaled a sharp breath through her nose and pulled herself together.

"They represent the four elements. A candle for Fire, the bell for Air, bowl of water for Water, and the crystal for Earth. Now *hush*, or she'll be cross with us. And believe me, you don't want Lìli cross with you."

He subsided, and Jade tried to relax into a normal state of being rather than a hyped-up bundle of inappropriate lust.

"Perfect!" Lìli crowed, provoking Jade to jump like a cat disturbed from a nap.

Malach soothed her by smoothing his palms up and down her arms. And while she appreciated the gesture, it did not help her state of mind one bit.

"You are nervous as a fennec vixen protecting her litter," he murmured.

"Gee, I wonder why?" From the corner of her eye, Jade spotted Lìli laughing silently. Hah. Good to know someone was amused.

"Pick me an apple from the tree, Jade. You will go with her to help her choose, Malach." Lìli bustled from the room before either of them could respond.

Malach slanted a quizzical glance her way and Jade shrugged. "I have no idea. Best do as she says."

"Indeed."

They wandered into the back part of the garden and stood before the fruit-laden apple tree. Malach's expression turned awestruck. He reached out to stroke one of the branches.

"She has green thumbs," Jade said.

He shot her a startled glance. "Truly? I had not noticed them colored such."

Jade smiled. "She doesn't *literally* have green thumbs. It's an expression. It means she's very good at growing things and encouraging them to thrive. And sure, her talent could be a result of her unique gifts, but it could just as easily be because she's a damn fine gardener." She indicated the tree and its bounty with a wave of her hand. "As this tree obviously demonstrates."

"Does the fruit taste as good as it appears?"

"It certainly does. This variety of apple may look similar to varieties you can buy in shops, but these aren't in the least floury or soft. They're crunchy and incredibly sweet."

Malach ran his tongue over his lips. He touched an apple, skimming his fingertips over the shiny, crimson skin.

"Anyone could be forgiven for thinking you'd never eaten an apple before," she said.

"Apple." He uttered the word slowly and precisely. "You are correct. I have never tasted one. To my knowledge such delicacies cannot be found anywhere in my homeland. We feasted upon *daktuls*, the small, sweet brown fruit of Daktulos palms."

"Well, what are you waiting for? Pick one and take a bite."

He stepped back, putting both hands behind his back like a small child trying his best to resist something tempting. "Your aunt instructed me to help you pick one of these fruits, and I would not go against her wishes."

"Look, it's just an apple. It's not like we're Adam and Eve, being tempted by a serpent with an agenda straight from hell. If you want to try one, go ahead. Nothing bad's going to happen, I promise."

"I prefer to err on the side of caution," he said.

"Fine." She could hardly blame him where Lìli was concerned.

She cast her gaze over the tree. "That one?" She pointed to a nice big rosy-red apple, and when he nodded, she stood on tiptoes to pluck the fruit. "Here." She tossed it to him, trying not to smile when he snatched it from the air, cradling it in his palms as though his life depended on it.

They entered the kitchen to find Lìli impatiently tapping an apple corer on a wooden chopping board. "Finally." She held out her hand and imperiously clicked her fingers.

Malach handed her the apple. She examined it, checking for imperfections and blemishes. Satisfied, she cored the apple and placed the removed portion to the side.

"Some believe that *píng-guǒ*—apples—are the fruit of passion and romance," she said, reaching for a wickedly sharp-looking vegetable knife. She sliced the cored apple in half. "They are said to be a favorite of the Goddess of Love." She handed half the apple to Malach and the other half to Jade. "Eat!"

"That's it?" Jade asked.

"Eat!" Lìli commanded, and they obeyed, demolishing their pieces of the fruit with unseemly haste.

Lìli scooped up the apple core and a small plastic container, and instructed them to follow her. Malach shot Jade a "What's going on?" look as they trailed after her, but Jade could only shrug. She hadn't the faintest idea.

Lìli headed for her herb patch. As anyone who knew Lìli would expect, the patch was freshly tilled with nary a weed in sight. Jade had always suspected none would dare her aunt's wrath by taking root.

"Niece, my trowel, please."

Jade opened the door to the small garden shed and retrieved the trowel from its hook above the potting bench. Despite having black thumbs, and struggling to keep even the hardiest potted plant from curling up and dying, she did know her way around Lìli's potting shed. As a child, she'd spent many an hour perched on the edge of the potting bench, swinging her legs while she watched her aunt plant seeds and strike cuttings.

They both watched Lìli bury the apple core and encircle the site with small, nipple-pink colored stones.

Lìli indicated a spot on the ground. "Sit here and repeat these words after me: Love will grow, sure and slow. Strong and true, this love will prove."

Jade hid a smile when Malach didn't raise a protest or question her orders. Lìli had mastered the art of ordering people around. A firm statement of her wishes, and the expectation she would be obeyed, was all it took.

Malach knelt, sitting back on his heels and resting his palms on his thighs. Even while supposedly relaxed he appeared ready to spring to his feet and defend himself.

Jade curled her legs to one side, tucking her dress beneath her so she didn't flash her panties. She shook her head when she realized she'd been so eager to head to Lìli's that she hadn't gotten around to ditching the dress and changing into more comfortable clothes. Unbelievable. So much had happened in the space of hours—not the least being that Malach had rocked her entire world.

"Concentrate, Jade!"

She winced. Trust Lìli to know her mind hadn't been on the job.

"Keep repeating the words," Lìli instructed. "As you say them, imagine them as energy bubbling up from the core of your being, then flowing out of your mouth and infusing the buried apple core with power. Repeat the words until you feel the magic."

Feel the magic? Jade cut her gaze to Malach to see how he was taking this, but he'd squeezed his eyes tightly shut and was muttering the verse with scarily intense concentration.

She felt instantly ashamed. His freedom—perhaps even his life—was at stake. Where did she get off letting her mind wander and possibly being responsible for this spell's failure? She shut her eyes and followed his example.

After the eighth repetition, she began to feel strange, as though her sensory channels had narrowed. She repeated the verse again, and by the time she'd finished the words "this love will prove", the only thing she could sense was Malach. He consumed her—memories of his body, the strength of his lean muscles, the scars marring tanned skin with pale puckers. She was drowning in his scent, and so she breathed him in and his essence coursed through her, enriching her as it invaded every part of her. He was everywhere, inside her mind and inside her body, quickening her heart and sharpening her breathing until she couldn't catch her breath....

She toppled forward.

She found herself caught and held in Malach's strong arms. He planted his butt on the ground, dragged her into his lap and cradled her.

"Love will grow, sure and slow," Lìli chanted. "Strong and true, this love will prove. May your love have the strength of a tree, be as flexible as its boughs in the wind, be as sweet as its fruit. May your blessings be as many as its leaves, and nurtured by the powers of both heaven and earth." She came toward them, placing her hands on their heads before uttering the final benediction. "If it harm none, so mote it be."

The instant Lìli finished speaking, Jade felt heat radiating from between her breasts. Her pendant. She drew it out, squinting down at it, trying to focus on the stone.

"What is wrong?" Malach demanded.

As the stone's heat cooled, the color seemed to lighten and....

Her blood chilled and the fine hairs on the nape of her neck stood to attention. "My pendant. It's changed color again." The disturbing blood-red hue of red jade had lightened to the exact shade of the flowers currently gracing the lavender bushes in Lìli's herb garden.

"Be calm, Niece," Lìli said. "No harm will come to you from your namesake crystal. It merely alters to reflect the journey you are currently undergoing."

"What has it become now, then? Tell me!"

Lìli gestured at Malach, who turned Jade to face him so he could get a proper look at her pendant. He fingered it, his hand resting intimately against her breastbone. Heat suffused her again. Not magical crystal-heat this time, but the heat of wanting him.

"'Tis lavender jade," he said.

"And?" Lìli prompted.

"Lavender jade lessens emotional hurt and trauma, bestowing the gift of inner peace and teaching subtlety and restraint in emotional matters."

"Very good. Tell me, Niece, when did the stone first change to red jade?"

Jade groaned inwardly and buried her face in the crook of Malach's shoulder. Of course Lìli would have spotted the change the instant she laid eyes on the pendant. Intriguing that her aunt hadn't immediately pelted her with questions about it, though. Almost as if she'd already known....

Jade shifted in Malach's arms, suddenly uncomfortable with such intimacy beneath Lìli's far-too-astute gaze.

Malach took the cue and lifted her from his lap, setting her beside him. She fussed with the skirt of her dress as she strove to recall the moment. "It was on my way home this morning, after—" Her face heated and she resisted the urge to fan her cheeks, certain they were now as red as her pendant had recently been.

"I see," Lìli said, and Jade was very much afraid that her aunt did. All she could hope was that Lìli wasn't getting vivid pictorials of anything Jade and Malach had gotten up to last night.

"How very fitting," Lìli said, and although her tone was carefully devoid of innuendo, her eyes twinkled.

"I believe so." Malach dropped his gaze, finding a very interesting blade of grass to observe.

Malach? Embarrassed?

That made Jade feel a tiny bit better. At least until she thought she heard her aunt mutter, "About time!"

"Pardon, Lìli Yíyi?" Surely she couldn't have said what Jade thought she'd said.... Could she?

"Nothing, nothing."

The silence became awkward, provoking Jade to say, "I guess the spell's worked, huh?"

Lìli smiled and shrugged. "It would seem so."

"What happens next?"

"You both let nature take its course."

Jade's gaze drifted to Malach. She wouldn't mind letting nature take its course again sometime. In the very near future would be good.

It crossed her mind to wonder whether her growing infatuation with him was because she'd starved herself of intimacy, and now she had a man on tap she felt compelled to indulge herself to the fullest.

Of course, it could also be Lìli's spell working its magic but right now, Jade didn't much care either way. Right now she just wanted to take Malach home and... let nature take its course. Not that it'd be easy to have a private moment, what with Mei and Grace acting as chaperones. But where there was a will, there was a way, and Jade was definitely willing.

She scrambled to her feet, brushed herself down, and offered her hand to Malach. "I guess we should be going. I need to get back home and check on Mei." There. Nice and casual. No hint of her true intentions in her voice.

Malach surged to his feet with that graceful flow of movement that never failed to affect her. A thrill clutched her heart. He was incredible. And for the next month he was all hers.

"Grace is more than capable of looking out for Mei," Lìli said, her tone mildly chiding. "But go if you like. Come back when you're ready to do some preliminary sketches. Malach, let us get you settled into your room before your session with Dai-soon." She linked her arm with his. "You can pick up your bag from Jade's house later."

"Huh?" Jade glanced from Malach to Lìli, wondering what she'd missed and when she'd missed it. "I figured he'd be staying with Mei and me."

"As I have a spare room, we thought it best if Malach stay with me for a while."

"We?"

Malach nodded. "'Tis unseemly for me to stay with you if

we have not made a formal commitment to each other."

"Unseemly?" Jade winced at the shrillness of her voice.

"People will talk."

Un-freaking-believable. "You're worried about what people will think of us?"

He nodded, his brows drawn together, lips compressed.

Jade couldn't contain her outrage. "What people might think didn't seem to matter last night, when Pieter shut us in and we ended up shagging each other senseless did it? It didn't matter when you ripped my knickers off me. It was just you and me, and what anyone else thought didn't seem to matter at all, then. Or was all that simply a means to an end, and now we're *bonded*, you don't want to screw me anymore? Don't I do it for you anymore, is that it?" She shook a finger at him. "You bastard! Do you think now you've had me, you can discard me like the whore you were so convinced I was?"

Her body shook with fury and shame, and she ducked her head, unwilling to meet her aunt's gaze. She'd gone too far this time. Not only would Lili be appalled by what Jade had done last night, she'd be appalled by Jade's swearing and her rudeness toward a guest.

She blinked back tears and stared at the ground, wishing it would swallow her up, wishing she could take back her angry words. And, as she waited for her aunt to dispense the tongue-lashing that she so richly deserved, Malach's boots blurred into view. His hand tilted her chin gently but forcefully, until she had no choice but to meet his gaze.

"You are not a whore. But even if you had been, you offered me a precious gift that I did nothing to deserve, and 'tis I who feel shame. I would take back my cruel words, Jade, if only I could find a way. But once uttered, such words cannot be recalled—only eased by gestures and deeds, so that in time they may be forgiven, and over time, perhaps forgotten." He pressed his lips to her brow. "I am sorry."

"Me, too." He folded her into his arms and held her exactly

how she wanted to be held at that moment. He comforted her with no expectations, and she loved him for that.

God. Just her luck that when she finally found a man who instinctively knew what she needed, he was in love with another woman and would only be sticking around for a month.

She sneaked a glance at Lìli. Rather than the disgust and disapproval she had expected, she found compassion and understanding and deep, abiding, unconditional love. And, more practically, when she disengaged from Malach, a handkerchief so that she could blot her eyes and blow her nose. Lìli, too, always seemed to know just what Jade needed.

"I am staying with your aunt to give us space, Jade," Malach explained. "I thought it better for us to *date*, as your world calls it, and get to know each other, rather than jump into the oasis feet first and live in each other's belt-pouch."

"We say 'pocket'. And you're right. We have gotten off to a rather rapid start considering we barely know each other." Except in a strictly biblical sense.

"So we are—as you would say—cool?"

"Yeah. We're cool." She smiled at him, and wondered how 'cool' he'd be if he knew how desperately she wanted to get him alone for a little one-on-one.

She tore her attention from Malach. "So what's this about a session with Dai-soon, Lìli Yíyi?"

"We discussed it while you were in the kitchen."

And doubtless lots more besides. But Jade knew better than to demand a full accounting from her aunt. She'd have to wheedle it from Malach later. "Well, you must have read my mind," she said. "I was going to mention the possibility of Malach attending a few sessions with Dai-soon. I thought it might be good for him to get a bit of a workout while he's here. Provided Dai-soon agrees to it, of course."

"It is already arranged, Niece. In fact—" Lìli glanced at her watch "—we are due at the school in fifteen minutes so we must hurry or we will be late for the lesson."

Jade narrowed her eyes. Her aunt hadn't phoned anyone since they'd arrived. So how had she arranged a lesson for Malach?

Aha. Light bulb moment. "You're hoping to surprise Dai-soon by turning up with Malach out of the blue, aren't you? You think he'll be so impressed he might concede to show Malach a thing or two, don't you?"

Lili winked at her. "What do you think, Niece?"

"I think Malach had better be as good as you think he is, or Dai-soon is never going to let you live it down."

Lili patted Malach's shoulder and then entwined her arm in his. "I am confident he is."

"How 'bout you, Malach?" Jade said. "You ready to meet a taekwondo Grandmaster?"

Malach cracked his knuckles, threw back his shoulders and stuck out his chest—a picture of self-assurance and confidence.

Jade winced. She'd seen Dai-soon in action. Malach was in for an arse-kicking he wouldn't forget in a hurry.

BY THE TIME Jade arrived at the school hall, she was red-faced and breathless—all her own fault, of course. The lure of capturing Malach in action had been too hard to resist and she'd run home to pick up her sketchbook and pencils, resulting in a dash up the street and a full out sprint the last few hundred meters to the hall, so as not to miss a second of Malach's taekwondo debut.

She shouldered through the doors and scanned the large room, intending to find Malach and wish him luck before the lesson began. He would need it. Dai-soon took no prisoners. Neither did his students, for that matter.

It took a minute or two for her to spot Malach among the bunch of students milling around the Grandmaster—someone had loaned him a uniform so he blended with the other students. And watching her aunt shake hands with Dai-soon distracted Jade from Malach's upcoming lesson. What was Lìli up to?

Catching sight of Jade, Lìli waved and left the floor. As she approached, a secretive expression curved her lips and excitement sparkled in her eyes. Something was definitely afoot.

"Dai-soon's given permission for Malach to participate in the lesson, huh? That's great! You must have done some fast talking." Jade juggled her sketchbook as she rooted in her shoulder bag for a charcoal pencil. "What was that handshaking business about?"

"Shhh. They're about to begin."

The crowd melted away, leaving two men standing in the center of the mat: Malach and Dai-soon.

Hang on. "Begin what?"

"Their sparring match."

"Their *what*?" Jade's shriek drew sideways glances from students gathered at the edge of the mats. She lowered her voice. "A match? Are you crazy?" She'd expected Dai-soon to give Malach a bit of one-on-one in a lesson, not an actual match.

"Shhh!"

Jade's heart jumped around like a mad thing in her chest. "What exactly did you tell Dai-soon about Malach, Lìli Yíyi?"

"I told him the truth."

"And that would be?"

"That Malach is an accomplished fighter who would appreciate the chance to match his skills with another accomplished fighter." She strove for nonchalance but Jade wasn't buying it.

"You didn't!"

"Shhh!" Lìli dragged Jade over to the bleachers and shoved her down before seating herself. She clapped her hands together gleefully, and then began to rub her thumbs over her fingers as if anticipating crisp banknotes crossing her palms.

"You made a bet with Dai-soon, didn't you?"

"One I am sure to win," her aunt said, oozing confidence.

"What were you thinking?" Jade couldn't suppress a groan as visions of tending a bruised and very battered Malach danced through her mind. "You seriously reckon he has a chance sparring against a Grandmaster?"

"Don't you?" Lili pinned Jade with a piercing gaze that arrowed straight into her soul.

Good question. And the answer?

She did believe Malach had a chance. A very slim, almost anorexic one, but a chance nevertheless.

Dai-soon was an accomplished taekwondo practitioner. He'd attained a Ninth Dan ranking—the maximum rank for members of the International Taekwondo Federation. His peers expected he would soon be awarded an honorary Tenth Dan for his contributions to the sport. And he'd passed the official Kukkiwon Instructor Program in Korea with flying colors, subsequently turning down the opportunity to remain in Korea and establish a new taekwondo school, in favor of returning to his adopted country.

In Sydney, Dai-soon was a living legend. So why did Jade believe Malach had even a slim chance of holding his own against him?

Because in this day an age, taekwondo was seen as a *sport*, and Jade knew that Dai-soon, for all his expertise, had never used it in combat. The military training and unarmed combat techniques of the past, had given way to a stylized form of taekwondo practiced primarily for self-defense, relaxation and recreation. And it was at this modern form of taekwondo Dai-soon excelled. He was good. Better than good: Superb. But to Jade's knowledge, he'd never been forced to defend his life using his skills.

Malach, however, was a warrior. Fighting had been a way of life for him. More importantly, he'd survived numerous battles. And that well-honed instinct for survival might just give him the edge. Or at the very least, allow him to walk from the mat with his pride intact.

She watched the two men warming up. Dai-soon, despite being in his sixties and barely five-foot-six, was one of those men who, by their very manner and bearing, could command the attention of an entire room. He flowed from one warm-up pattern to the next in a seamlessly woven symphony of movement that was thrilling to watch.

In direct comparison, Malach appeared almost clumsy as he rotated his shoulders and proceeded to perform a set of very basic stretches that had Dai-soon's students snickering and whispering among themselves.

Trepidation trickled down Jade's spine and made her shiver. She'd never been one to enjoy watching grown men fight. She couldn't bear to watch boxing—it was too brutal. And although she appreciated taekwondo for the artistry involved in its incredibly disciplined, intricate patterns, she was also aware it was often lauded for its kicking techniques, which allowed the execution of powerful strikes.

God help Malach if he got in the way of one of those.

And then her blood chilled in her veins. Dai-soon also taught his students how to use pressure points and grabbing self-defense techniques he'd borrowed from other martial arts. Oh no. This wasn't good. She bit her lip against the need to call a halt to what she was very much afraid would be a debacle. She could cope with the thought of Malach sporting a black eye or cuts and bruises, but what worried her was that despite Dai-soon's expertise, Malach could still get hurt. Badly.

Dai-soon bowed and Malach followed suit.

Enough. Jade tried to jump to her feet but Lìli hung on to her arm. "Lìli Yíyi!" she hissed. "Let go, please. I have to stop this before Malach gets hurt."

"*Joonbi!*" one of the students called. "Ready!"

"Watch and learn, Niece. Have faith in your Malach."

"But—"

The words, "*Si jak!* Begin!" rang out, echoing from the

walls and muting Jade's protests with the inevitability of it all.

It was too late and far too dangerous for her intervene now. The sparring had begun and oh boy, all she could do was watch and wince. And hope Malach would live up to Aunt Lìlì's expectations without the props he was accustomed to—namely a bloody great sword and a horse.

There was one other thing she could do, and that was sketch Malach in action. At least it would take her mind off the increasingly violent-looking direction this sparring match was taking. She whispered her intention to her aunt, whose gaze was glued to the two men, and made her way to the edge of the mats. Recognizing she was there in some artistic capacity and therefore unlikely to interfere, she remained unchallenged by the students. And, as Malach arched backward to avoid a snap kick that had looked powerful enough to take his head off, instead of closing her eyes and refusing to watch, Jade sketched him.

As the sparring match progressed, her fingers flew madly, covering page after page with charcoal lines and smudges in her search to capture the essence of the man. A corner of her mind noted that it was not taekwondo that Malach used, nor any recognizable form of martial art as Jade knew it, for that matter. His moves were more like a bastardization of every form ever devised and a few never before seen on this earth. It was effective nonetheless, despite Dai-soon never giving Malach an opening to press an attack, and forcing the younger man into more of a defensive mode.

The watching students murmured their approval of Malach's tactics and determination. Pride that he was holding his own bloomed in Jade's heart, chasing away some of her fears.

When Dai-soon paused, presentiment skittered down her spine. Abruptly she stopped sketching, her gaze riveted on the two men. "He's gonna try something," she muttered. "Don't just stand there and wait for it!"

But Malach stood with his feet firmly planted on the mat, his hands held at chest-level, palms facing outward and fingers bent, his elbows tucked in close to his sides, waiting and watching Dai-soon with an intensity that made Jade swallow to moisten a mouth gone suddenly dry.

A number of things happened simultaneously.

Dai-soon raised his right knee and swung it forward and up, while at the same time pushing his hips forward to generate more power. "Nae-ryuh Chagi," Jade heard one of the students whisper. "Axe Kick!" and she had time to think "Oh no!" as Dai-soon's leg extended almost completely and arced upward, his foot heading toward Malach's head in a blur of movement that was so fast Jade's brain could barely register it and—

Somehow, Malach's hands shot up to grab Dai-soon's foot, stopping the movement dead.

Jade instinctively understood that it was barely within the realms of human possibility for Malach to have reacted that swiftly.

But somehow he had.

"Impossible!" the man standing next to Jade blurted, his jaw sagging in stunned amazement.

Jade held her breath, wondering what Malach would do next. Or Dai-soon, for that matter. But the two men did not move nor make a sound. They were frozen in a tableau of silent wills and hidden strength, with Dai-soon perfectly balanced on one foot and Malach gripping his other foot.

Abruptly, Malach released him and Dai-soon lowered his leg, bouncing experimentally on the balls of both feet. The two men backed away from each other, then stilled, each searching the other's face for answers.

"*Keu-man*," Dai-soon declared, his voice echoing in the silence of the hall. "Finish!"

The combatants bowed and the students applauded. Dai-soon approached Malach, clapping him on the shoulder and grinning widely. "A worthy opponent, indeed!"

Muted approval swelled to open respect as the students crowded around Malach, congratulating him and pelting him with questions.

Jade allowed herself to breathe again.

"I told you he would prevail." Lìli materialized next to her, grinning triumphantly.

Dai-soon must have seen her aunt gloating for the Grandmaster approached them, linking his arms in theirs to draw them away from his rowdy students. "Good to see you again, Jade." He gave her an affectionate peck on the cheek. "I have missed you at our classes. I hope to see you back at training one day soon."

When she only smiled and neglected to reply, he gestured to the sketchbook beneath her armpit. "Did you manage some good sketches?"

She blinked. "Er, I'm not entirely sure. I hope so."

"May I see?"

"Of course." She thrust the pad at him, embarrassed by his interest.

He flipped page after page, studying her work, and Jade found herself surprised by the number of sketches she'd managed. She'd been working purely on auto-pilot, completely at the mercy of her muse. Here's hoping her muse wasn't having an off-day, and she hadn't filled half a sketchbook with useless scribblings.

She chewed her lip, screwing up her nose as she tried to gauge Dai-soon's reaction. But the Grandmaster remained as smooth-faced and enigmatic as Jade's aunt could be.

"Who did he learn from, Lìli?" Dai-soon glanced up from the sketchbook to pin Jade's aunt with an intent look.

"I have no idea. He tells me he last underwent formal training as a boy."

"Impressive."

"I'll say," Jade blurted, and flushed when Dai-soon chuckled in a knowing way.

"I understand from Lìli that you are in Malach's employ for the next month, Jade."

"I wouldn't exactly put it that way, Dai-soon. His, uh, *uncle* has commissioned me to paint him and show him around Sydney while he's here."

"Oh? And how long is he here for?"

"A month for certain. After that…. It depends. Why the interest in Malach, Dai-soon?" Jade caught Lìli's raised eyebrows and remembered her manners in a big hurry. "If you don't mind me asking, of course."

"I would take him on as my assistant if he was prepared to stay for a longer term. He shows much promise."

High praise indeed. "Why don't you ask him? He's his own man, after all."

"Is he?" Lìli asked.

Jade's gaze flew to her aunt's face, but right now Lìli rivaled Dai-soon for inscrutability.

"This one perfectly captures the man, Jade," Dai-soon said, tapping one of the sketches. "It is a raw, powerful rendition—the best of all of them. Don't you think so, Lìli?" He held the sketchpad out to her.

Lìli scrutinized the proffered page. "Ahhh," she breathed. "His soul, his essence shines through. It is him. Beautiful work, Niece."

Jade made a grab for the pad. "Let me see that." And when Lìli gave her superb evils muttered, "Pretty please?"

She studied the head-and-shoulders sketch she'd dashed off while Malach had been poised motionless, waiting for Dai-soon to strike. She tried to view it objectively, dispassionately, as she'd been taught when self-critiquing her work at art school.

Malach's face sprang from the page and the impact of the sketch struck Jade like a physical blow, overpowering her with the power and honesty of those hastily drawn pencil lines. She wondered if Dai-soon and Lili saw everything that *she* saw—Malach's inner strength and the single-minded determination in the jut of his jaw, the pain of losing someone he loved etched in the deep lines bracketing his mouth, the longing for redemption shadowing his eyes....

They were both right. It was brilliant. She'd even go so far to say it was the best work she'd ever done. That single sketch, each of its stark charcoal lines and subtle shadings and smudges, was the culmination of everything she'd learned thus far. She'd drawn something unique and utterly compelling. Silently she gave thanks to the muse who had taken control of her pencil for that short but significant span of time.

She flipped page after page, scanning the other sketches. They were all good. Very good. She would be proud to call them her own under any other circumstances. But Malach didn't live and breathe in those drawings. There was some essential aspect of the man himself missing from those pages. She hadn't truly captured *him*.

"Jade!"

She tore her attention from the drawings and glanced up to see the real thing striding toward her with a dangerously predatory gleam in his pale blue eyes. If he'd been a big cat in a zoo, he would be prowling his enclosure and eying up members of the public for their suitability as snacks right about now. Or perhaps eyeing up a potential mate. He was hyped, high on adrenaline, in the throes of a typical male animal's reaction after a good, hard, fight. He wanted her. And from her body's instant response, her dry mouth, racing heart, flushed skin, dampened panties, she didn't mind a bit.

"Jade." He grasped the hand she had unknowingly stretched toward him, pulled her in to his side and pressed a kiss to her cheek. It was a chaste kiss, unlikely to offend even the most prudish person. A perfectly acceptable public caress. But it rocked Jade to her core.

Her sketchpad dropped from suddenly nerveless fingers,

unnoticed in a heady rush of comprehension.

The impossible had happened. Aunt Lili's spell had been a complete success. She loved Malach.

And, as she inhaled his scent and clenched her fists to prevent herself ripping open the front of his borrowed uniform and nuzzling his chest, Jade realized something else. Truly falling in love with Malach, without the aid of a love spell, would have been a complete disaster. If she truly loved him, how on earth would she bear knowing he loved someone else? And when the time came to set him free, how would she survive it?

Thank God what she felt for Malach was an illusion.

Oh, it might feel terribly real to her, and she might be suffering all the textbook symptoms she'd read about, dreamed about, yearned for, but it wasn't real. And thank God for that.

Chapter Eleven

Jade trundled past the snazzy pizza joint on Burns Bay Road and mulled her choice of workplace. Since no one ate pizza for breakfast, working there would have meant more of a sleep-in every morning. Still, she couldn't complain too much. Starting work at a sparrow's fart had its compensations. Namely a three-thirty in the afternoon finishing time, and an understanding boss who didn't throw a tantrum if she had to whiz off to deal with a crisis—provided she made up the hours some other time, of course. Carlo might be understanding as heck when it came to family emergencies, but he was first and foremost a businessman.

Even at the unholy hour of six forty-five in the morning, the hum of traffic was steadily building to its usual ear-grating fever-pitch, and Jade once again found herself extremely grateful her family home was close enough to the café that she could walk to work. Even breathing exhaust fumes was preferable to the frustrations of sitting in nose-to-tail peak time traffic.

Despite the traffic, Lane Cove was a nice place to live—an area she would never have been able to afford to buy into under normal circumstances. For Jade, it had always been a suburb of contrasts. Although primarily a residential area, it was also home to several large businesses. Its extensive shopping area, which snaked across both Longueville and Burns Bay Roads, comprised small specialty stores, numerous restaurants and cafés, and a pub: The Longueville Hotel. No points for originality when they named that one.

The area boasted a few historic properties but there was a general impression of modernity. And despite close proximity to the city, the townhouse complexes dotted along the main road simply shrieked suburbia.

The restaurants and cafés in the area were somewhat ethnically diverse, to say the least. Chinese, Middle-Eastern, Thai, Italian, Malaysian, Indian—even a Japanese sushi bar and seafood restaurant. And the people who infused their passion for food into the cuisine they served up to eager patrons, represented a melting pot of ethnicity, too. Even so, they contributed to a true-blue community feel in Lane Cove that Jade thought was often lacking in other Sydney suburbs.

She spared a smile for the trio of caffeine-eager customers waiting for the café to open, and rapped on the door to let her boss know she'd arrived.

Carlo's mustachioed face peered through the window. He opened the door wide, and flipped the café sign to Open. "Whaddya doing here, Jade? Bit early for *you* ta be wanting a coffee fix, innit?"

"Ha ha. Are you gonna let me in or am I going to have to walk over you?" She lifted a foot to display her chunky-soled black shoes. Hint, hint.

He merely grinned and tugged one drooping end of his luxuriant moustache. "Oooh. Feisty. I like that."

"I know." She pushed past him to enter the café and stopped dead in the act of reaching for her apron. It wasn't hanging on the hook, as it usually was. It was around the waist of the stacked, twenty-something blonde behind the counter. "Who's the newbie, Carlo?"

"That's Gemma, our new barista. I hired her yesterday. Gemma!" He clapped his hands imperiously. "One extra-strength latté for the lady whose shoes you haveta fill. Chop chop! And it better be good or *you* get the chop! Hahaha, just joking, hey?"

Gemma eyed him with trepidation, visibly gulped, and "chopped" to it. She thumbed the grinder, filling the café with an ear-piercing whine and the aroma of freshly ground coffee beans.

Jade swiveled to confront her boss. Hands on hips she pinned him with the most evil glare she could summon. "What's going on, Carlo? Is hiring this Pammie Anderson lookalike, your not-so-subtle way of telling me I'm fired?"

He shrank beneath her accusing glare. "'Course not. You're like another daughter ta me, Jade. But you're supposed ta be taking a month's leave. So whaddya doing here?"

Her stomach cart-wheeled. "What? A month's leave? Who told you that?"

Carlo steered her to a chair, pushed her into it with one meaty hand, and plonked into the chair opposite. "Old guy. Name'a Stone. Came in yesterday morning soon as we opened for brunch, and told me you was needing some time off. Is it Mei? She taken worse?" He grabbed Jade's hand across the table and squeezed it hard. "You shoulda told me, Jade. I woulda cut back your hours, given you time off—no questions asked."

"It's not Mei. She's fine." Jade swallowed and dropped her gaze to the saltshaker. "Well, not fine but... you know."

"Yep, I knows." Carlo sagged back in his chair, obviously relieved. "That's good. I'm glad she's hokay."

"Yeah. Me, too." Jade dragged her thoughts from Mei to smile at Carlo's daughter as she brought over the coffee. "Thanks, Maria."

"You're welcome," Maria and Carlo responded simultaneously.

Maria dimpled and then scurried away to serve a customer. Jade picked up her cup and was about to take a sip when she realized Carlo was watching her with worried eyes. Beads of sweat pearled on his brow and he blotted his forehead with a large striped handkerchief.

"Well? Did she do good? Is it hokay?"

"What? Oh, the coffee!" Jade put down her cup and scrutinized the brew with a critical eye. "Nice silky microfoam, good color." She took a sip. "Ratio's perfect. Temperature's about right." She put him out of his misery and smiled. "Yeah. It's pretty good. She'll do fine."

Carlo beamed. "Good."

Jade took another sip and tried to focus on why she was here, sitting at a table with her boss, instead of standing behind the counter serving early morning customers. "So what exactly did this guy look like, Carlo? Was he say, seventyish? Average height, slim build, white hair, English-y accent?"

"That's him."

Figured. "Made you feel instantly at ease? Like, whatever he said made perfect sense?"

"Yep, yep." Carlo's bushy eyebrows drew together and he stroked his moustache, the beginnings of suspicion dawning on his tanned face. "This guy, he know all about you, Jade. Stuff you keep private, yanno? Seemed legit. You telling me he's some whacko and I shouldn'ta listened ta him?" He drew a deep breath, his chest swelling with outrage.

Jade sighed inwardly. "No, Carlo." She patted his hand. "He's legit. But I wanted to come by personally and tell you what was going on, okay? I owe you that for being such a great boss. Only I didn't expect Mr. Stone to be so quick off the mark to… to… sort everything out for me."

Carlo clicked his fingers at Maria and bellowed, "Espresso. Pronto."

"Right away, Papa," she called back.

"This Mr. Stone. He give you any trouble, you tell me, hokay? You and Mei, you are like family." He thumped his barrel of a chest. "I take care of this Mr. Stone for you."

"Pieter—Mr. Stone—doesn't need to be taken care of, Carlo. He's paying me to paint his, ah, *nephew*. And he's paying

Grace to look after Mei while I work on the portrait. If anything, I should be grateful to him for giving me such a great opportunity."

Carlo's ears had pricked up at the word "paint". "But this is wonderful!" he cried, lurching to his feet and addressing the café's patrons with outstretched arms. "Our Jade is finally becoming a famous painter!"

"Sit down, for goodness sake, Carlo," Jade said, mortified by all the attention she was getting from Carlo's customers. "I'm taking a month off, and then I'll be back knocking on your door, demanding my job back. So I sure hope you've told Gemma her position's only temporary."

"Of course."

Maria rushed up with Carlo's espresso and he grabbed the cup, downed the contents in one gulp and handed it back to her. "Ah. Espresso. Nectar of the gods." He patted Jade on the shoulder. "See you back in a month, Jade." He winked at her. "Unless you become rich and famous in the meantime. Then you must remember your old boss, Carlo, and paint a portrait of me to hang in my café."

He glanced over at the counter and frowned ominously. "That Gemma—she is not smiling enough. Customers like ta see smiling faces—it makes them happy. I gotta go teach that girl how ta smile proper."

Poor Gemma. Jade vividly recalled Carlo's how-to-smile boot-camp—and her aching facial muscles—from her first week working for him.

"Bye, Carlo."

He bent to plant a smacking kiss on her left cheek. "That for you. And this—" he planted another kiss on her right cheek "—for Mei. You tell her Uncle Carlo expect ta see her soon. I will brew her something special—make her feel better. You bring her soon, hokay?"

"I will," Jade promised. She reached into her bag for her wallet.

"On the house, Jade," Carlo said, looking very pleased with himself. "You are my official coffee quality control inspector. It is very important job, so you must come drink my coffee often, hokay?"

He was such a sweet man. "Thanks, Carlo." She pecked him on the cheek before he bustled off to harass Gemma.

Jade sipped her coffee and wondered what she was going to do for the rest of the day. She'd never had the opportunity to be young and carefree, and indulge in the things carefree young people supposedly did. Her parents had been very strict, and she hadn't been allowed to go to a party unchaperoned until she was sixteen. Even then she'd had a totally humiliating curfew of ten-thirty.

Grace had taught Jade practically everything about being a girl in this day and age. But Grace's sage advice about boys and sex, and all the other stuff she thought Jade needed to know, had been a poor substitute for the thrill of discovering it for herself. Hence the Murray disaster. Grace had warned Jade about him, but Jade realized now it had been impossible for her younger self to be discerning about boys when she had been just so darned grateful to be noticed by one—especially a good-looking, popular jock like Murray.

By the time Jade had semi-recovered from that first disastrous attempt to spread her wings, high school was over and she had the rest of her life to have fun. Except Murray had put her off boys big-time, and she no longer wanted to have *that* sort of fun. Boys sucked. All they wanted was sex. And all *she* wanted to do was paint.

Her wonderful art teacher had done some miraculous fast-talking, and convinced Jade's parents to let her enroll full-time at a prestigious art school. There, she'd spent a blissful few months immersed in the wonders of life drawing, life painting and portraiture during the weekdays, and working weekends at Carlo's to help pay her tuition fees. She'd been far too busy to have "fun". But hey, at eighteen she had plenty of time.

Right?

Wrong. Not long after Jade's parents had learned Mei's ongoing health problems might be serious, they were killed. And Jade had to grow up overnight. She had no time for frivolous pursuits of any kind. Getting Mei well again was the only thing that mattered. Being there for her sister whenever Mei needed her, and seeing she had the best care Jade could afford, replaced painting as Jade's all-consuming passion. Life was not about having fun and doing what you wanted. It was deadly serious. And her penance for being the healthy sister was to turn her back on her own dreams.

Mei was her life, her responsibility. But now Mei had Grace looking after her full-time, and Jade no longer had a day job to keep her occupied. She could do anything she wanted—within reason.

Ironic that all she felt like doing was insisting Grace back off and let Jade resume the role of primary caregiver. Yeah, like that would go down well.

Grace would tell Jade to go have fun, but what did girls these days do to have fun? Manicure? Massage? Get her hair done? No way could Jade justify spending actual money on any of that stuff. Sure Pieter had given her twenty-five grand, but it wasn't truly hers yet. She hadn't earned it—wouldn't until she'd finished Malach's portrait. Besides, she would only feel comfortable dipping into that pot to pay urgent bills. And so, as she wandered along the footpath at eight in the morning, with a full day stretching ahead of her, Jade didn't consider going shopping or catching up with friends for lunch or whatever it was girls her age did. She dreamed about the portrait she was going to paint of Malach.

She no longer considered this commission a chore. Malach tantalized her. Glimpses of him swirled through her brain like a reflection playing hide-and-seek amid puddles on a pavement. One moment vibrant and real—touchable—and the next, shimmering, distorting, sliding from her view.

Her heartbeat escalated. Her stride quickened and lengthened, became a half-walk half-trot until, finally, she couldn't hold back any longer. She gave in to the compulsion urging her onward and broke into a run that quickly became a flat-out sprint the rest of the way to Lìli's house.

She was red-faced and gasping for breath when she reached Lìli's front porch. As she toed off her footwear, she opened the door, and beneath the curtain of her tangled sweat-soaked hair she sought him out.

Malach, drawn by the sound of an unannounced entrance, loomed large and deadly from the shadows, his stance shrieking his intent to protect and defend Lìli from whoever might dare threaten her. Then, seeing Jade, his fierce expression softened into a smile.

He opened his arms.

It was an invitation it never crossed Jade's mind to refuse. She walked into his embrace, laying her cheek against his chest and sighing as he enfolded her. And in that instant, she knew she was home.

AS JADE SIGHED and burrowed close to him, Malach felt a flare of warmth that centered in his heart and spread outward until it engulfed him. He held her delicate frame in his arms, rubbed gentle circles on her back. She purred like the Little Cat her aunt had named her, and for the first time since being catapulted into this world, Malach felt no pressure to remain hyper-alert and vigilant.

He could hear Lìli humming to herself as she dusted the rear rooms of the house. Outside, the warbles of birdlife warred with the drone of vehicles and the occasional chatter of passersby.

It was a soft, easy world, far removed from the brutal harshness of his desert homeland. And rather than sneer at the weak inhabitants of this world, or mock them for their complacency, he'd slipped into the day-to-day routines as easily as a sidewinder slithered over grains of sand.

He felt relaxed and content, at peace. He knew it wouldn't last. It couldn't be this easy for him to shed his past and shrug off the soul-destroying horrors of his imprisonment. Nothing in his life thus far had ever been easy.

Malach had never known his mother. She had died bearing him, and he had been given into the care of a group of older women who were past childbearing age, and therefore not eligible for the Choosing Block. Many of the group had been content with their lot, preferring childcare duties to life with a warrior, or the constant drive to earn coin enough to set up their own business or household. But some of the women had been bitter. They had withheld kindness, blaming their small charges for their aging bodies that made them useless to men who required children to boost a dying population.

As a child, Malach had mourned the lack of a mother's love. As a stripling, he'd been thankful for the lack, for it had made him self-sufficient, aware from an early age that he could rely on no one but himself.

He'd never held any ambition to be a Lord Keeper. He had recognized early on that his skills lay not in decision-making, but in dispensing advice to his superior, and then conveying that superior's orders in a way that was palatable to the men of his troop, while still garnering their respect. Many a time an underling had bridled at a command, and been on the brink of telling his superior where he could shove his orders, only for Malach to talk him down and smooth the way, while still leaving both men with their pride intact.

Malach had harbored little respect for the Lord Keeper of his own fief, however. The man had been an arrogant fool, whose incompetence had resulted in the injury, and even death, of many a warrior beneath his command. And Malach had known as soon as he spotted Wulf during a trade negotiation between local fiefs, and witnessed the respect the young man commanded from his peers, that Wulf would make an excellent commander. He'd had the makings of a Lord Keeper without parallel. So, after much soul searching, Malach had forfeited everything he owned—including his hard-won reputation as the best man to have at one's back during a skirmish—and, with the jeers of his Lord Keeper ringing in his ears, he'd departed his fief.

It'd taken him a month on foot, walking only in the cool of night, sheltering in shallow dugouts during the heat of the day, to reach the outskirts of the Shifting Sands fief. Despite exhaustion and dehydration, he'd overpowered the outriders patrolling the perimeter, and fought tooth and nail for the right to be adopted into the Shifting Sands fief. He'd worked his way through the ranks and proven himself in many a skirmish. He'd waited patiently for the time when Wulf was able to select his own men, and then he had presented himself before Wulf and presented his case.

He'd been proud of his daring, prouder still to be named tehun-Leader by the new Lord Keeper of the Shifting Sands fief. And for many years, Malach had believed himself fulfilled by strategizing with Wulf, and getting the best out of men such as Wulf's kinsman, Kyan, who enjoyed causing trouble by questioning orders. He had believed himself content with a life that essentially boiled down to fighting and fucking. But only now, with Jade in his arms, did Malach finally understand true happiness.

He pressed a kiss to her temple, inhaling the subtle jasmine fragrance of the shampoo she favored. His balls tightened and his cock swelled. Lust. Unsurprising, for she could incite him with a sway of her hip or a glance from across a room. But there was something else, too. An ache in his chest—a good ache, like that of a well-used muscle after a sparring session. An overwhelming sense of knowing that this young woman in his arms felt *right*, that she fit him like no other woman had done—not even Francesca.

Could this be love? Or was it merely gratitude for this respite from the hell the Crystal Guardian had condemned him to. If this *was* love, could it be real, what he felt? Or was it false and untrue, the result of Lìli's clever spell.

Regardless, Malach liked the feeling. He liked it very much indeed.

His arms tightened about Jade, and as she lifted her face to his, her lips slightly parted as though begging for a kiss, he silently thanked Pieter's goddess for giving him this memory to treasure. Even if the worst came to pass, he would still have this one precious moment

He kissed Jade then, savoring the honeyed sweetness of her lips, the eager press of her lithe young body against his. And when she whispered against his mouth some of the things she wanted him to do after her aunt had retired for the night, Malach shrugged off all thought of the future, all thought of the vow he'd made if passing the Testing seemed hopeless. Right now there was only Jade. Nothing else mattered.

Chapter Twelve

Jade shifted in Malach's embrace, and pondered how adeptly humans managed to adapt to significant turning points and changes in their lives—events and deeds so shocking to their fundamental belief systems, that one would expect them to be quivering, shell-shocked heaps, barely capable of functioning. She contemplated some of those significant recent changes in her own life as she settled his encircling arms more comfortably beneath her breasts.

He stirred, and she caught her breath. Please God, she hadn't yanked him from the peace he so desperately needed. And deserved.

When his breathing steadied, muscle by muscle she allowed herself to relax. And, as if impatient with her controlled efforts, her entire body shuddered and abruptly went limp. If only her mind could give in as easily—quit angsting over everything and just accept what was happening to her. But lately it was becoming increasingly difficult to trust anything she'd done, or even thought.

How much of it was *her*, instinctively reacting, and for the most part coping, with whatever was thrown at her? And how much was due to Pieter's interference? After all, despite her dwindling savings, seriously contemplating becoming a prostitute had been pretty "out there" given her upbringing, her morals, her values, and her extreme lack of experience. Heck, she could have auctioned off her virginity over the internet and made a mint. But that idea had seemed so tawdry when she'd thought of it that she'd immediately discounted it.

She'd thought long and hard about her decision to place that ad in the local paper—what it would mean to her personally if anyone responded and she went through with it. She'd considered all the negatives, weighed her options, and still decided it was the right choice. Her choice.

But perhaps she'd not *chosen* that path at all. Perhaps it had been Pieter's choice all along, all part of his grand plan.

"Boy, you better have some answers to some hard questions when I next lay eyes on you, old man."

Malach jerked, and she realized that she'd spoken aloud. "It's nothing. Go back to sleep. Everything's fine. Sleep now." She crooned the words in a singsong voice.

When he'd settled, she curled up beside him with her head pillowed on his chest, and closed her eyes. She concentrated on breathing slowly and evenly. Just as she'd hoped, his breathing quickly slowed until it matched hers.

She listened to the steady, even thump of his heart beneath her cheek. He'd become such a huge part of her life she couldn't imagine being without him. She'd even moved in with him. Temporarily of course. Just until they passed the Testing, and their love spell was broken, and she could help him contact Francesca, his true love.

Jade had decided that although she might live to regret it, she couldn't hide that she'd located Francesca from him. She couldn't live with the guilt.

"Jade?" he murmured, his arms tightening around her as though sensing her disquiet.

"Shhh." She silently cursed herself for disturbing him.

He nuzzled her ear and she felt a jolt of pure lust spear through her. He had that effect on her. All the time. Even a careless touch had the power to reduce her to a wanton creature, ready and willing to give him whatever he wanted. It was disturbing and a little scary how much she wanted him. And magical, too.

Magic. Curses and spells. Warriors from other worlds. All part and parcel of her life now. How quickly she'd accepted the unbelievable.

Lìli, Grace and Mei had all accepted Malach, too. In fact Lìli hadn't batted an eyelash the first time Jade stayed the night in Malach's room, in his bed, with him. It'd been unintentional, of course. Jade had far too much respect for Lìli to deliberately throw her relationship with Malach in her beloved aunt's face.

It'd happened when Malach had dragged her off sightseeing after a morning of painting. "I want to walk over the bridge," he'd declared, his eyes glinting with excitement.

"Some fresh air'd be nice," she'd agreed, fondly imagining the small bridge spanning the stream in the park not far from her home.

The view from the Sydney Harbor Bridge had been picturesque, all right—not that she'd been in much of a state to appreciate it until she could breathe without seeing spots dancing before her eyes, and stand upright without her thigh muscles quivering. And afterward, when they'd returned to Lìli's, Jade had been so emotionally and physically wrung out that she collapsed on the spare bed to recover, leaving Malach to make himself useful by massaging her aching legs and feet. She'd intended to walk home as soon as she could move, but she must have fallen asleep. And Malach had joined her.

Even in the cool of the night, days after the incident, her cheeks still burned at the recollection of Lìli's knowing grin as her aunt had awoken them the next morning bearing a substantial breakfast on a tray.

"Lucky I made enough breakfast for three, heh?" Lìli had chortled. "Malach has a big appetite, Niece. So if you're hungry, be quick or he'll eat everything." She'd patted Malach on the shoulder, obviously approving of his hearty male appetite. And when she slanted a gaze at Jade, a grin had split her face and there had been a suspicious gleam in her eyes.

Malach had taken Lìli's waggling eyebrows in his stride, murmuring that she was a gracious hostess.

It could have been worse, Jade supposed. At least Lìli had known they hadn't "slept together" slept together because they were both still fully clothed.

Speaking of sleeping together, Jade had snuck Malach into her bedroom on a couple of memorable occasions so she could enjoy his attentions without fear of discovery by her aunt. But the knowing looks Grace and Mei exchanged, and their not-so-covert whispers and giggles, were too humiliating. Plus, the spare bed at Lìli's was larger and sooo much more comfortable than Jade's own lumpy, poor excuse of a mattress. So after much soul-searching, she had dared ask permission from her aunt to stay overnight in Malach's room.

She'd been granted it—along with the added embarrassment of Lìli's blessing, which went something along the lines of, "Niece, I give you my permission to have sex in my spare bed. But please try not to make too much noise because I'm an old lady and I need my beauty sleep."

Embarrassing, much? And to spare herself further comments from her worldly-wise aunt, Jade had very quickly learned how well pillows muffled moans of pleasure.

She carefully shifted over to her own side of the bed, and stretched out on her back, staring into the inky blackness that shrouded the room. Malach had seamlessly insinuated himself into her life. Even Grace was taken with him, and made no secret that she thought he was hot stuff.

She complimented him outrageously one minute, and then threatened his balls in hair-raisingly imaginative and graphic ways if he dared make Jade miserable the next. And the teasing never let up. "Hey, lover-boy, I've been meaning to check on a pet theory of mine, and Jade absolutely won't tell, so I'll go straight to the source. How big is your willy?"

"Willy?"

"Your dick. Or penis, if you prefer—though I reckon that's such a whiny, unattractive word. Must be pretty impressive size-wise, huh? I mean, get a load of your hands! And as for your feet—you could paddle across the harbor with those puppies. I'm a nurse, so it's okay to talk to me about this stuff, by the way. I've seen plenty of men's bits before."

"Grace. Enlighten me please. What do the size of my hands and feet have to do with the size of my male parts?"

"Well, some people reckon you can gauge the size of a man's dick by how big his nose is, but I reckon that's a crock. I once dated a guy who had a beak like you wouldn't believe but man, was I disappointed when I got his gear off."

Malach, once he'd gotten over the shock of the topics Grace was willing to discuss, always gave as good as he got. And boy, warrior-types like Malach sure knew how to make a girl blush. Come to think of it, Jade had never seen Grace blush before. Being a nurse, Grace had pretty much seen it all, so it'd been a singular delight to see the occasional flush spread over her friend's face and watch her struggle to think of a suitable comeback.

And Mei….

Jade's sister adored the man in Jade's life. He'd slotted right into the role of the big brother Mei had always yearned for. In between sittings for his portrait, lessons with Dai-soon, and making Jade bite pillows, Malach regaled Mei with fascinating tales about his world. And when Mei's energy levels permitted, Malach would browbeat Grace until she gave in and drove them to the park, or to visit Carlo at the café.

In return, Mei had taken it upon herself to teach Malach to read, and Jade often found them giggling over children's books such as *A Bellbird In A Flame Tree*—the Aussie version of The Twelve Days of Christmas—or the wonderful Dr. Seuss classics Mei had so adored when she was a child.

Each and every significant person in Jade's life—her sister, her best friend, her aunt, her boss, and even Dai-soon, who'd undertaken to mentor Malach—had stamped him with their seal of approval and made it abundantly clear they heartily approved of Jade's "older man".

Jade chewed her lip and wondered if Malach understood the true significance of this unequivocal acceptance. He'd have to really screw up big-time for them to change their minds about his suitability as her partner. So how would they react when she pushed him away and handed him to another woman on a platter?

Two words: Not well. She sighed and willed herself to sleep.

JADE AWOKE WITH her heart leaping about in her chest and a sense of foreboding that made her shiver and curl up into a ball. Beside her, Malach inhaled a harsh breath that abruptly choked off.

God. Not again.

A small, terrified part of her didn't want to see, yearned to pretend nothing was wrong. Her hand shook as she reached for the bedside light, and she shuddered with half-relief half-trepidation when its pale glow pushed back the darkness. She firmly told herself that she could deal with Malach's nightmares. She'd done it before. She could—would—do it again.

She turned to him, expecting to see his body tensed and writhing as he fought to break free from his demons. She expected to see his face twisted, eyes wide and sightless, mouth gaping in a silent scream as he was forced to again endure the horror of his crystalline prison.

She didn't expect to be confronted by a ghastly tableau that captured the pure desperation of a man who'd suffered so much, that he could find no other way to escape his fear and despair. And what she saw would forever haunt her.

"Malach!" She threw herself at him, screaming his name over and over as she grasped his fingers and tried to pry them from his throat.

His complexion was mottled. He was doing an excellent job of trying to throttle himself to death. Commonsense, or perhaps something she'd read somewhere or heard on TV, told her he would pass out before he suffocated, and then his muscles would relax and he'd be able to breathe again. But she couldn't merely watch and do nothing. She couldn't!

"Malach, please!" Doing her best to avoid his flailing legs, she maneuvered herself until she sat astride him, and dug her fingernails into his hands, inflicting small sharp pains that she hoped might get through to him and interrupt this nightmarish loop he'd been caught in.

She succeeded in prying one hand from his neck, and held tightly to that wrist with both hands while he fought her. He lashed out, delivering her a glancing blow to the cheekbone as she struggled to hold his arm still. When she didn't let go of his wrist, he elbowed her hard in the ribs. She gasped with shock and pain, and loosened her hold. And then he picked her up and threw her on the floor.

"Let me die!" His fevered gaze met hers as she struggled to her feet, and Jade couldn't find a trace of the man she knew. That man was gone—subdued, or perhaps finally overwhelmed, by his mind's insane desire to put an end to the nightmares, put an end to any possibility he would be returned to hell of his malachite crystal for a third time.

He wrenched his maddened gaze from her face and threw himself back against the mattress. His hands were like creatures possessed as they crept to his throat again.

Jade cradled her bruised ribs. She watched helplessly as he choked off his breath. His spine bowed, and his heels dug deep depressions into the mattress as his powerful warrior's body refused to succumb and continued fighting for oxygen.

She'd failed him. And her heart twisted at what tomorrow might bring when Malach awoke and found himself still alive.

The door to the bedroom slammed open and Lili rushed in. "Quickly, Jade! Help me hold him down so I can give him this."

Jade had no idea how two featherweight women managed subdue him so Lìli could pour the sleeping potion down his throat, but somehow they managed it. Perhaps deep inside Malach truly didn't want to die, and chose to let them help him. Or perhaps Lìli's indomitable will finally overcame him.

Thankfully, he didn't spit the potion out. They pinned him, Jade lying on his left arm, Lìli on his right, as he howled his anguish to the night. And, as the potion took hold and his howls diminished to hoarse gasps, Lìli nodded to Jade. Cautiously they released his arms.

Jade sagged with relief when he lay still. She brushed the tears from his face and held him until his eyelids drifted closed and finally he slept.

Malach. Her lover. Her flawed warrior. She'd been a fool to ever believe that she alone would be enough to save him.

Chapter Thirteen

THE PORTRAIT OF MALACH was almost finished, just a few minor touch-ups and a final protective glaze to administer. Jade wished she could keep it, but didn't hold out much hope of that coming to pass. Doubtless Pieter would commandeer it for some archaic, magical reason known only to himself. After all, he'd paid a small fortune for it.

She wondered whether he'd think it worth the money he'd forked out. He'd bloody better. It was the best work she'd ever done.

Walking into the tiny room she used as a studio and laying eyes on the painting was like a blow to her gut—in a good way, the kind that left her clutching her middle, breathless because she was so damn proud of what she'd accomplished.

She'd captured the essence of her subject, his soul. And the man himself had captured her heart. She wanted to save him. She wanted to truly love him. But even if that were possible once the spell was broken, she was doomed.... Because he loved someone else.

Jade stroked her fingertips lightly down Malach's thigh, tracing the long, lean muscles. For a few more days he was hers, and she refused to think about what the future might bring. That way lay misery. Instead, she sighed, snuggling into his warm body, breathing in his intoxicating male scent, wishing he'd wake up and make love to her so that afterward, she could drift off into the pure, easy slumber of a well-pleasured woman.

One more week until the Testing—whatever that entailed.

Don't think about it. Don't think about what Pieter might have in store. Put it firmly from your mind. Concentrate on the positives...

One more week and they'd both be free.

Jade teetered on the edge of near-sleep. One more week—

Her eyelids flew open and she stiffened as the importance of that date smacked her upside the head. In exactly one week it would be her birthday—her twenty-first birthday, to be precise.

This Testing, with a man's life at stake—only like, the highest stakes ever—was taking place on her twenty-first birthday? "Shit!"

"What is wrong, Jade?" Malach's voice wasn't the least bit sleepy-sounding. He'd been awake for some time.

"Nothing."

He huffed a breath that was half-laugh, half-exasperation. "You are a terrible liar. Tell me what is worrying you."

"How do you know I'm worried about something?"

"'Tis obvious, *Xiǎo Māo*," he said, calling her by Lìlì's favorite nickname of Little Cat. "You have been twitching and jumping about in the bed as though you are infested with fleas."

"Very good," she purred, raising her head from its oh-so comfortable position on his chest to look him straight in the eye. "Your pronunciation is near-perfect. You've obviously got a talent for languages." Might as well try a diversion. "You've been such a good student I believe you deserve a reward."

He shifted, hooking his leg through hers and clasping her tightly to him as he rolled, and ending up on top, positioned comfortably between her thighs. "Languages are not all I happen to be very good at," he murmured.

Yay. Her diversion tactics seemed to be working. "Oh really? Enlighten me. What else are you very good at?"

"This."

He nibbled her earlobe. A delicious shiver tickled down her spine and she pressed closer to him. "Oooh."

"And this." He brushed aside her hair and butterfly-kissed his way down her neck and across her cleavage. He sat up and back on his heels, still straddling her, to cup her breasts and pay homage to them with a heated gaze that had her biting her lips to stifle the pleas that hovered on her lips.

He bent forward, and as his long hair obscured her view, she felt the warm wetness of his tongue darting across the sensitive skin beneath her breasts. Her nipples tingled, puckering, and she squirmed, arching her back and offering them to him.

"And this." His tongue swirled over her nipple, laved it, then suckled deeply.

"Ahhh." She writhed between the tight clamp of his muscular thighs as his clever fingers attended to her neglected breast. "Oh yes. You're very good, indeed."

"Mmm." The vibration of his lips over her now ultra-sensitive breast caused her to squirm even more. "And you are very tasty, indeed."

His fingers continued their skilful manipulations while his lips and tongue traced a trail down her belly to the juncture of her thighs. His hand left her breasts to part her thighs still more and she gasped, tensing, aware of what was to come, wanting it, aching for it.

He parted her labia and breathed gently on her clitoris.

She jerked right off the mattress, the overload of pure sensation blowing her mind and fizzing through her blood, setting all her nerve-endings alight. He held her down, chuckling smugly as only a male confident of his sexual prowess and effect upon a woman could do.

Jade came back to earth. Her clit throbbed as though he'd spent the last hour or so teasing her and bringing her to the brink of orgasm, only to pull back and leave her wanting more.

She levered herself onto her elbows to stare at him, this man who had so much power over her. How could he do that to her with merely a breath?

And then her breath caught in her throat. She knew exactly why. Because he was Malach. Powerful and determined. A risk-taker, a warrior in full control of his body and its strength. Sensitive, generous, vulnerable. A skillful and caring lover. And a patient and gentle caretaker to Mei.

The numb terror that lurked inside her would never be entirely eased—not until Mei was out of danger—but it eased when she gazed at the man before her. He was magnificent. Especially now, with his thick, hard cock jutting from his heavy scrotum, his chest expanding with each breath and highlighting his tightly packed abs and impressive musculature. And then there was the hungry "I want you, you, and only you" expression darkening his eyes that made her heart thrill and race.

"Malach."

"Jade." He bent his head again, giving her more of what she craved. And, as the night progressed, he gave her another gift that was even more precious than his worshipful fulfillment of her body's needs: Relief from her worries and fears, and the comfort of his arms as he held her until at last she slept.

IN THAT EERIE period before dawn when darkness still lingered, the insistent blaring of the phone sucked Jade from sleep. She full-body shivered, somehow knowing to expect the worst even before Lìli snuck into the room and bent to whisper in her ear. Grace had rushed Mei straight to Royal Prince Alfred Hospital and left a message that they should meet her there.

Shocked mute by Lìli's news, Jade could only nod at her aunt and gesture her from the room. She slipped from the bed and the security of Malach's arms, feeling scared and bitter and full of shame at the hold he had over her.

She squinted in the gloom at his peaceful face, thankful he still slumbered, thankful he couldn't gaze at her and witness her guilt that she'd allowed him into her heart at her sister's expense. Because of him, Jade had become a woman so caught up in her own desires, so enamored by a man, she'd ignored her own sister's illness. If not for him, she would have been at home with Mei when her sister needed her the most.

She shoved herself into her clothes, her skin icy-cold, her heart aching, and stumbled from the bedroom into the almost unbearable brightness of Lìlì's kitchen. "How bad is she?" she asked, her throat so raw and tight the words were a raspy whisper.

Lìlì avoided her gaze under the pretext of brewing a pot of tea. "Her prognosis is not too bad."

"Don't bullshit me." Jade hissed the words through teeth clenched so tightly her jaw ached. "Grace wouldn't have taken her to hospital if it wasn't serious."

Lìlì's complexion was ashen when she raised her gaze, and the anguish in her eyes cut Jade like a blade. "Grace simply thought it best to get her checked by—"

"I'm not a child, Lìlì. You can't protect me from all the bad stuff anymore. Tell me."

Her aunt's breath sighed out in a shudder. "Nausea, vomiting, swollen ankles."

Jade's heart thundered in her chest. The symptoms she'd hoped never to hear echoed over and over in her mind.

Nausea. Vomiting. Swollen ankles. Taken singularly, not serious symptoms. But together, and when applied to Mei....

"Nothing else?" She had to ask, despite knowing that Grace would never put Mei at risk. She'd have watched Mei like a hawk, noted each symptom's appearance and severity, consulted with the specialist by phone, and then gone with her gut instinct—even if that gut instinct resulted in her carting Mei off to hospital and facing off against a doubtful specialist. Jade trusted Grace, but no one knew Mei better than Jade. She should have been there.

"Grace didn't mention anything else."

"Oh."

"We'll know when we get to the hospital and speak to Mei's specialist," Lìli said.

"Right. I'll go straight away."

"I'm coming with you." Lìli sounded determined.

"Right. Okay."

Jade couldn't get her brain to function properly. She knew it was shock, but she couldn't beat it back. How was she going to get to the hospital?

Home. She needed to get home. Grace's car was at home. But what if Grace hadn't waited for an ambulance and had taken Mei in her car?

"When's the next bus or train, Lìli Yíyi? Where've you put the timetables?"

A corner of her mind noted Lìli exhorting her to be calm, felt her aunt's hand plucking at her sleeve, smelled the sourness of fear emanating from Lìli's pores. And her aunt's fear shredded the last of Jade's tenuous control.

"Where's the fucking timetable?" She yanked open drawer after drawer, rifling through recipes and old letters in her search for a bus or train timetable that might not even exist.

"Sod it!" She heard her voice rising to a wail. "We'll fucking well walk or hitch a ride!" In her mind she whirled and rushed headlong from the room. In reality she was rooted to the spot, unable to move, and it was as though her soul had disengaged and continued its mad dash onward, leaving behind a shell that was too afraid to take the next step. Too afraid to take any step at all.

Strong, capable hands soothed her, gentling her panic into something more manageable. His scent engulfed her and she breathed him in, letting him sweep her away. And by the time she'd beaten back the nightmarish scenarios of her sister dying alone in some hospital bed, and could breathe without panting, she was seated in the back of a taxi with Malach holding tight to both her hands, and Lìli sitting up front with the driver, urging him to hurry.

The journey to RPA went by in a flash, so quickly Jade could almost imagine some benevolent god taking pity on her and transporting them instantaneously to the hospital car park. And then the reality of where she was, and why, smacked her again and it was all too much to bear.

She vaguely remembered being ushered from the cab, walking into the hospital and waiting, still clutching Malach's hand, while Lìli asked a receptionist to locate Mei. She recalled flashes of Grace's pale, tightly controlled features as she flew from the lift and rushed toward them. She remembered Grace's lips moving, the tic in the muscle by her left eye, the stricken expression that Grace couldn't hide as she explained everything. And Jade remembered nodding—not because she understood, but because a part of her sensed a response of some sort was required. Other than that, she couldn't bring herself to move unless someone coaxed her into motion.

Her lifeline, the one thing that kept her from shutting down and shutting out the world, was the firm pressure of Malach's hand gripping hers. And she knew with every fiber of her being that if he let go, some essential part of her would drift away and be lost.

They were waiting again, this time for the specialist to arrive and explain the situation before they could see Mei. More talking heads. Words spilling from mouths, entering her ears, penetrating her cotton-wooly brain and dispersing without sinking in. It was like living a dream—a nightmare.

And then Jade was ushered in to Mei's room.

She'd last seen her baby sister only yesterday morning, but it was as though in that short space of time all the life had been drained from Mei. Only then did the harsh reality of Dr. Rothwell's words—the ones Jade had been refusing to process—hit her. "Your sister's CRF, chronic renal failure, has progressed to end-stage kidney failure. Dialysis isn't sufficient anymore. She needs a kidney transplant immediately. And unless we find a suitable donor in the next few days, she'll likely be too weak to survive the operation. She's been fast-tracked to the top of the transplant list and we'll do everything we can. I'm very sorry."

Jade could no longer deny those words. They stared out at her from Mei's face. And worse, so much worse, was the acceptance dulling Mei's eyes.

ALL JADE COULD DO was wait, and watch Mei's body fail her. And wonder how, after years of fighting and living, her sister could have deteriorated so quickly.

Pain was Mei's constant companion, now. Chest pain, stomach pain from the gastrointestinal ulcer no one had suspected she suffered from, even pain in her bones. She bore it all with stoicism and dignity, even amid the humiliation of constant nausea and vomiting.

Jade had to swallow bile after she stupidly asked a nurse why Mei's skin looked so weird, and was informed the powdery white substance coating her skin was caused by the high concentration of urea crystallizing from her sweat. And those were only the immediately obvious symptoms. Levels of parathyroid hormone, calcitriol, phosphorous, calcium, triglycerides…. Jade's brain ached from trying to make sense of the medical-speak concerning the endlessly increasing list of hidden nasties.

She pelted Dr. Rothwell with questions, refusing to let him out of her sight until she understood his answers—as far as she was able. He was a patient, kindly man. He assured her he would do everything in his power to help Mei survive this.

Jade believed him. Just as she believed his assurances to Grace, who seemed bound and determined to shoulder the blame for Mei's sudden downhill slide.

"I shouldn't have pushed for peritoneal dialysis. Maybe if

she'd been on haemodialysis…." Grace turned her face away, struggling to keep it together, doubting her own training and competence.

"Haemodialysis wouldn't have prevented this," Dr. Rothwell told her. "No one could have prevented this. You and I both know it happens, Grace. No one knows why. You must stop blaming yourself."

Cold comfort for Grace, who, despite experiencing similar instances with other patients, couldn't stop herself from voicing the "maybes" and the "I wishes" and the "if onlys".

Grace loved Mei like her own sister. Of course she would blame herself for Mei's sudden deterioration. Jade knew it wasn't her friend's fault. Deep down, she knew there was nothing *she* could have done to prevent this either. But she couldn't forgive herself for being happy with Malach while Mei was quietly, secretly, becoming more and more ill.

Lili coped in her own way, kneeling at Mei's bedside and praying to whatever deity, or deities, she believed in. To Jade's surprise, Grace joined her aunt. "I'll take all the help for Mei I can get," Grace said.

But Mei was having none of it. "None of us should be praying for someone's death so that I can live. It's wrong and I won't do it. And neither should any of you."

They ignored her, and continued their prayer vigil.

Jade refused to join them. She knew prayer was useless. Mei wouldn't be here, dying in this hospital bed, if prayers were answered.

As she dozed in the chair beside Mei's bed, she found herself wishing her parents had been able to have more children, so maybe one of her siblings might have been a match for Mei. She knew it was a ridiculous wish, because if her parents had been able to conceive another child, they wouldn't have adopted Mei in the first place. But she couldn't help wishing it.

She wished they'd been able to trace Mei's birth parents—maybe one of them would have been willing to help her by donating a kidney if they'd known of her illness.

She wished for a hundred impossible things, and when she'd stopped torturing herself with impossibilities, she wished for a disaster with a high death toll and a wide choice of organ donors. Heck, if she'd had some psychic power that enabled her to walk up to a person and know their blood type—know for certain their kidneys would be suitable for Mei—she'd have fallen on them, ripped a kidney from their body with her bare hands, and personally carried it to the transplant team.

Malach spent his time charming the nurses, bringing endless cups of coffee or tea for Grace and Lìli, and piles of trashy gossip mags for Mei. Whenever Mei was awake, he made her laugh by perching on the side of the bed and haltingly reading aloud the outrageous headlines, and "true-life" reader stories and letters. And then, after coaxing Jade, Grace and Lìli down to the café for lunch, he disappeared.

It never occurred to Jade to wonder where the man who'd been her entire life for three weeks had disappeared to. All her energy and focus was on Mei. She had no time for lovers. And when Lìli finally consented to head home in a taxi, provided Grace promised to ring her if there was any change in Mei's condition, all Jade could feel was relief.

Part of her hoped Grace would go, too. Another part of her was grateful Grace stayed, but only because it meant she had someone to fetch food and drink, or talk to the nurses and doctors out of Mei's earshot, so Jade didn't have to leave Mei's room. She wasn't prepared to risk leaving her sister's side for even a minute. Their time together was far too precious. And Jade knew it was running out.

Chapter Fourteen

Dr. Rothwell gently shook Jade awake. Her stomach twisted into a tight knot. Questions she wasn't sure she wanted answered had already formed on her lips when she noticed the mile-wide grin on his face. She exhaled slowly through her nose and dared to hope again.

He gave her a thumbs up before turning his attention to Mei, who was still sleeping. He pulled the bottom of her sheet free from the mattress to expose her feet, and gently tickled her soles until she twitched and pried open her eyelids. "Excellent news, Mei. We've found you a donor kidney!"

Jade watched the hope light up her sister's eyes, transforming Mei's features into something ethereal and angelic, otherworldly... and then reality bit, leaching away the beauty to leave sunken eyes and sallow skin stretched over frail bones. Mei buried her face in her pillow and refused to look at either Jade or her doctor.

Anxiety gnawed at Jade, chasing away her relief. What if Mei was too weak to survive the operation? What if she refused to have the operation at all?

She couldn't think like that. Not now. Not ever. "Don't tell me you've discovered my blood tests were wrong and I'm a match?" Her sad attempt at humor fell flat.

"It's good news, Mei," Dr. Rothwell insisted. But Mei didn't respond.

He tried again. "No one died so you could live, Mei. We

have a live donor."

Mei stilled. She turned her head and stared at him. "We do?"

Dr. Rothwell beamed from ear to ear. "Yes. All the tests show we're good to go. We're prepping him now."

Jade snagged his sleeve as he straightened from the careful hug he'd given Mei. "Who?"

"Friend of yours, as I understand it. Malach—" He glanced at the chart tucked under his arm. "Malach Stone."

For the space of a heartbeat Jade's world ground to a halt. And when time resumed, she was left with a startlingly clear insight into Malach's character.

He'd been off on his own, with no one to hold *his* hand while he put his trust in strangers wielding needles and vials and a bewildering array of alien equipment. There had been no one to comfort him while he gave himself over to technology that had to have seemed terrifying and godlike. There had been no one to reassure him while he conferred with Mei's specialist and struggled to comprehend a procedure he'd probably never in his wildest dreams imagined possible. There had been no one standing by his side, telling him how much they loved him and cared for him, while he prepared to risk his life to give a young girl another chance—a girl he'd met three weeks ago, who wasn't even of his world, who had no claim on him whatsoever.

Here was a man she would be proud to spend the rest of her life with—a man she could love for real.

"Interesting name for an interesting man," Dr. Rothwell was saying. "Healthiest forty-one year old I've ever seen in my life. Seems he's never touched a drop of alcohol, his cholesterol is so low even *I'm* in awe, his blood pressure's superb, and aside from a few interesting scars he's in peak physical condition. He tells me he got those from some mock battle that got out of hand." The doctor snorted his disbelief. "A likely story. My bet is that he was SAS or Special Ops. Anyway, he's a compatible tissue type. And regardless of how those scars were inflicted, there's nothing wrong with his kidneys. Even better, he's more than happy to give one up to you, young lady." He chucked Mei under the chin. "So stop moping and hug your sister. She looks like she needs one. I'll be back in a little while, okay?"

It had never even crossed Jade's mind to consider Malach a potential donor. But it had crossed his. And he'd acted upon it.

"Hang on!" Jade's outburst had Dr. Rothwell turning back to her with a worried frown. "I thought it took months to do a full work-up for a live donor cross-match?"

Dr. Rothwell's frown etched deep lines between his brows. His gaze lost focus. From the way he tilted his head to the side, he seemed to be waging some internal debate. Then his expression cleared and he smiled. "We fast-tracked it. We're nothing if not efficient here at RPA, eh? But rest assured, we've been extremely thorough. HLA tissue type, CDC cross-match, flow cytometry cross-match, ABO blood-group compatibility, renal function assessment, complete blood workup, renal angiogram." He ticked each one off on his fingers. "We've done 'em all, Jade. Anything else you need reassurance about?"

She shook her head. She sensed Pieter's gnarly old paws all over this… and knew there was no point cluing Dr. Rothwell in to the sheer impossibility of having all those tests performed, and the results confirmed, in the space of twenty-four hours. Jade had no doubt the hospital records would show all the necessary tests had been completed and that Malach had passed with flying colors. She only hoped Pieter knew what he was doing.

"Thanks, Dr. Rothwell," she said. "Sorry to be such a pain in the bum."

"No problem, Jade. Completely understandable." He bustled from the room, and the instant he'd cleared the doorway, Grace burst in.

"You've heard the news?" she demanded.

"Malach's donating me one of his kidneys," Mei whispered, her face shining with hero-worship-style awe.

"Yep!" Grace kissed Mei's cheek. Then she snatched Jade into her arms and pulled her into a clumsy little dance of joy.

"How on earth did you find out so quickly?" Jade managed to ask. Grace had dashed off to run some errands yesterday, but had otherwise stayed glued to Mei's bedside before finally heading home to bed about midnight.

She gave an evil cackle. "I haf vays of making zem talk. After Malach confessed his intentions and I got him in to see Rothwell, I strong-armed one of the lab staff into texting me when the results came through. Let's just say he owed me one and leave it at that, shall we?"

Yes, Jade thought. *Let's*.

Grace released Jade to dance over to Mei and hug her again. Jade stumbled to the chair, sinking into it, her brain awhirl. Malach had confided in Grace but not her? Why?

Grace answered her unspoken question. "Don't get upset, J." She reached over to squeeze Jade's wrist. "He didn't say anything because he didn't want to get your hopes up. That's why I didn't mention it, either. Please don't be angry."

"It's okay. Better this way, huh? Especially since it's turned out to be the best news we could have, and—" An unwelcome thought slapped her and she wrapped her arms around her middle.

Malach's suitability as a donor might be the result of some magical behind-the-scenes manipulation by the Crystal Guardian, but what about Malach's desire to be a donor in the first place? She had to believe that was all him. To believe otherwise was too horrific for words. To be given no choice in the matter....

Then an even worse thought struck her, leaving her choking down panic. Had the Testing come early? Was her bond to Malach about to be Tested in an operating theater beneath a surgeon's scalpel?

She dug her fingernails into her palms. Could this vengeful goddess of Pieter's be so cruel that, if they failed the Testing, the price she intended to extract would not only be Malach's life but Jade's baby sister's life, too?

There were only two people she could talk to about the intentions of goddesses and the like, without risking being dragged off to the psych ward. And since Pieter was conveniently absent, Jade borrowed Grace's cell phone and excused herself to ring Lìli on the pretext of telling her the good news.

Lìli listened silently until Jade had run out of words.

"You need to talk to Malach, Jade. You love him. And you must tell him so before he goes into surgery."

Jade's heart shattered into teeny tiny pieces, and she clutched the receiver so tightly her knuckles ached. "You don't think he's going to make it, do you?"

"Tell him, Jade. He needs to know. A man who has suffered as Malach has suffered, needs to know he has someone who cares for him—someone who loves him."

"What do you know, Lìli Yíyi? What aren't you telling me?"

"Just tell him you love him, you foolish girl!"

"But I—" The phone clicked in Jade's ear as the line went dead. "She hung up on me? She hung up on me!" she announced to no one in particular.

What the heck was the point of telling Malach she loved him if she wouldn't know for sure it was the truth until Lìli's spell wore off? If she confronted him now, and told him to his face how she felt, would Pieter's goddess hear a lie as soon as Jade uttered the words "I love you, Malach"?

She couldn't risk it. She couldn't risk Mei. She had to play this out and hope that if what she felt for Malach *wasn't* real, she would still manage to fool Pieter and his goddess.

Better to keep her declarations of love bottled up inside her. Better to let Lìli's spell do its work and hope that actions spoke louder than words. Jade sure acted as though she were head-over-heels in love with Malach, and vice versa for that matter. It would have to be enough.

She leaned her forehead against the wall and hoped with all her heart that if it all turned pear-shaped, Malach would forgive her for failing him. She hoped that if the worst happened, Pieter would be swayed by Mei's innocence in all this, and petition his goddess for Mei's life. And she hoped Pieter's goddess would listen and grant Mei mercy.

JADE COULDN'T HANDLE it any longer—the waiting, the powerlessness, the overwhelming terror something was going to go terribly wrong. Despite all the practice she'd had in hiding her worries from Mei, now it was hard—desperately hard—not to fall apart. Because now she had two people to worry about. Two people for whom she would willingly trade places on those operating tables in an instant.

She appreciated Grace and Lìli's unstinting support but she dearly wanted time alone to shriek her fears at the top of her voice, beat her fists on the nearest wall, or collapse in a quivering heap on the floor, without subjecting her best friend and her aunt to more worry. Instead, she was forced to do whatever it took to keep it together for the sake of appearances.

Twice already Grace had asked her to quit beating a tattoo on the linoleum with her heels and— Oops, she was doing it again. She shot Grace an apologetic look and hooked her ankles around the legs of her chair. She glanced at the clock on the wall and then quickly looked away, vowing not to look at the damnable thing again. Every passing minute seemed interminable, torturous, and she couldn't help dwelling on Malach, trapped for centuries in his crystal prison. Powerless. Conscious of nothing but the passing of time, willing to do anything to escape or make it end. How had he borne it without losing his sanity?

"Jade, please!"

She blinked back to here and now reality to find Lìli gripping her shoulders and pressing her hard against the back of the chair. "Huh? What's the matter?" *God. What am I doing now?*

"You're doing it again. Rocking. Please, Jade, try to relax. You will help no one if you work yourself into such a state."

"Sorry." She gripped the seat of her chair so tightly her hands ached, all the while keeping her back stiffly upright, knees and feet pressed neatly together. She probably looked like some macabre ventriloquist's dummy, but she was beyond caring. Focusing on the jabbing ache in her back and the cramping of her fingers was better than the alternative. Sooner or later, though, Jade suspected she was going to lose it big-time. And she probably wouldn't even be aware of it until she was racing pell-mell down a corridor waving her arms about like a madwoman. Or grabbing the next intern who wandered past and threatening to throttle him unless he told her how Mei and Malach were faring.

She caught herself before she started with the rocking thing again and groaned, pinching the bridge of her nose.

Grace nudged her with an elbow. "You all right, J?"

"Yeah." No. No way. She needed to do something—anything—rather than sit here, at the mercy of time and surgeons and fate. "I'm going for a walk."

"Want some company?"

Jade shook her head. "'S'okay, Gracie. I need some fresh air. Need to clear my head."

"Okay. Here, take this." Grace thrust her cell phone into Jade's hands. "I'll have them call you if anything—" Her mouth twisted. She ducked her head and resumed staring at her feet.

"Thanks." Jade thrust the ridiculously tiny, state-of-the-art mobile into the pocket of her jeans and strode off down the corridor.

She found herself heading not toward the lifts, to find her way outside, but toward Reception. And, as she walked, the credit card she kept for emergencies burned a hole in her pocket. It wasn't until she reached the front desk that she realized what she intended to do. That realization froze her into immobility, causing her to stand there, openmouthed, until a nurse asked if anything was wrong.

The woman was so kind Jade didn't feel too embarrassed by her lapse. She guessed everyone here was used to seeing people lose it. Transplant wards were hardly the kind of place people would normally choose to spend their time. And despite this ward's cheery colors, and the bright paintings adorning its walls, to Jade it seemed tainted by the pain and anguish of all the people who'd been left behind, despairing, when things didn't go to plan.

The nurse directed her to a row of payphones that took credit cards. Jade snagged the most private corner booth, and fished around for the printout from the People Finder website that she'd secreted in her handbag. The fee had been a small amount to pay for such potentially life-changing information.

She unfolded it, smoothing out the creases. She stared at the address and phone number printed on it for a long time.

Should she or shouldn't she? Would it put Mei at risk? Would Pieter's goddess exact retribution, or would it count in Jade's favor that she could be so selfless as to offer Malach a choice?

With shaking hands, she inserted the credit card into the slot, lifted the receiver, and slowly, carefully, dialed the number.

As soon as it started ringing she realized she didn't have the foggiest clue what time it was in the States. Oh God. Maybe she should hang up—

"Hello, Francesca speaking."

"Oh! Hi. It's, um, Jade Liang calling from Australia. Is... is...? God! Sorry." She took a deep breath and started again. "Is this Francesca Laureano-Owens?"

"This is she."

Francesca came across all terribly polite and distant, but Jade thought she detected a faint curiosity, too. "I'm calling about a man you used to know."

"Oh, really?"

Her clipped tone warned if Jade didn't explain herself quickly, Francesca would disconnect. And if that happened, Jade knew she wouldn't have the guts to ring her again.

"His name's Malach."

Silence.

"Do you remember him?"

More silence. Really awkward, elephant-sized silence.

"Well, anyway, he sure remembers you."

"What did you say your name was?"

"Jade. Jade Liang."

"Oh. *Jade.*" Said with heavy emphasis. "Pretty."

"Thanks. I—"

"Well, good try, Jade. But I'm not buying. Chalcey put you up to this, didn't she?"

"Who?"

"Chalcedony. My daughter." Francesca sighed. "I wonder what I've done to upset her this time."

She sounded so resigned Jade's heart twinged. "I don't, uh, *personally* know any Chalcey or... or... Chalcedony. But chalcedony's a crystal, right?"

"It is. And it happens to be the crystal I named my daughter for, back when I was going through a... stage."

"Oh. Well it's a very pretty name, too."

The woman on the other end of the line gave a light little laugh. "Far better than Beryl."

It took Jade a few seconds to understand the reference. "Ah, got it. Your first name is Beryl, but you go by your middle name, Francesca, right?"

"Look, Jade, I don't know what the purpose of this call is, but—"

"I'm calling to tell you that although Pieter chose me for

Malach and we've, um, you know, *bonded*, I think Pieter's made a big mistake. I'm afraid Malach and I are going to fail the Testing, and Malach's going to be returned to his crystal. I don't think he's going to survive another round of imprisonment in—"

"Malach's alive?"

Her shock snaked down the phone line and suckerpunched Jade right where it hurt. Francesca still had feelings for Malach. Just as he did for her. If Jade hadn't gotten in the way, they might have met up and lived happily ever after—well, except for the inconvenience of Francesca having a husband, of course.

"Yes, he's alive but—"

"Pieter didn't kill him?" The question was almost a shriek.

Uh oh. "No, thank God. But he might as well have. The second stint in the crystal has really screwed Malach up. He has nightmares and—"

"Why are you ringing me, Jade?" Cue heavy, panicked breathing, like Francesca was struggling for control. "I've put that period of my life behind me. I've moved on, tried to forget—"

"That you chose to stay with your husband, and condemned Malach to be imprisoned in his crystal for another two decades or so, until the Crystal Guardian found another woman to take your place? Yep. Got that part already." *And Malach's got the scars on his soul to prove it.*

Jade heard Francesca's pained gasp and hurried on before the woman could start up with the excuses again. "And I know you were married at the time, and your husband was dying so you opted to stay with him. Malach doesn't blame you for that. He understands."

Not so long ago, Jade hadn't blamed her, either. She'd thought Pieter and his goddess cruel to choose Francesca for Malach in such circumstances. But knowing Malach intimately, knowing how dreadfully he had suffered because of

Francesca's decision, Jade sure was inclined to blame the woman now. Yes, her husband had been dying, but she could still have bonded with Malach. They might not have passed the Testing, but at least she could have tried.

"He was supposed to die!" Francesca wailed. "Pieter was supposed to kill him! He wasn't supposed to stay in the crystal and suffer!"

Jesus. "And that's the only reason you could live with yourself? Because you thought he'd *died*?"

"No! Yes. I mean…. God. You must think I'm a terrible person."

"No." Well, yes, but deep down Jade knew she was being incredibly unfair. Jade was, after all, rooting for Malach and firmly on his side.

"I'm glad he's alive," Francesca said. "He didn't deserve to die. He was a good man."

"*Is* a good man," Jade bit out. And resisted the need to fish Grace's phone from her back pocket to check it for messages… and confirm that Malach hadn't perished under the surgeon's knife due to unforeseen complications. He wasn't dead. He couldn't be.

Not yet, a spiteful little voice whispered in her ear.

"So, you're really the woman Pieter's chosen for him."

"Yep. That'd be me."

"I don't mean to be rude but you sound awfully young, Jade."

"I'm twenty."

"And Malach's what? Still in his early forties? Or has he aged since then? God, please don't tell me he's now in his sixties."

"He's forty-one. He hasn't aged since you last saw him."

"Still. What was Pieter thinking?"

"I'm sure I have no idea."

This conversation was not going at all how Jade had planned. Not that she'd really planned what to say, but she sure as heck hadn't expected to deal with Francesca questioning her suitability for Malach.

"Malach didn't fight for me once I'd made my decision," Francesca said, interrupting Jade's musings. "He stopped pursuing me to make it easier for me to stay with Benigno, my husband. I—we—were both convinced Pieter would kill him once he was returned to his crystal. He sacrificed himself for me and told me to forget him. So I did. Or I tried to, anyway." She paused, her silence weighted with past decisions and consequences. "You know I married again."

"Yes."

"Then what's the point ringing me to tell me that Malach is alive? Are you so cruel that you'd torture me all over again with a choice I don't have? I wouldn't leave my husband even if I—"

"Even if you still loved Malach," Jade finished for her. "Do you? Still love him, I mean?"

"I don't know. Maybe." Another pause. "Not that it matters now he's got you."

It mattered all right.

"And what about you, Jade? Do you love Malach?"

She closed her eyes. "It's… complicated."

"It always is. What Chalcedony went through with Wulf…."

Jade's ears pricked up. "Wulf? He's another one, right? From Malach's troop, I mean."

"Yes. Wulf was in charge, and Malach was his second-in-command." She laughed, but there was an underlying bitterness that made Jade suspect all was not fine and dandy in Francesca's world.

"Ironically, my daughter ended up bonded to Wulf. Or should I say, Wulfenite, Lord Keeper of the Shifting Sands fief. And they now devote a large portion of their spare time to tracing other Crystal Warriors. They've been married a while. I have three grandchildren—not that I get to see them very often. Chalcedony and I have... issues."

"I'm sorry." Lame, but what else could she say? At least Francesca could talk to her daughter and her grandchildren if she really wanted to. At least her daughter still *had* a mother.

"Francesca, I rang you because I thought you'd want to know Malach's undergoing a serious operation right now. He's donating one of his kidneys to my adopted sister to save her life."

"How typically Malach. Self-sacrificing and so noble it makes my teeth ache."

What a *bitch*. "Yes. Well, I'm sure your husband, being a dentist, will be able to fix that for you."

"Ouch!" That light laugh tinkled down the phone-line again. "I guess I deserved that, didn't I? It was very insensitive of me, and I'm truly sorry, Jade. Malach's the kind of man who wouldn't hesitate to help someone in need, and I'm glad he's there for you and your sister. Where's the operation being performed?"

Jade's heart began to pound and she felt lightheaded and ill. This was it. Francesca was going to catch a plane and—

"I'd like to send something to him, if I may?"

"Uh, sure. We're at the Royal Prince Alfred Hospital in Sydney, but I'll give you my address in case your letter, or whatever, arrives after he's been discharged." Jade gave Francesca the details, wondering whether the woman really believed that writing Malach a freaking letter, or sending some bloody gift, was going to put this issue to bed.

She'd been stupid to imagine Francesca might be so grateful to learn the man she'd once loved was alive, that she would hop on a plane and fly out to see him. Realistically, there'd been a high probability of no happy ending whatsoever for Francesca and Malach. But Jade had kind of pictured Francesca doing something drastic. Like ditching her husband to take up with Malach and live happily ever after.

She should have felt awful for Malach. Instead, all she felt was a lightening of her spirit—relief, she guessed, that now he was all hers….

If everything went to plan. If he survived. If she still wanted him once Lìli's spell wore off. If he still wanted her….

"When's the Testing due?" Francesca surprised her by asking.

"Technically it's only been three weeks since Malach showed up, but I think something's out of whack because surely what he's going through now is the Testing."

"The operation, you mean?"

"Yeah."

"Mmm. Perhaps. Jade, I get the sense that it's difficult for you but for Malach's sake, please don't fail him like I did. He deserves a life with a woman he loves. He deserves to be happy."

"But that's where it's tricky. He's still in love with *you* so how could he ever truly fall in love with me?" Her voice wobbled and she bit her lips to stop from tearing up.

Francesca was silent for a very long time. "You have no choice but to make him love you," she finally said.

"Yeah, we're trying our best. We had my aunt cast a spell to make us both fall in love until the Testing's over."

"Really? You did that for him?"

"Yeah. Sounds pretty stupid, huh?"

"Not at all. Desperate people do desperate things."

"Yeah. And I'm pretty desperate to save him. So here's hoping Pieter and his bloody goddess are fooled, and Malach will finally be free of the crystal. And here's hoping if it doesn't work, my sister doesn't end up caught in the middle of something that's nothing to do with her."

"It will be all right, Jade," Francesca soothed. "You'll see. Have faith."

"Yeah." Jade wiped her eyes with the back of her hand. "Thanks."

Francesca rang off, leaving Jade with that awful churning

in the pit of her stomach she got when she suspected she'd only made a bad situation worse. She tried to justify what she'd done. Surely ringing Francesca had been the right thing to do. But she couldn't help feeling she'd just made the biggest mistake of her life.

She stood clutching the phone, resting her head against the cool Perspex of the phone booth's partition. Too late now. Francesca knew Malach was alive and the rest was up to her.

As she replaced the receiver, the chorus of The Fray's *How to Save a Life* rang out.

What the—? Who was the dickhead with the warped sense of humor?

Jade had craned her neck to locate the source when she realized the song was coming from the pocket of her jeans. And that it was the ringtone of Grace's fancy mobile phone.

Chapter Fifteen

Jade had done enough research, and talked to enough specialists, to know that kidney transplantation wasn't a walk in the park. It was a major operation. And with a live donor, there were two patients to look out for.

So far as Mei was concerned, Jade been fully versed in what to expect. The surgeon would make an incision through Mei's pelvis, place the donor kidney inside her, and attach it to her blood vessels and bladder. As long as her non-functioning kidneys weren't infected or causing uncontrollable high blood pressure, they'd be left in place. She would have to take immunosuppressants for the rest of her life. And live with the specters of side-effects or contracting a severe infection.

Many kidney transplantation patients went on to lead normal, active lives, but there were a host of things that could go pear-shaped. And Jade knew them all. She knew all the percentages pertaining to rejection of a kidney after transplantation by heart. She knew it could happen shortly after the operation, or gradually, over many weeks or even months. But she refused to consider anything other than one-hundred percent success right now. A part of her believed that to dwell on any of the big bad nasties was to invite it in to their lives.

Mei had survived the first hurdle, and her prognosis was good. End of story. Jade had perfected the art of not dwelling on what the future might hold a long time ago.

Malach, too, had come through the operation with flying

colors. And as Mei was still being kept doped up to the eyeballs, Jade left her sister with Grace and chose to hang out by Malach's bedside. He'd been moved from Intensive Care into his room, and she wanted to be the first person he saw when he woke up.

She felt ashamed that she had no clue what might be in store for Malach now he was one kidney down. When Grace had tried to explain it to her, she hadn't taken any of it in. She didn't even know whether his kidney donation and recovery was covered by the public healthcare system. Hopefully, Pieter would have made provisions for that eventuality—as he'd done with everything else.

If Jade were brutally honest with herself, she had been a mess—almost paralyzed by fear that she was going to lose one or both of them. She had, in Grace's professional opinion, been a total cot-case. But it was time to get her shit together so she would be there for the people she loved when they needed her. The people she loved label included Malach. He'd given up a kidney for Mei. He was Mei's savior, *and* Jade's, too. Because before Malach, Jade's life had been a sham. Before Malach, she'd only been pretending to live. And now, he was everything to her….

He groaned and his eyelids fluttered.

She leaned forward to smooth his hair back from his brow. He seemed so pale and colorless, so unlike himself that she had to blink multiple times to hold back her tears.

"Francesca?" he murmured.

Her hand stilled. She was about pull back when he opened his eyes and focused on her face. He smiled. "Jade."

Too late now to beat a hasty retreat. She would have to nurse her hurt in the deepest recesses of her heart and pretend nothing was the matter. "Hi. How're you feeling?"

"Like crap, as you would be saying."

She chuckled. "Yeah. That's what I would be saying. Want some water?"

"Please."

She poured him a cup and held the straw to his lips. He took a couple of sips and then waved it away.

"Dr. Rothwell says your operation went like a dream," she told him. "Because your kidney was removed laparoscopically, with that little fiber-optic telescope device he told you about, you've only got small incisions and you'll be out of here quicker than you might expect. He wishes all his patients were in as good a physical condition as you."

"'Tis strange," he said, "to be put to sleep in such a fashion. I was afraid I might dream, as happened during my imprisonment in the crystal, but I remember nothing."

"Probably just as well."

"Indeed."

"That was it, you know. We've succeeded and you're free, Malach."

He frowned. "I do not understand."

"The Testing. We've passed it. You're free."

His eyes narrowed to slits and Jade could almost see him calculating the length of time that had passed in his head.

"It has only been—"

"Three weeks. I know. But this has to have been the Testing, right? You put your life at risk to save Mei's, and you both survived."

He pursed his lips, a picture of doubt.

"Where is it written in stone that it has to be four weeks?" she demanded. "Look. It's over. You're safe from the crystal forever. Lili's spell won't be affecting us anymore, and we'll know what's real. We'll no longer be living a lie. We've beaten Pieter's curse, Malach. You're free. And now you can do whatever you want." *Like... leave me to search for the woman you truly love.*

The unspoken words loomed over them both.

She knew Malach was thinking about Francesca, too, when the distant expression darkening his eyes cleared.

Jade's stomach plummeted to her toes. How would he feel when he found out Francesca had remarried and wouldn't even consider a relationship with him?

The stress she'd been enduring finally had its revenge, and her heightened emotions burst forth with a vengeance. "Oh God, Malach!" She couldn't bring herself to confess how she truly felt about him when he was thinking about another woman, so she opted for a lesser truth. "How can I ever thank you for what you've done for Mei?"

"Anyone would do the same, Jade. There is nothing to thank me for." He reached for her, and as she leaned into him, he cupped her nape and drew her down onto the bed beside him.

She sobbed her heart out while he held her, and she released all the long held fears she'd harbored for Mei. And when she'd finished crying for Mei, Jade cried for Malach. She cried for him because she'd done what she promised and found Francesca for him. She cried for him because even though Francesca still loved Malach, she would never leave her husband.

And, before she drifted off to an exhausted sleep, she even cried for herself. Because now that Lìli's spell had ended, Jade knew she loved Malach with all her heart and soul. But once he contacted Francesca, if he did end up staying here in Sydney, with *her*, it would be from a misplaced sense of obligation, nothing more.

Jade would be the consolation prize, always trying to measure up to Malach's first love, always hoping that he would eventually grow to love her as much as she loved him. And the bitch of it all was, she loved him so much she would take whatever tiny piece of his heart he had left to offer.

FOR THE NEXT few days, Jade was in a holding pattern, endlessly chasing her tail and unable to take the plunge that, for better or for worse, would move her life forward. During visiting hours, she carefully avoided the bigger issues. Such as love. And whether she had a future with Malach. Or whether now that she'd given him Francesca's contact details he would ring her.

She didn't tell him much about her conversation with Francesca, but she did tell him about Wulf, and how it'd been Francesca's daughter who had freed him from the crystal's curse. And afterward Malach's features were carefully expressionless, giving her no clue what he might be thinking.

Mei continued to make excellent progress. Her rate of recovery delighted Dr. Rothwell no end, and he in turn delighted Mei by announcing he didn't see any reason why she couldn't go back to school sometime this year. Mei didn't notice that her doctor was carefully vague as to exactly when that might be. Just as he remained cagey as to when Mei would be discharged.

Outside visiting hours Jade had time on her hands. Too much time. Grace had decamped to her apartment until Mei was allowed to come home, leaving Jade rattling around by herself in a too quiet, empty house. She kept in touch with her aunt via phone, but for now she couldn't bring herself to face Lìli—that would mean facing up to the consequences of Lìli's love spell.

So Jade busied herself with banking Pieter's money, paying outstanding accounts and putting all the finances in order, while waiting with trepidation for the first of the hospital bills to arrive. Thank God her parents had taken out health insurance for Mei and Jade when they were babies. Mei's insurance plan would only cover some of the costs, however, and Jade needed to save every penny. With this in mind, she placed another ad for a temporary caregiver for Mei. Doubtless Grace wouldn't be too impressed but Jade couldn't afford her friend's usual rates once Pieter stopped his payments, and she absolutely refused to let Grace charge mate's rates on a long term basis.

The next order of business was to clean the house from top to bottom, and despite her best efforts to eke out the chores, she could only make them last a day and a half. Even tidying up the garden only took a few hours. Jade's mother had also suffered from a black thumb, and she'd planted with low-maintenance in mind. It was simply a matter of pulling weeds and trimming a few straggly bushes.

When Jade could bear the empty house no longer, she visited Carlo to fill him in on how Mei was faring… and to make a point of letting him know she wanted her old job back as soon as Mei was home and settled. That done, she retrieved Mei's portrait from the gallery, and touched up a couple of chips on the frame where it'd been knocked about during transit. She hung the painting in Mei's room, where it belonged, and dreamed of the day when her sister would again resemble the healthy, glowing young girl in the portrait.

She had one more task to complete: Signing her name to Malach's portrait. And once that was done, there was nothing left to do but brood.

She stood the painting on an easel in her bedroom, and spent hours lost in contemplation of the reality it represented—the man who held her heart in his big, capable hands.

When exhaustion finally drove her to her bed, she lay there, turning the halves of Malach's crystal over in her hands. He'd given her the two pieces of malachite, requesting she dispose of them as she saw fit. But despite his hatred for the hunks of stone, Jade felt a deep connection to them. They were a part of him. And once Pieter had claimed the portrait, if Malach chose to walk away, Jade would have only these pieces of crystal to remind her of the man who'd burst into her life and seduced her into loving him.

If Malach chose to walk away, she didn't know how she would let him go.

THE DAY BEFORE Jade's twenty-first birthday, Malach was

discharged on the condition he didn't undertake anything "too physical". Yeah. Riiight. Like he was going to pay heed to that.

He reluctantly allowed himself to be ensconced in Lìli's spare room, and Lìli insisted on coddling him to within an inch of his life. Jade wondered how long he would put up with it.... And smothered a smile when he lasted all of twenty-four hours. By lunchtime the following day, the endless tasty tidbits Lìli had plied him with "to fatten you up", and the vile-tasting herbal concoctions he was forced to drink "to build up your strength" had finally taken their toll.

The way Lìli told it—in a most affronted tone over the phone to Jade—he snuck out of the house while she was in the garden picking apples to bake him a pie. And she had a message for Jade to give him the minute he turned up... which he did not five minutes after had Lìli had hung up the phone, still grumbling beneath her breath about stubborn males who didn't know what was good for them.

He greeted Jade at the door with a kiss that made her insides melt, and a box tucked under his arm. "'Tis a gift for you. For your Birthing Day." He tugged her into the lounge and thrust the gift into her hands.

"You shouldn't have," she told him as she opened the box.

Inside, nestled amid pale pink tissue-paper sheets, were the sandals her mother had brought her, their heels reattached and miraculously mended.

Jade's hand crept to her lips. "Oh my God! I take it back. You definitely should have! How did you—?"

He grinned from ear to ear, pleased by her delighted reaction. "I retrieved the heels of your sandals from the waste bin in the hotel room. I know not what compelled me to do so, only that I kept recalling the misery on your face. And then I found the sandals themselves beneath the chair where you had kicked them, and with Grace's aid, I located an excellent cobbler."

"Ah. So that's where they got to. I figured Grace had

thrown them out to save me any more upset."

"Are they acceptable?" His pleased smile turned anxious.

Jade took the sandals from the gift-box to examine them more closely. "The man's a genius. I can't even see where they were damaged. Wasn't it costly to have them fixed, though? They were in a shocking state and—"

Malach held up a hand to halt her mid-fret. "Pieter provided me with plenty of money, Jade."

"But—"

"Yes, it was costly, and perhaps cheaper to buy new footwear, but that was not the issue. Besides, when I explained the situation to the cobbler, he lowered his quoted price and put much time and effort into his repair—a true craftsman, I think."

"I'll say." Jade stood on tiptoes so she could kiss him lightly on the mouth. "I think I'll wear them tonight. Lili will expect us to dress up a bit. She loves to stand on ceremony."

He sighed, looking rather glum.

"What's wrong?"

"Your aunt is smothering me and treating me like an invalid," he grumped. "As much as I esteem her greatly, I would willingly walk into the sands during the Storm Season than put up with her clucking over me any longer."

"I take it a stroll at that time of the year wouldn't be a very sensible thing to do in your world?"

"Nay. 'Twould be most unwise indeed. Quite likely fatal."

She bit back a giggle at his disgruntled expression. "You know she's going to have some rather uncomplimentary things to say to you tonight when we head back there for dinner."

"I do know this, but—"

"It'll be worth it?"

"Indeed. If only so there is room remaining in my belly to fit the feast she is preparing in honor of your Birthing Day. She has stuffed me so full, I fear I am in danger of exploding. But I fear offending her if I refuse to sample at least a portion of each dish. She is a most determined woman, your aunt." He rubbed his abused stomach.

"You know," Jade said, eyeing the offending portion of his anatomy. "It does look like you've put on a bit of weight around the middle. Maybe you need to go on a diet."

He squinted at his stomach. "Do you truly think so?"

She bit the inside of her cheek to keep from laughing. "No."

He glared at her through slitted eyes.

"Gotcha!" she crowed.

He made a grab for her, doubtless intending to extract some form of dastardly revenge, but she danced out of reach. "Uh uh! No roughhousing. You heard what the surgeon said. And, truth be told, you've actually *lost* weight and could do with fattening up. I could whip you up an omelet."

He groaned. "Please, I beg of you, do not ply me with food or I swear I will go on a fast and restrict myself to bread and water." He frowned and reconsidered that statement. "After tonight's celebration, that is. Lili is baking apple pie—my favorite dessert. And as she has taken so much trouble, I must force myself to eat at least one piece."

"Speaking of Lili. She figured you'd turn up here so she left a message for you."

"Oh?"

Jade watched him pace the threadbare rug. He radiated the need to burn off some of his excess energy, and she knew he wasn't going to be happy with what Lili had to say. "She said to tell you she's already spoken to Dai-soon and clued him in about your specialist's instructions. So don't even *think* about trying to cajole Dai-soon into sparring with you."

Malach's expression reminded her of a mutinous child who'd hatched a brilliantly cunning plan, only to be thwarted before he could put it into action.

"Sorry. I imagine it's hard to swear off exercise after you've been confined to bed for the best part of a week. I'm sure you can think of something less strenuous than taekwondo, though. How about we go for a walk?"

"I have done enough walking up and down Lord Alfred's infernal corridors to last me a lifetime. I do not want to go for a walk."

"Just for the record, those 'infernal corridors' are named after a royal *Prince* not a Lord. And you'll do as you're told or I'll tell Lili *and* Grace on you."

He lowered himself into an armchair and scowled. "I am perfectly fine."

"Sure you are."

"I have made a complete recovery."

"Aha. And I'm sure you know better than your surgeon, right? You being such an expert in removal of kidneys and how long it takes to recover after *major* surgery—which, I might add, doesn't even exist in your world. But of course you would know best."

He glowered at her.

It was an impressive glower, one that might have had a lesser mortal beating a hasty retreat, and it didn't move Jade in the slightest. He was still feeling the effects of his operation, even though he'd rather die than admit it. Typical man.

"Stop grinning at me and come here," he growled.

"Who made you my boss, huh?"

"Come here."

She raised her eyebrows.

"Please?" he amended.

"Since you asked so nicely." Jade had fully intended to perch on the padded arm of the old chair but Malach grabbed her and plonked her in his lap.

"Hey!" She struggled but he merely wrapped an arm around her hips and had no trouble holding her still. Of course, she could have jabbed him in the stomach, but that would be playing dirty, and she couldn't bring herself to hurt him.

"I have thought of one thing I can do to quell my desire for physical activity." He tunneled his fingers through her hair, angling her head so he could nuzzle her ear. He bit gently on the lobe. And when his lips nibbled the sensitive little spot just below her jaw-line, Jade found herself trembling instead of struggling.

"Ahhh... do you really think this is a good idea?" she managed. "Mightn't it be a bit too strenuous?"

"Easily solved," he murmured, flicking open the buttons of her blouse and easing the garment back from her shoulders. His lips found her breast and he drew one lace-covered nipple into his mouth, suckling deeply.

Sharp pleasure pooled in her pelvis. *Whoa. Happy Birthday to me!*

He pulled back just long enough to say, "I will just take my ease here, in this comfortable chair, leaving you to do all the hard work. I am sure that will more than satisfy my surgeon."

She couldn't think of any reason to scotch that suggestion, especially since he'd turned his attention to tormenting her neglected breast and her brain had decided to take a hike. She moaned, wriggling in his lap. He took that as a "Yes", and shifted her until she knelt astride him.

"Malach, you're supposed to be careful!"

"I promise to be very careful indeed—once you divest yourself of those ridiculously short trousers before I am forced to rip them from your body."

He was dead serious. Jade climbed from his lap and unbuttoned her shorts. For good measure, she shed her bra and panties, too.

His eyes darkened as he gazed at her. And he held her gaze as he slowly rose to shuck his track pants and t-shirt, before lowering himself back into the chair. She didn't wait for him to ask again. She supported her weight on her knees and lowered herself slowly onto his erect cock. When she leaned in to kiss him, she was careful not to graze the healing incisions on the lower left side of his body.

It was strange, this feeling of absolute control, the realization *she* was the one setting the pace. Increasing it, then slowing it down, squeezing and releasing his hard length with her inner muscles, teasing him unmercifully until he lost control. And then she reveled in his tight grip on her hips, his hoarse whispers urging her to come with him, insisting she let go and tip over into ecstasy with him.

And she did.

She thought she heard a car door slam as she lay slumped across his chest with only his arms across the small of her back preventing her from slipping bonelessly to the rug. Probably the neighbors.

The harsh blare of the doorbell jolted through her. "Bugger. That'll probably be Grace. Talk about bad timing." She slithered from his lap and grabbed her clothes.

The doorbell chimed again. "Coming," she called, blushing at her choice of words. "Won't be a minute."

She shoved herself into her shorts and blouse, threw her bra and panties at Malach, and ran to answer the door. She glanced over her shoulder before she exited the lounge, just to make certain Malach was decent. Lucky she did, for she spotted his briefs lying on the rug.

"Malach!" She pointed to the offending item, and he grinned at her before snagging them with his toe and kicking them up to snatch them out of the air.

"Show-off." She knotted the front tails of her blouse in an effort to disguise her braless state, and opened the door with a grin.

The grin faded the instant she recognized the tall, elegant, immaculately-dressed blonde standing on her doorstep.

Chapter Sixteen

Jade escorted Francesca Laureano-Owens through to the lounge. She copped one glimpse of the stunned expression on Malach's face, and the tears pooling in Francesca's expertly made-up eyes, and bolted to her bedroom, muttering about giving Malach and his visitor some privacy.

She sprawled on the bed and tried her utmost not to torture herself by guessing what Malach and the love of his life were discussing right now. But wondering ate at her soul. And when she'd counted all the blotches of discoloration on the ceiling, and the walls of her room had closed in on her, turning her sanctuary into a prison, she gave up and crept from her room.

She had no intention of eavesdropping. She had no desire to hear anything Malach needed to say to Francesca. She tiptoed down the hallway, and as she flit past the slightly ajar door, she couldn't help glancing through the gap. Seeing Malach with his arms around Francesca, comforting her, and Francesca burrowed into his embrace, was the final kick in the teeth. Head down, numbed beyond coherent thought, Jade stole from the house, down the path, past the top-of-the-line rental car parked in the driveway, and kept on walking.

Time passed. Jade had no idea how long it had been since she'd fled the house. The numbness had spread, encasing her in a protective, emotionless shell.

She tried to fight it because this time she *wanted* to feel—

needed to feel. She had been so afraid to truly feel anything for so very long that she wanted to wallow in the overwhelming loss she knew lurked inside her, waiting to pounce. She wanted to fully experience the shame of knowing she'd been a coward, and the despair of knowing it was now far too late to tell Malach how she felt about him. She wanted to despise him for choosing another woman. And, most of all, she wanted to hate the poised, perfectly dressed, beautiful woman who'd had the courage to do what Jade had not, and claim the man she loved before it was too late.

She leaned on the wooden rail of the bridge, and stared into the clear, reflective depths of the water below, wishing she could wind back time and have her chance over again. Sure, even if she had bared her soul and confessed her love for him, Malach might have dumped her like last week's takeaways the instant he laid eyes on Francesca. But maybe, knowing Jade loved him would have made a difference. Maybe, knowing *that*, he would have politely shown Francesca the door. Maybe.

Francesca.

God. What a piece of work. She'd screwed him not once, but twice, and then balked at completing the bond with him.

Francesca had never allowed her relationship with Malach to progress as far as the Testing. Whereas Jade had given herself wholeheartedly to Malach, and gone all the way right from the start. Jade had been there through it all. And if the Testing descended here, now, Jade would still fight for him.

Francesca had never given him the slightest chance to escape the crystal—had believed she was condemning him to death, gotten over him, and gotten on with her life. Jade had fought. She'd gone so far as to have Lìli cast a spell on them both in an attempt to fool the Crystal Guardian's goddess.

Francesca had had her chance with Malach and abandoned him. So why should *she* have him now? Why should *she* have another chance when she'd screwed up the first one? It wasn't fair. It wasn't bloody fair.

"Whoever said life was fair?" a gentle voice enquired.

Jade glanced up and discovered Pieter, standing not two feet from her, leaning nonchalantly on the railing.

"You." The numbness fled, supplanted by rage. Her hands clenched into fists as she considered her options.

Option one: punch him in the nose and watch him bleed.

Option two: grab him and toss him over the bridge rail into the water where, with any luck, he'd drown.

Option three: shake him 'til his teeth rattled and... and....

And insist he guarantee Malach's happiness or she would lop off his balls with a blunt instrument, and feed them to the swans for a snack.

The rage drained away, leaving her cold and weak and shaking. Her eyelids drifted shut and she faced up to the unvarnished truth. She would leave Pieter unscathed, and get down on her knees to plead for Malach.

When she opened her eyes again and dared focus on the old man, he handed her a small bundle wrapped in an all-too-familiar golden scarf. All the careful, reasoned words she'd been planning to utter fled. With hands that trembled, she clumsily unwound the scarf, already knowing what she would find within its silken folds.

"How did you get these?" she whispered.

He didn't answer, merely held out his hand. Jade handed back his scarf, and cupped the two broken pieces of Malach's namesake crystal in her palms.

They had never looked more beautiful to her. It was as though her artist's eyes, always quick to appreciate details and nuances others missed, had somehow been enhanced. The crystal pieces were so highly polished they gleamed, and among their encircling bands of emerald, and rosette-like splashes of jade, she noticed other shades of green she had never imagined could exist.

A tear ran down her cheek, unnoticed until it plopped onto one of the crystal halves she cradled in her hands. Another tear welled, spilled, and began the journey down her cheek to plop without ceremony atop the second piece of the crystal. As Jade watched, enthralled, the crystals absorbed the moisture and her tears became part of them… just as Malach was now inexorably a part of her.

Without knowing why, she fitted the two halves of crystal together. They warmed in her hands. And….

Fused into one whole, unblemished crystal.

"The portrait you did of Malach is the best work you have ever done, Jade." Pieter's words sliced through her shock. "It exactly captures his essence, his soul. You know him better than he knows himself. I did not err when I chose you. Francesca could never love him as you do."

She was too overcome to form words. Her soul sang with emotions too powerful to name and her body thrummed with an urgency she could not ignore. She tore her gaze from the malachite crystal to demand that Pieter tell her what she should do, but the old man had vanished. And, without consciously moving, she was running back toward her house. Back to the man she loved.

As she ran, Jade realized she'd been so very, very wrong. The Testing hadn't taken place a week early, as she'd believed. Mei's deteriorating health and Malach's sacrifice had been purely incidental. *Now* was the Testing—this precise, precious moment in time. And it was *her* Test, not Malach's.

For better or worse, Malach had already been Tested, and now it was up to Jade.

JADE BURST THROUGH the doorway into her lounge, skidding to an untidy halt when she saw him. He sat slumped in the armchair, elbows resting on his knees, head held in his hands. His head jerked up at her unannounced entrance, and Jade glimpsed shiny tracks of moisture on his cheeks.

Tears?

Her heart plummeted and she gasped, wrapping her arms

about her middle. Tears for Francesca, of course. She'd left him again, the cold-hearted bitch.

Jade didn't know whether to keen with joy that Francesca was out of the picture, or weep with anguish for Malach's pain. Her knees wobbled, and she fought the need to throw herself at his feet and beg him to stay with her.

Then she noticed that the portrait Pieter had commissioned had been propped against the wall nearest Malach's chair. Pieter hadn't claimed it, after all. And for the first time Jade felt true gratitude toward the old man. No matter what happened now, he'd left her something precious to remember Malach by.

She sucked in a deep, painful breath. "Malach, I have something I need to say to you. I-I...." Her tongue felt huge, like it had tied itself in a big knot. She was about to tell a man who had just lost the woman he loved, that *she* loved him for real. Like that was supposed to make it all better. Like he was supposed to jump up and down and shout "Yippee! Lucky me."

Shit. She grabbed a fistful of hair and tugged it until the sharp pain made her wince. "I'm going to say it, okay? I know you love Francesca, and I wish it'd worked out for you two, but—"

He made a slicing motion with his hand, and Jade shut her mouth with a snap.

She waited, on edge, a sinking feeling churning in her gut. But when he didn't speak, she couldn't remain silent any longer. "Don't tell me she's gone to pick up her stuff and you're going back to the States with her? Christ! She's got more guts than I thought. Well... that's... great. Congratulations, I guess."

She searched Malach's face, attempting to read his carefully blank expression. No hints there. She was on her own.

Even a simple inhalation felt like she'd swallowed knives that were now shredding her heart. "I'm happy for you,

Malach. Truly, I am. But even though I know how much you love her, I have to do this. It's part of the Testing, you see, and I can't risk fucking this up and being responsible for you ending up back in this stupid crystal." She waved the piece of malachite in his face. "I love you. And I'm not going to let this bloody thing take you again."

"What did you say?"

"I said, I refuse to let you end up back in this hunk of rock."

"No. Before that."

Jade hopped from foot to foot, itching to throw herself at him, to crawl up his big body and press kisses all over his face. "I love you, Malach."

There. She'd finally said it. Twice, even. And it was true.

She waited for something momentous to happen, for Pieter's voice to boom out from the ether and declare in portentous tones that Malach was forever free of his crystal prison. She waited for his goddess's cruel laughter to ring out as she informed them they were fools for thinking that a love spell cast by a mere mortal could ever fool a deity. She waited for Malach to become transparent, to be drawn back into the crystal, while she stood by, useless and helpless, her ears ringing with his torment—torment that she would relive over and over in her nightmares. But the malachite crystal remained whole. And so did its namesake human, the Crystal Warrior who'd suffered so terribly in its cold, unfeeling depths.

"Say something!" Jade pleaded, her heart twisting as she gazed at his face, as always so achingly strong and beautiful to her, but now so cold and unfeeling, too... just like his crystal.

"Mother of all gods, thank you," he said. "I love you, too, my Jade." He stood and held out his arms, inviting her in, smiling as she stumbled over her feet in the rush to be enfolded in his embrace.

After five whole minutes of pure, unadulterated bliss, Jade couldn't help it: She had to ask. "Where's Francesca?"

"I told her to return to her husband," he said. "And I believe she was relieved. For although she and I still have feelings for each other, we both know my love for her is but a pale copy of the love I have for you, Jade."

She smiled up at him, misty-eyed with such intense happiness she felt like she might burst. "I loved the shoes but what you just said? Best birthday present ever."

"I have an even better one." His mouth swooped down to capture hers.

"Ow!" She eased away from him to rub the skin between her breasts where it felt as though something had scorched her.

"What is the ma—? Ah." Malach lifted her pendant and held the piece of jade so she could see it. The stone had just undergone its third metamorphosis. Instead of lavender, it was now a vibrant burnished gold.

"Let me guess. Golden jade?"

"In truth 'tis known as *yellow* jade," Malach said. "Though that name does it little justice." He bent to kiss the still reddened patch on her cleavage before replacing the pendant and settling the chain around her neck. "And 'tis now the perfect crystal for you."

"Oh? Tell me about yellow jade, Malach."

"'Tis energetic and stimulating." He emphasized the last word as he tugged her against his torso.

Jade felt her cheeks flush. Mmm. Something sure was stimulated. "Anything else?"

"It also bestows a quality of mellowness, that brings joy and happiness—much as I feel at this very moment."

"Aw, you say the sweetest things."

He kissed her again, with such passion that it crossed Jade's mind to wonder how rude it would be to arrive terribly late for her own birthday dinner. Somehow, she didn't think Lili or Grace would mind.

Epilogue

Lìli sensed his presence and turned to face him with a smile that warmed his heart. "Hello, Pieter," she said. "I've been expecting you."

"How do you fare, Lìli?" he asked.

"Quite well—no thanks to you," she grumbled. "Fake love spells... bah! The lengths I had to go to, to help those two realize they were in love. You have a lot to answer for, Crystal Guardian. I am an old woman. And what with worrying about young Mei, and fretting whether that Francesca woman would steal Malach away from my niece, I have aged ten years in four weeks. If I'd had any sense, I should have washed my hands of it all and left *you* to deal with it."

He bowed. "To me, Lìli, you could never be an old woman. However, I must humbly apologize for the stress I have put you through this past month. I have no doubt I could not have convinced Malach and Jade that they were soul mates without you. I owe you a great debt."

"Mind you remember that, Pieter. You owe me a favor—no, *two* favors for this."

"My dearest Lìli, you have no need to extort favors from me. If it is within my power to grant your wishes, you need only ask."

Her eyes crinkled with mischief. "I will hold you to that, Crystal Guardian."

Pieter smiled. "I would expect nothing less from you." He

linked arms with her and escorted her into the kitchen.

"Tea?" Lili asked.

"Please. But allow me." With a gesture, a pot of tea, two teacups, a jug of milk, and a plate of sliced fruitcake appeared on the bench, all neatly arranged on a tray.

Lili clapped her hands. "Ah, Pieter, you're a useful man to have around." She fluttered her eyelashes at him and his pulse raced. "How long can you stay this time?" she asked.

"Only until tomorrow, I'm afraid. Now that Malach and Jade are happily settled, I must resume my search."

"No rest for the wicked," Lili murmured.

Pieter sighed. "That is very true. However—" he waggled his eyebrows at her "—one may as well be hanged for a sheep as a lamb."

She slanted him a cat-got-the-cream smile. "Over the years I have learned that is very true, indeed. Eat up, Crystal Guardian, for tonight you will need your strength."

Lili was right. Tonight he would put aside all thoughts of his terrible mistakes, and the other Crystal Warriors he had imprisoned. Tonight he would not think of the terrible price both he, and the warriors he'd cursed, had paid. He would give himself up to Lili's tender ministrations and lose himself in the comfort of a woman's arms.

Lili's smile grew sultry, and Pieter's weary heart beat faster, anticipating the night ahead. Obediently, he crammed cake into his mouth and as he chewed, Lili's sly laughter chased the chill from his soul.

~*~

About the Author

MAREE ANDERSON WRITES paranormal romance, speculative fiction romance, fantasy, and young adult books. She lives in beautiful New Zealand, home of hobbits, elves, and kiwis—both the fruit and the two-legged flightless variety. Her first novel for young adults, the multi-award-winning Freaks of Greenfield High, was optioned for TV by Cream Drama, Inc., Canada. She recently released the fourth book in her Crystal Warriors series, and is currently working on a third book in the Freaks series.

For more information about Maree's books, please visit her website at: http://www.mareeanderson.com

Other books in The Crystal Warriors Series

THE CRYSTAL WARRIOR
(Wulf & Chalcedony's story)

RUBY'S DREAM
(Kyan & Ruby's story)

OPAL'S WISH
(Danbur & Opal's story)

~*~

Made in the USA
Lexington, KY
04 August 2017